Utopian can
work. Thanks for
being just you.
B xx

The Women's Press
science fiction

This is one of the first titles in a new science fiction series from The Women's Press.

The list will feature new titles by contemporary writers and reprints of classic works by well known authors. Our aim is to publish science fiction by women and about women; to present exciting and provocative feminist images of the future that will offer an alternative vision of science and technology, and challenge male domination of the science fiction tradition itself.

We hope that the series will encourage more women both to read and to write science fiction, and give the traditional science fiction readership a new and stimulating perspective.

SALLY MILLER GEARHART

Sally Miller Gearhart was born in the mountains of Virginia in 1931. She received an M.A. in Theatre and Rhetoric in 1953 and a Ph.D in Theatre in 1956. Between 1957 and 1970 she taught at various colleges in Texas, and she is now a full professor of Speech and Communication Studies at San Francisco State University. Her publications include *Loving Women/Loving Men: Gay Liberation and the Church* (with the Reverend William Johnson, 1974) and *A Feminist Tarot* (with Susan Rennie, 1976). She is now involved in the Animal Rights Movement, studies Aikido and sings bass in a lesbian–feminist barbershop quartet.

SALLY MILLER GEARHART

THE WANDERGROUND

Stories of the Hill Women

The Women's Press

sf

First published in Great Britain by
The Women's Press Limited 1985
A member of the Namara Group
124 Shoreditch High Street, London E1 6JE

Published in the United States by
Persephone Press, Massachusetts, 1980,
and by Alyson Publications, Inc., Massachusetts, 1984.

Some of the stories in this book have appeared in *Ms.*, *Quest: A Feminist
Quarterly*, *The Witch and the Chameleon*, and *WomanSpirit*.

Text illustrations by Elizabeth Ross

British Library Cataloguing in Publication Data

Gearhart, Sally Miller
    The wanderground: stories of the hill women.
    I. Title
    813'.54[F]   PS3557.E2

    ISBN 0-7043-3947-1

Typeset by AKM Associates (UK) Ltd, Southall, Greater London
Reproduced, printed and bound in Great Britain
by Hazell, Watson & Viney Ltd, Aylesbury, Bucks

My particular thanks to Jane, Dorothy, Amanda, Elizabeth and the Persephone women who struggled at crucial times with this manuscript. From the beginning, though, these stories were inspired and supported by hundreds of women and in the deepest sense they come from all of us.

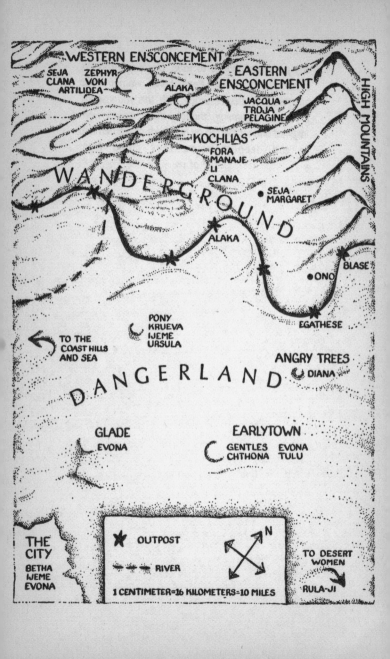

Contents

Contents

Opening

Jacqua stood above the Eastern Ensconcement gazing across the high meadow. Far below, anger was being spoken. She knew that anger came from two older sisters who had overvisited with each other, but she could grasp no words – only intentions. Suddenly from a completely different direction, she heard in her head the clang of armour. Not the jingle of horse bridle and bit, but armour. How did she know it was armour? Who in the world wore armour any more? It sounded as if the wearer walked at a good pace. With each step the armour sighed and creaked, rattling a bit. In the background were the winter forest noises. She listened harder. Was it two? Twenty miles away? No mind invitation. She attempted to move to visual. No luck. Too far for taste and smell, still so comparatively underdeveloped anyway in her and among all her sisters. All she could do was listen. The armour seemed to be moving faster now, the squeaks coming more frequently.

Then suddenly, nothing. Silence. She checked her listenspread and found it still operating. The forest noises continued. The person had stopped – not sat down or fallen, but stopped short. Could the person have heard her hearing her? No chance. Was her own breathing too loud? Was the armour-wearer breathing? If so why couldn't she hear her?

Still she waited. Minutes went by. Silence. Then it seemed an hour. Jacqua grew impatient. She was only beginning to train herself. Perhaps she was making some mistake.

'You're doing fine.' The thought was enfolding her.

'Diana?' she asked.

'Yes. I've been worry-reading you. And you've been open. What you're hearing is really happening.'

'Can you hear it too?'

'I did. I don't now. I'd call up an extended ear and pay attention elsewhere. A person can stand still only so long. Particularly in regalia like that.' Diana passed off and away.

Jacqua was relieved. Gingerly she summoned her extended ear – not like the more deliberate fanlike spread, but nevertheless a field sensitive to unusual noises. She opened it toward the armour's sounds. Still the silence. Now she was free to revisit her own thoughts. Could it be that it wasn't a woman at all but a man? One from the City, standing stock still there within their Wanderground? She tried to recall the lessons from the remember rooms: the stories, the mind pictures, the pain of some not-so-ancient days when the men owned all things, even the forests and hills. 'It is too simple,' she recited dutifully to herself, 'to condemn them all or to praise all of us. But for the sake of earth and all she holds, that simplicity must be our creed.'

She dropped back into her first-tellings, when she was only a girl-child and sat at gatherings with her mothers. In the singing and the playing of the tales of men there ran the thread, 'We once had hope for them, but even that hope they snuffed out.' Rage. Sadness. All mixed with tenderness and love. Love men? The idea did not fit. It was uncomfortable and backwards in her mind. She tried it on from every angle but it would not adjust; some of its bulk stuck out over the edges while other parts of it were too short to approach the edges. Yet somehow once it had been so. 'Maybe it was a different kind of love,' she mused. 'Or maybe they were gentles.'

Gentles. Men who knew that the outlaw women were the only hope for the earth's survival. Men who, knowing that maleness touched women only with the accumulated hatred of centuries, touched no women at all. Ever. Once, she remembered, some gentles had come to the Wanderground, stricken and dying. Unwilling to return to the City where they might have been revived, they came to the hill women. They came for help in their dying. They cried for the ministrations of the women. 'Minister to yourselves,' they were told. Yet always the women stood by, friends from a distance, the midwives of death who would ease their passing.

'Why can't we help them?' Jacqua had asked.

'They must help themselves,' her mothers answered.

'But they're dying!'

'Yes. They are dying. That is the most important thing. That is exactly what they must help themselves to do. When they touch their own bodies they know that. Only when they disconnect do they cry for our help and curse our hardness.'

Jacqua had seen them die there. Four of them. One by one over the days while she and the other women talked with them and sang with them but never touched them either with mind or hand. They had been unable to sustain their man-ness, and, though they had tried, unable to grasp their own woman-ness. It was too late for them now to reach down and lift themselves up. And these were the gentles of the men. What were the others like?

'They are driven,' Wenadi would say. 'Driven in their own madness to destroy themselves and us and any living thing.'

'Their madness. Is it like Clea's?'

'No. Hers was the madness of too full a vessel. Theirs is the madness of power.' Jacqua pondered all that.

The meadow below her was green with its own form of winter. There were some signs of life. Briefly she checked her extended ear. Still no sound. It must have been minutes now. How can a person stand so still?

She turned back towards the ensconcement where the anger and the pain had come from earlier. The rhythms were quieter there. Two older sisters had spent too many days together without speaking their hearts to the rest. She knew the pattern, as young as she was. In fact, probably because she was so young. It was one of the first lessons for them all.

Lightly in her memory she touched her long-ago warm soft days with Ursula, Ursula who had been her learntogether. She had not forgotten the feeling of needing for life itself Ursula's simple presence. They did not speak their warmness beyond each other to their sisters. They had become hidden with it. It began to eat away at their freestanding selves. Hence the saying, 'There are no words more obscene than "I can't live without you". Count them the deepest affront to the person.' Jacqua had not forgotten. In the end she had understood the importance of never feeling that way again.

The present matter was all the more difficult, though, because the two women were city-born, had found each other there, had fled together, been separated, and for more than a year now had been reunited. Among many of the sisters there was the feeling that they held too hard to each other and to the old ways of trying to love. Jacqua would be anxious to know how the talking had come out.

A clank disturbed her. The person was moving now. Jacqua turned her listening to the resumption of sound. There was someone else there, too. Again she tried other senses and mindstretches. No avail. She turned as Diana came up behind her.

'Look with me,' said Diana.

They locked minds, Diana's eye-seeing pushing outward and away, expanding with her power. As always, Jacqua was astounded and exhilarated.

'I'll never be able to do it alone!' She squeezed in the thought before Diana could stop her. Diana chastised her sharply, calling her up short. Jacqua took her deserts and began to focus with Diana to the scene so far away.

There was the source of the squeak: a metal headpiece whose raised visor jiggled with the slightest motion. Beneath the armour and the headpiece there was a woman. Fear sprang to her eyes as Jacqua sighted a familiar figure: Seja, from the Western Ensconcement. Seja was looking squarely at the stranger. The sudden noise of the helmet had been caused by the woman drawing her arm – and a smooth stick – across her chest. Seja stood only a yard from her.

'You are not open,' Seja said.

The woman's eyes blazed.

'You don't need that armour. Or those weapons,' Seja said.

The stranger spoke no word and her eyes were hard. It was clear

4

to Jacqua that the woman had been walking fast, as if fleeing, when she encountered Seja. The two were very different: Seja with her short curly hair, cotton shirt, soft trousers and sandals, her frank face and large hands open and out to the newcomer; the stranger, larger in stature, ludicrously garbed in the costume of a range of eras, as if she had robbed the wardrobe of some theatrical company. She was guarded and burdened by the weighty chain mail that clung to her torso, and by the old-fashioned helm. Thin skilfully worked metal formed her shoes; they were meant for feet much larger than her own. Her legs were bare up to mid-thigh except for leather greaves. She wore a short kilt-like skirt made up of loose metal-covered leather straps. Over its waistband was a belt and wedged into the belt at the side was a large kitchen carving knife. In her hand was the polished stick which she now held as if to strike Seja.

Slowly Seja moved. She sank before the other woman, knelt before her and bowed her head. The stranger stared.

'If you do not understand my words or my mind, then understand my body. I do not wish to harm you. You may kill me if you like. I trust that you will not.'

Still the strange woman stared. Quietly Seja raised her head, looking up into the other's face. Then her hands and head turned to the leather on the stranger's legs. She reached out to untie one of the thongs that held the shin protection in place. The woman let out a cry, stepped back and raised the stick above her head. Seja stopped. Then she pointed to the stranger's knife. The woman's eyes narrowed and her head turned a bit to the left. She seemed to understand something. Still holding the club above Seja's head, she drew the knife from her belt.

Jacqua gasped. Diana held her and with shortstretch urged her to silence. Now Seja was lying on the ground on her back. She forced a piece of an old log beneath her head. Jacqua was incredulous. 'She must be crazy,' she whispered. Seja, in the face of danger and even death, was lying down as if to sleep. In silence Seja looked at the woman with the weapons, then with deliberate calm she closed her eyes and pushed her head back over the wood so that her neck was fully exposed.

How long they stayed there – the armoured woman and the vulnerable hill woman – Jacqua could not tell. She dared not breathe lest the stranger leap forward and slash Seja's waiting throat. She held fast to Diana.

Then it happened. There was a change in the eyes of the larger woman. She lowered her hands – the knife to one side, the club to the other. Seja opened her eyes. At that, the standing woman looked to each of the weapons and with intentional slowness dropped each upon the ground.

Seja rose to a kneeling position. The woman did not move. It seemed to Jacqua that they looked at each other for an eternity. Then, very deliberately, the stranger thrust forward her leg toward Seja. With like slowness, Seja untied the thong. The unburdening began. Piece by heavy piece, Seja took the armour from the body of the stranger: the greaves, the thick belt, the monstrous helmet – so the long hair flew in the wind – then with some difficulty the chest mail. The woman moved only to straighten her arms so that Seja could remove that vest. Seeing she wore nothing beneath the chestpiece, Seja immediately removed her own shirt, baring her breasts in equal fashion.

They stood looking at each other for a long moment. Then the face of the strange woman broke into an amazing smile. It leapt from her face to Seja's and back again. They stood grinning at each other. Then both began picking up the armour and weapons from the ground. Seja extended her hand. The woman took it. Together they ploughed through the underbrush towards the ensconcement.

Jacqua was breathless. Her relief slid into exhaustion. She sank to her knees and then curled upon the brown grass.

'I may sleep a bit,' she said to Diana.

'May your dreams ease your wakefulness,' said Diana. She kissed the cheek, passed her hands over the young body and rose to descend the path.

Red Waters

Alaka was matching frostbreaths with her hound companion when something brushed the edge of spoken. Automatically she spanned other frontiers before responding to the outskirts of her southern stretchfield. All was well. She thrust a slim, taut enfoldment upwards and out along the forest top, knowing even before the contact itself who the caller was: Evona, in the City. She was risking a stretch. That could mean trouble.

'Evona?'

'Alaka. Yes. It's me. I had to touch.'

'Are you in fallaway?'

'No. But would have been if I hadn't extended. Wait until you do a rotation. You'll understand better. It's got worse.'

Alaka nodded, absently stroking the dog's cheek.

Evona's touch continued, sending now, 'Is it a bad time for

you to stretch?'

'No. But I'm just ending my watch, so if I drop out now and again you'll know I'm spanning. You feel diffused. Do you need earth?'

'Yes, I do. Is that Sophia with you?'

'No. Cassandra.'

'She is not ranging clear for me.'

'She singed her nose today. She's probably healing and not open.'

'Grant her root touch for me.' A pause. Then, 'Breathe with me, Alaka.'

'Of course. Wait a moment.' Alaka spread fan-fashion over half her horizons. Folded. Spread again. No disturbance. As she removed her warm boots and wool socks, she rigged a half-power-open condition, full circle, and slid a monitor into place. Briskly then, she began scraping aside the crisp leaves and broken sticks. 'Help me?' she shortstretched to Cassandra. The dog fell into rhythm beside her, nudging and scratching the leaves away. When they had uncovered a patch of dirt about the size of a moderate fire ring Alaka placed her bare feet firmly on the cold earth, legs apart in an accustomed wide stance. She caught Cassandra's eye.

'Oh, okay. Come on,' she smiled, motioning the dog onto the cleared space beside her. Cassandra flopped to a full-length prone position on the ground, her head draped over Alaka's toes. Once more Alaka overrode the monitor in an assurance sweep, then re-set it. She leaned down, touched the dark dirt with the palms of her hands, then straightened. To Evona she sent, 'Ready?'

'I'm ready.'

'Breathe with me, Evona.' Alaka closed her eyes. She dropped her consciousness to her stomach and locked into Evona at diaphragm level. They began. First in counterpoint, then in harmony, finally in unison. In the miles between the City and the forest's edge, the breathing, the moving, the earth-surging among the three of them structured a voiceless liturgy.

When she again felt the bite of the wind, Alaka heard Ursula, her watch relief, breaking through the brush by the path below. She turned back toward Evona's steady, now less frantic contact.

'Are you there, Evona?'

'Yes. Thank you. Fully given and well taken. Soon, Alaka.'

'Or deep, Evona,' chanted Alaka.

8

'Soon.'

'And deep.'

'Red waters.'

'Deep.'

'Deep.'

'Deep.'

'Deep.'

They spoke together. 'Deep. Soon.'

Alaka withdrew slowly. She was spreading a final span and putting her boots back on when Ursula appeared.

'All quiet?' Ursula sent.

'Here, yes,' Alaka sent back. 'Evona needed earth.'

Ursula nodded.

Alaka gave over her monitor to the other woman and turned to go. She sent to Cassandra, 'Coming?'

The hound looked with a question to Ursula. Ursula, taking up her watch position, nodded and waved. Cassandra looked to Alaka who spread her arms in a shrug. Cassandra rubbed with her nose the soft knee-spot of Alaka's trousers and then bounded back to share Ursula's watch. Alaka made her way down the mountainside.

Alaka's Journey

Alaka had made good time over the Wanderground from the outpost. Without rest it was nearly a full day's travel. 'I'll have to learn to ride wind yet', she thought, panting up a rise toward the noisy stream. As she had suspected they would, the mountains had drawn her eastward above the Kochlias so that now to reach Seja she was turning west again, meeting for the first time the south-westward flowing waters. She rested a moment on the side of the wooded hill, ranging out once more to the full circular expanse of her mindchannels. All was well. 'I can relax here,' she told herself. 'Why am I so cautious?' Tired. Tired and anxious to reach Seja. 'That's when my safety is best monitored,' she explained.

Now as she was approaching the water she would have to choose: to swim or to climb. She searched above her for the sun of day's ending. She knew even as she did so that it would be making its customary dramatic exit beyond the far mountains. 'Swim,' she decided. With renewed energy she began a lateral movement over the hillside towards the stream. A rock-bounded pool marked the river's sudden disappearance here under the ground. A denser growth harboured the quiet pool. Alaka knelt in the gravel by the river's edge and removed her boots. She sheltered them under a low ironwood tree and noted its location for her return. Then, with a deliberate mustering of courage, she turned to the pool.

'Earthsister,' she said aloud to the water, 'I want to join you.'

The word seemed to come from all around her. 'Join.' A simple response. Alaka knew better than to stand in converse with so fundamental a substance. Such elements were to be moved with or felt into but never accosted or confronted. She bent groundwards to scoop her lungs full of the rich air that rested near the earth and moved among the wet grasses there.

With a tilt of her head, she dived beneath the icy water, pushing down, downwards towards the river's bottom. She knew the course and her destination beyond the cave. The only question was whether or not her lungs would sustain her for the minutes without air. Smoothly, with unerring quickness, she moved into the colder deep-flowing current, adding her own broad strokes to its speed.

She was under the hill now, into the cave. No sunlight here in the mid-depths. Darkness was complete. Still she pushed forwards with the stream. Steady glide. Pull and kick. Glide. Pull and kick. Glide. She no longer felt the water as cold, only as an environment and as a swift suction carrying her forwards. In one strong and wide stroke her hand encountered a fish. Just the brisk touch of a mutual greeting. There were other touches, too. She particularly welcomed the river dwellers bold enough to swim with and about her.

Her lungs began to feel too full. She forced herself to hold the air another moment before slowly oozing out a tiny stream of breath into the water. Where would it bubble up, she wondered, if the river were all underground here?

Now, she thought. Now she could begin to push the air out faster. Surely the river was about to emerge again and she could surface. But where was the light? She did not dare to glide upwards while the water still ran underground; there might be no air when she came up. No air, only earth. She felt tiredness throughout now, and in one effort she both gathered and centred her strength. The only task was to reach the other side of the hill. The only task was forwards. How long had she been under? Four minutes? Five?

She increased the force of her strokes. Where was the light, the familiar opaqueness of the water that would tell her the stream had burst from the mountainside? She was pushing out the breath faster now. Only a few seconds left and then she would be on supplemental air. There at the bottom of her breathing cycle she could survive for more than a minute, perhaps longer. But she dared not risk letting all her air go until she could see the light. In a sudden decision, Alaka shifted to her lonth, to that deep part of her kinaesthetic awareness that could take charge of her bodily movements in involuntary fashion. Her change-over was uncertain at first. She wondered briefly why she was always so reluctant to give over any control to her lonth; it was, after all, a genuine part of herself. Why did she feel lonthing somehow to be an inauthentic way of being? She knew very well, for instance, that while she mistrusted her lonth she would never learn windriding or even scudding. 'Pelagine would say I'm biting off my nose to spite my face,' she mused. All this passed in the moments of gradually growing confidence, as she was consigning her kicks and glides to that other less familiar part of herself.

'More trust for you in the future, lonth,' she pledged. Now as the lonth moved her still steadily forwards her attention was freed for the full addressing of her plight. With only tacit awareness now of her swimming, she shortstretched to the companions who swam with her.

A whole school responded as if one fish. 'You are in trouble?'

'Yes,' she sent back. 'I need air and light.'

'Not far away,' assured the fish. 'A few more of your strokes.'

Alaka almost exploded the remainder of her air in relief. Instead she forced herself to release it slowly. 'Thank you, water-ones. May you go well and come again!'

'And again. And again. And again,' sang the fish. The refrain seemed to echo forwards and back in the surrounding water.

There. Had she risen or was the current really warmer? Warmer for sure. And yes, there was the light, the greenish-brown translucence spread out before her. She tilted her head towards the top of the water, fighting even now the urge to open her mouth and drink into her lungs all the rivers's murkiness.

Her head broke through the smoothness of the river's surface.

The small splash echoed over dark rocks and hanging vines. Alaka swept air into her body, pushed it out, swept it in again. She had made it. There in the distance was the outside, and in a twist of nature, the water seemed bathed in the south-westward setting sun. The sun. She praised it silently. Always bright even if too rarely warm these days. The sun, having led her there, greeted her again on this side of the mountain.

Back in her own conscious control now – after proper gratitude to her lonth – she floated forward until she was sure she would be able to stand up on the shore. Silently she swam and then silently waded. A large tree root helped her out of the water. She did not shake the drops from her hair or her body. It might be too soon. Quietly she stood by the giant who had helped her up. Was it a cypress? Too big. A kind of willow maybe. Its roots were almost completely undercut now by a swift bend in the river.

'Thank you,' she said in mindstretch to the tree.

'Again if you need me,' responded the tree.

'Stay well,' she chanted inside.

'Go well,' said the tree.

Time to explore. Even as she began to warm herself she stretched to listen. Stock still, standing with her back against the tree, she spanned her immediate territory. Rabbits. Or some small animals just below the cold ground. Above, strangely quiescent starlings. Or sparrows? Around her, fallen branches, deep moss, damp grass, red-brown mud, dormant brambles, layer on layer of thicket, the sun passing behind the far rise, the river moving slowly by and swirling faster beneath the giant tree, the far-off promise of a midnight frost. Quietly she swung her stretch further to full circle at a distance beyond the rise. Less intense sounds and smells now, but more of them. By swift montage she listened to and felt one at a time, every thing, every oxygen-breathing thing, every other-breathing thing, every non-breathing thing. They felt her attention and told her all was well.

She drew back full into her own body, into her hardself and sent out a short automatic sweeping channel while she physically shook the water from her hair.

'I will warm you,' she heard. Laughing, she turned to the tree. Gently she laid herself against the heavy bark, spreading her legs and arms about the big trunk.

'I take when you give,' said the tree.

'I know,' she said. 'And I take when you give.' She inhaled slowly, pressing her viscera against the tree. As she released her breath, the trunk pushed against her. Slowly, with no visible motion, the two set a rhythm of pneuma exchange. Alaka's trousers became dry and warm. So did even her soft shirt, a chamois given her by Olu, her long-loved antelope when Olu changed form. Her hair swung free now and dry. All her insides felt comfortable. 'My feet,' she said to the tree.

'No boots?'

'No. I swam.'

'Can you torpor them?'

'Will you help me?' Alaka dropped her eyes to her feet, encasing her toes, her arches, her heels in heavy wood soles. She held fast temporarily while the tree wrapped warm breeze about them. 'That should do. I have less then twelve kilometres to go. I thank you.'

'Again if you need me.'

'I take you with me.'

'And I keep you with me.'

Alaka smiled the tree a touch. The sun had disappeared now and she tasted the coldness that her warm body was refusing to know. She spread before her a wide mindstretch, allowing its field to reach to her left as well as before her. Quietly still she set out towards the rise where the sun had set. 'I'm early,' she thought. 'I could have taken the long way over the hill and down.'

'Never too early, Alaka.' The voice burst into her awareness.

'Seja!'

'I'm coming from the ensconcement, moving towards you.'

'Is that a clear wish?'

'Yes.'

'Then may you always come with ease and care.'

'With your care I come with ease.' Seja completed the ritual. They laughed a mutual laugh. 'The others also greet you,' Seja continued, 'but I wanted to meet you fully first.'

'Good.' With Seja's energy the governor now of her direction, Alaka moved more and more eagerly through the brush. Even as she walked she stretched, 'I don't want to interrupt the twilight ministrations. I can wait here.'

'We sang all day. It's mid-moons and the eggs are passing down. Remember?'

'I forgot,' Alaka sent, reminding herself that that might explain her edginess today.

'Anyway,' continued Seja, 'everyone's exhausted. Yelena declares she will not sing one more note even if her worthy egg never passes.' There was an excitement in Seja's sending that signalled Alaka of a change. Seja was about to lapse into her narrative mode. Alaka could always tell when Seja had a story coming on – usually an entertaining one.

'Wait!' she sent. 'Wait please until I get there!' She could feel Seja pull herself up short and move back to more immediate matters.

'Well, anyway,' Seja was sending, 'we'll need no twilight tones tonight.'

'Will you sing with me, then, since I've missed singing entirely today?'

'Of course. Maybe tomorrow after you've rested.'

'Good.' Alaka came to a clearing where sandy soil was covered with small stones. She was aware that her feet were feeling the cold earth again and that occasionally a stone seemed to bruise her unnecessarily. Still she walked on, pacing herself to the rhythms set by Seja's voice and by her own, even as they talked without words.

'If she's willing I'll bring Clana from your ensconcement with me to the Kochlias when I leave,' Alaka sent conversationally. Then more slowly, 'I have to return in three days.'

There was short pain from Seja. 'That's very soon.'

'It's the closing in of winter. Some expect intruders.'

Alaka walked without thoughts for a while. She was channeljoined with Seja now and each was enfolding the other over the distance between them. She made her way over uneven ground.

Seja returned to the thought. 'We expect some, too. We found a woodland buck in the outland scree. It had been shot-killed.'

'Shot and left?' asked Alaka.

'Yes.'

'Not even the head taken?'

'No. They want only does.'

Alaka stopped suddenly, dizzy. She eased herself to the

ground with an audible cry.

'Alaka!'

'Yes. I'm not in retrosense. Only stricken.'

'I'm very close,' Seja sent. 'Do you need earthtouch?'

'I don't know. I don't believe so.' Alaka could feel Seja's physical presence now, not more than a few kilometres away. She checked her spanners for double safety and then drove a cool blast into her lowest energy base. Seja was breathing with her. The pain, the rage, the dizziness subsided. She breathed freely again. Seja was apart from her but shortening the distance between them.

'That's what you get,' Seja was saying, 'for not shielding. Are you up?'

'I'm getting up.' Alaka felt a tinge of resentment. Seja knew how such news always affected her. 'I didn't know I'd have to shield,' she sent back a little stiffly.

'It was yours, sister, and not my own,' Seja was quick to rejoin her.

'It was mine,' Alaka said after a pause. She felt the resentment fade. She began walking, slowly at first and then more quickly. 'I will ready myself better tomorrow and you can tell me more about the buck.'

Seja seemed closer. Both women held fast to the channel connecting them as they came eagerly towards each other. The day was hanging between darkness and light. Here where the stream began a smaller fork there was steadier ground. Alaka, concentrating on her feet in order to hold them in warmth, scarcely noticed the dwindling of the day. She would welcome darkness as she welcomed dawn. Now her outranging spanners touched on the birch brake that surrounded the Western Ensconcement. The nests there seemed calm, as if in their exhaustion everyone slept. Seja had made good time. Even as she stretched toward the ensconcement, trying to draw upon its comfort, Alaka stayed in firm touch with the approaching woman.

Suddenly, a blaze of colour stunned her mindstretch. Such force! She stopped, pulled in her spanners and her channel-reach to Seja. With her first ears she heard someone striding through the brush. Leaving the lower ground, she moved towards the noise, smiling. Seja, too, had drawn in her mindstretch, moving only in her hardself. She laughed aloud. Alaka laughed back. They were foolish, perhaps, to strike their protection in this way, both at once. Some would say that they could endanger both ensconcements. But Alaka knew and understood how others had risked in the same manner, risked even a whole colony for a few seconds of old-fashioned, unsophisticated, unguarded greeting. It was like allowing themselves to be children again. Each leaned towards the other, not yet in her sight.

Alaka was the first to catch a glimpse of Seja. 'You there!' she said aloud.

'I here and you there!' Seja responded. Alaka lifted herself over a log and stood waiting for Seja's breathless hug. It spun her around in a merriment long suppressed. They were loud and free in their laughter, in their voices, in their holding-close-and-soothing.

'You've grown taller,' Alaka said.

'Impossible. Only skinnier,' said Seja.

'Or maybe I'm just bigger,' said Alaka.

Again they grinned and each stood quietly holding the other. The darkness softened the lines of their touching. They soon breathed out together and silently pulled apart to stand side by side. Alaka threw out an enfolding spanner to her left and up and counter-clockwise. Seja did the same to her right and up in clockwise fashion. When their spanners met and joined, they smiled and gathered their fingers together into a clasp for walking together up rugged terrain.

The darkness was deep when they reached the sleeping ensconcement. Only Beula, on guard, broke their silence with her kiss and words of welcome for Alaka. They shared food and drink in the comparative warmth of Seja's nest and though they did not sleep immediately, when sleep came it was no less sweet and deep than their loving.

A Morning Together

In the summer Seja's nest had no walls at all, only a roof against occasional rainfall and a view in every direction of countless subtle greens and dancing sunlight. To sleep with Seja in the summer months rarely meant sleeping only with Seja; usually there were at least three bodies in her thick pine-needle bed and frequently four or five. Alaka had grown to expect not only the ensconcement animals that sought out Seja but the creatures of the wilder forest as well, from chipmunks and squirrels to lizards and, once, a black bear cub.

But it was another season now, one that Alaka had not shared with Seja. So her waking on the morning after her arrival had in it a quality of surprise, of strangeness. Her short circle stretch upon first reaching awareness was as natural to her – to all the women – as breathing. In it she found safety and quiet but some unfamiliarity.

'Earthtouch to you, Alaka.' Her sweep had brushed the night watch and opened now to a welcoming enfoldment.

'And to you. Are you Beula?'

'No. Notu-ka. After your rest we'll meet. We both cook this evening.'

'Good. A broad deep day to you, Notu-ka.'

'And to you.' As the woman's mind-touch gently fell away Alaka strained in the slow dawn to inspect Seja's nest, a nest very different from that of her summer visit.

First of all, she realised that there were no animals beside her or, as she recalled with a smile, between her and the sleeping woman a few centimetres away. Then there were the walls – structures heavily draped with broad sweeps of cloth and apparently well-insulated, though with what Alaka could not yet imagine. The walls were secured between the four round poles which in summer supported only the low roof. An undersized dutch door faced her in the south wall and its open top offered the room its only possibility of light.

Finally, there was the floor. She remembered the floor very well from the summer when Seja had been rearranging it. Books. Hundreds of them, stacked at different thicknesses within rectangular wood sections. 'Best insulation ever,' Seja had said, 'and quite an experience to be walking on all that knowledge.' To Alaka's amazement Seja had demonstrated a remarkable recall of what books were where and could quickly lay hands on any title she had. Now she noted that Seja's reading had rendered the floor pretty uneven in places. Two children's books, open by the door, had left a gap that a French grammar was failing to fill and next to two texts on plant diseases right near her reach was a long hole whose bottom, Alaka could see, was the dark earth itself. She picked up a book and examined it. There was no sign of mildew. Seja must bathe them in dryness every day, she thought.

The books were an acquisition from the deserted library at Earlytown. Seja had claimed all that the women in the remember rooms and others had not wanted. It had not been entirely satisfactory, Alaka recalled Seja's saying. At first some women had insisted on burning all the books. Seja and others had spent long hours in sister-search with these women before any clear wish had been reached. Then, after that, sisters from both ensconcements and the Kochlias had taken Seja for the local librarian – stretching to her at all hours to ask about some obscure title. Now that she examined more carefully, Alaka noted that behind the hangings books were also the primary wall insulation. She surveyed all the details of Seja's living quarters, feeling the nest's uniqueness. As she lay warm and at ease in the simplicity of the room, she puzzled over whether the soft quilts were Seja's forever or a rotated possession. She marvelled at the care that had gone into the winterising of the tiny space. Particularly was she marvelling at the floor, wondering what treasures of literature their bed was covering, when a bright fresh mindstretch enfolded her, inviting her attendance. Seja was awake.

'Morning!' Seja announced. Alaka opened, and at the same time turned to hug the grinning head above the snuggling body.

'Cold?' Seja was sending.

'No. You?' Alaka responded aloud.

'No.' Also aloud. 'I never had it so good. Never had such fine walls, never had such a warm floor, never had such a soft body beside me . . .'

Alaka cut her off by stretching her bare self top to toe against Seja. 'Even your brown bear cub?'

'Couldn't hold a candle to you,' Seja assured her.

Alaka's mood altered only a bit as she shifted back to the swifter communicative mode. In her mind she showed Seja that she missed the animals. Seja promptly formulated in her mind the sensations and categories and connections that told Alaka how in winter any strays were welcomed in the ensconcement's half underground barn – or if the social relations became strained there, how they then were taken in at the main hall which was at night given over to shelter for anyone who needed it. Still, Seja observed, she had occasional animal visitors.

Thus their day was beginning.

Even within so comparatively young a relationship as Alaka and Seja's there had grown between them certain rituals of loving, rituals of working, rituals of eating and sleeping. The early morning ritual of beginning together proceeded that day along familiar lines: in mutual mind effort from across the room they enfolded the tea water, requesting it to boil, aiding it, with its consent, in doing so; they swung the door closed and ignited a glow lobe to make a softer dawn within the nest; they propped up their backs against the books on the north wall, balancing tea cups on the quilts as they shared in silent recall the dreams of the night and fantasised at will wherever dreams seemed incomplete; they talked aloud and with frosty breaths about whatever news needed telling.

This morning that news began with Seja's description of the comedy being planned by a group of women at the Western Ensconcement. She ended the monologue on that subject by saying, 'They're all in wood-readying this month and apparently rehearse as they cut and gather. They claim they're tired of sober epics and the agonies of *The Purges and The Hunts*. Supposed to be pretty funny.'

Out of the embryonic uneasiness that had lurked for days just below her consciousness Alaka sensed in Seja's words a diminishing enthusiasm. Some pall seemed to overtake them both, dulling any high spirits. They sat motionless for a long moment, inwardly tempting a quiet despair.

Alaka articulated it first. 'There are rumours that potent men are outside the cities.'

Seja's sudden grasp shook her physically. 'How do you know,' Seja was almost shouting. 'How do you know that, Alaka?'

'Ease,' thought Alaka closing her eyes. 'Soothes and ease.' She enfolded Seja in a care curl, desperately trying to handle the turmoil that was bubbling out of her lover.

'Birdnews.' She made a deeper cradle of her arms. But Seja was up, up and out of bed now. She paced. She talked as she paced, and then threw on her clothes without interrupting her stride or her sentences.

'I've told no one, Alaka. I'd hoped it happened to her long ago – not recently. Or I hoped it was only a nightmare that she had made real in order to purge it. Or something.'

'Who, Seja? What are you talking about?'

'Margaret. The crazed woman I met in the clearing near the Eastern Ensconcement two weeks ago. The one wearing all the armour. She'd been raped. And not in the City. Do you hear that? Not in the City, Alaka. There hasn't been a potent man outside the City in our living memory. These reports – and Margaret's story – have to mean that the effect isn't holding. As soon as they discover that the country no longer drains their drive, they'll be back, right on us again.'

Alaka was trying to convince herself as much as Seja. 'Only one man, Seja. Maybe a fluke . . .'

But Seja was shaking her head. 'Two men. She was taken by two men. In the short hills far east of the City. Then they dressed her in that armour as a joke. Took it out of some school museum and set her loose laughing and throwing rocks at her as she scrambled away from them through the brush. She didn't tell me any of this. She couldn't talk. Or mindstretch. But she opened to me and let me read her recalls.' At that, Seja kicked loose an oversized book. She had been clenching and unclenching her fists and now with a stark sustained throat noise she put both her hands into her thick curls and pulled fiercely as if to uproot both her hair and the memory.

For the second time in a day Alaka realised that she had failed to shade herself. In grand old-fashioned female style she had tried to protect Seja, but she'd left her own lower channels open. As Seja re-knew Margaret's horror and outrage, Alaka, too, was absorbing the full force of the armoured woman's experience. She was aware that she was going to be deeply and violently ill. In the split second before she grasped that knowledge, she reminded herself of some irony: that she, a remember-guide, should herself fall so near retrosense and that she, who characteristically hesitated to give up any personal control, should now be in the grip of an emotional turbulence so strong that it racked her body.

The room was reeling. Even as she crawled toward the door Alaka was nattering in her head about what great literary masterpiece might fall heir to her vomit. She made only a superficial note of Seja who still stood, head-in-hands, galvanised against the east wall. Thrusting one knee in front of the other, one hand in front of the other, she crawled slowly forward, holding in delicate balance the urge to faint and the urge to empty the whole world out of her stomach. Another wave of nausea propelled her to the door. She achieved the fresh air but not the earth. As she baptized Seja's step, choking and heaving, she tried to be glad she had made it thus far. Then she wasn't glad of anything. Or sorry. She gulped some of the sharp air and with a huge sigh felt her head fall forwards on the doorsill, there to be transformed into a puffy white cloud floating up to the top of the sky.

She really didn't care that Notu-ka's mindstretch was enfolding her, frantically asking for explanation. Or that Seja was now screaming, or that the taste of last night's late supper was with her again. She drifted high above it all, wearing a top hat and mesh stockings, smoking a long white cigarette with a ruby-red filter in a slim sexy holder. Besides there was a sunshine tree draped over her left shoulder and she was busy distributing the day from its dripping leaves.

'Rowena and Beula are both coming. They'll be there right away.' Notu-ka's mindstretch aroused Alaka.

'No!' she sent. 'Wait. It's not over and we are all right.' She was sobered now and brought harshly back to the present.

In the few short seconds that Alaka had been out, Seja had dropped to the floor into a foetal posture. Her scream was still in the air. Alaka sent spanners out to catch the approaching women. She found them open – one coming from the watchpost, the other hurrying from the barn.

'Rowena, Beula,' she sent. 'It will be good that you come but stay back. She has not yet touched her anger and she needs to go alone until then.'

'Are you well, Alaka?' Beula was sending.

'No. Not at all. We're a pretty sight here, both of us. Vulnerable and wiped out. But I'm beyond it now. Stay quiet if you come. Seja needs to finish.' Beula and Rowena assented and Alaka turned back to her lover.

Seja had yielded entirely to the memory, yielded with no protection. She was clearly in full retrosense, tensed in rigid paralysis there on the floor by the book of plant diseases. Inside her head Margaret's ugly drama was still raging; apparently even the remember rooms had not prepared Seja for this more visceral experience of rape. 'What would we do if it were happening in our hard-selves,' Alaka wondered, 'when we are this overwhelmed by a memory?' Even as she asked she knew the answer, or knew at least what she, Alaka, would do.

She was constructing her own shield now, regaining control,

moving in the familiar patterns of a remember-guide. She did not try in her hard-self to reach Seja, though she was less than a short metre from her. She was not sure she could have done that at this moment even if it had been called for. Instead she enfolded Seja in a steady shortstretch of drenching greens and blues, of major chords and leading tones drawn to consonancy, of coolness and of sturdiness. As she enfolded, she sent the constant message, 'The facing of the fear is yours. But you are not alone.'

She was regaining her centre. She sat up now, leaning against the door frame, still soothing, still sending. There was nothing else to be done for now. In her function as a remember-guide Alaka had re-channelled thousands of rapes, thousands of killings and tortures, re-channelled them hundreds of times, scenes of the most sordid and grotesque nature, atrocities she had not dared to experience without memory shields. It was in fact the job of a remember-guide to call up and re-play, for those who did not know it, all or any part of the hill women's violent backgrounds. Decades ago each woman who had escaped to the hills had offered – usually with great pain – the memory of her city experience, however dramatic or mild, however heroic or horror-ridden. Her experience as she had known it had been added then to the vessels of memory kept within the person of every hill woman. 'Lest we forget how we came here.' From countless seemingly disconnected episodes the women had pieced together a larger picture so that now they had some sense of what had happened during those last days in the City. Over the years as women had joined them the memory vessels had been added to: more and more stories, more and more horrors, and sometimes a narrative that brought with it some hope or humour. As a woman shared, she became part of all their history.

Regularly now women went to the remember rooms in the Kochlias to watch as remember-guides re-channelled the old stories. Often they elected not to shield or to shield only partially as they watched so that they might experience a story, a description with more nearly its full reality. That was when they needed the remember-guides' greatest skill: the skill of allowing with patient and calm attention the intensity of retrosense (and sometimes the intensity of madness) to run its course.

The stories of outrage were the deepest, always, and usually the oldest. Now Margaret's would take its place with others. It would do so more significantly, Alaka feared, because of what that story might mean to them all.

Alaka looked over at Seja. Even if she had not been sustaining contact with the turbulence that was in that curly head Alaka would have recognised the signs of an uncontrollably rising anger. In her experience that anger inevitably followed any recall of rape, particularly if the recall had been even slightly unguarded. Seja was stirring, breathing hard, beginning to move her fists in soft steady blows against the floor.

Even with her shield Alaka almost recoiled from the starkness, the unequivocal purity of the ragings she found within the other woman: a naked and unadulterated desire to kill. Alaka scooted across the floor and covered Seja with her whole body. Placing her neck on the other woman's neck and holding the side of her head against the wet cheek she made a strong appeal for attention.

'Seja!' she shortstretched.

Seja responded as if to an interruption.

'You're about to move into murderous energy. If you need to do that we'll go through it with you.' A hesitation. Alaka knew that Seja's eyes were open now, and that they were sparkling far too brightly. She held and waited. She ached with Seja's outrage, cried with Seja's crying.

Suddenly there was a strong tensing of muscles as a writhing body attempted to break from under her hold. 'I'm no match for her,' Alaka thought, and at the same moment openstretched to Beula and Rowena. 'Come!'

With a shriek Seja threw her over, almost easily, reversing their positions. As she sensed the violence being turned towards her, Alaka feared for the first time for her own safety. A shield was hardly relevant now. Things were moving too swiftly and anyway they were too physically close, already deeply mixing their auras. 'Fighting and lovemaking,' Alaka flashed. She might even have smiled if Seja's hand had not at that moment been trying to separate her head from her body. Alaka was holding Seja's other hand – a fist – out and away from her own face. That hand, too, sought to hurt.

Alaka eased the pressure on her throat but was having trouble containing Seja's upraised arm. The fist escaped once, and then

25

again before she recaptured it; each time it sought to land a heavy killing blow on her head. Alaka was amazed at her own calm. She was aware that a mindstretch cradle was supporting them now from Beula and Rowena who must be approaching. Seja was having none of it.

'Too mild a soothing,' sent Alaka. 'Bring your hard-selves, and fast!'

The two struggling women were in the corner by the bed now, and Seja's arm was breaking free for a third time. 'She could kill me,' Alaka thought.

Then, as if the earth had decided gracefully to cease its turning, all motion seemed to stop. In a frozen moment Alaka saw the woman above her not as lover, not even as crazed and outraged sister. It all seemed mock heroic at first, and Alaka could almost hear a militant musical score in the background. But it became very serious.

Seja was a warrior – strong, righteous, brave, committed. She rode bare-breasted under a brilliant helm of crescent horns and flanked by bold and bright-clad sisters. Stonefaced, powerful, beautiful, highly-trained and self-disciplined, she was the virgin, the one-unto-herself, the spirit of the untrodden snow, whose massive hands were as unflinching in battle as they were gentle in love. And her sword rang on the shields of men who dared to violate the sanctity of womankind. Here was no passive damsel, here none of the forgiveness of the soft supine woman. 'He who rapes must die.' A simple maxim by which to live your life, by which to die yourself if that is necessary. Now there was the fighter, flushed with valour, sworn to death or triumph and now here was the calm victor, not rejoicing in the kill but looming over her vanquished enemy at this very moment about to let fall the fatal blow.

'My enemy by definition cannot receive my love. My enemy by definition is the one I kill.'

'It is not in his nature not to rape. It is not in my nature to be raped. We do not co-exist.'

Seja, the woman-of-war. Seja, the righteous killer. The ringing battle cry, 'Enough!' and the thunder of defiant hooves, the slashing of avenging swords.

The earth began to move again. The vision vanished. There was Seja's hand about to descend on her own immobile face. Alaka had no strength to turn aside again. She closed her eyes and waited.

The blow never fell. Instead she was breath-robbed by the sudden pressure of a collapsing mountain. Seja was crushed against her, and on top of Seja two other figures were piled straining and grunting as they brought wild arms and legs into a tense control.

Alaka, barely breathing, set her attention to a shortstretch. Rowena and Beula were there. So was a murderous defiant Seja. Her low sustained struggling cries undergirded the four-way mindstretch.

'Your choice, Seja,' Beula was saying. 'Your choice. We release you and you go free to do whatever harm you wish to yourself – but no other – or you yield to us here and let us hold you, give you earth. Your choice.'

'Your choice,' repeated Rowena.

'Your choice, Seja,' Alaka sent.

The mound of bodies moved less feverishly. They waited. Seja tried in vain to move. Alaka cried quietly. Still they held and waited, Alaka clasping Seja from below, Rowena and Beula pinning her from above.

'Your choice,' they all sent. 'Your choice.'

Silence. Holding.

The bodies began to quiver. Then they shook. Then they were rocking up and down, rising and falling as Seja's sobs grew louder. Her heaving intakes became more elongated, her releases each a series of short, rough declining coughs. She screamed. The three women around her sent quick thick shields to their ears. She screamed again. And again.

'The whole nest is shaking,' thought Alaka, crushed beneath her sisters. Seja released another body-racking cry. Alaka thought, 'Oh I wish I had some of that air!'

She did not get a deep breath for quite a while. Seja continued coming down for a long time and Alaka would not have broken the releasing for any reward she could imagine, nor for any threat save her own untimely death.

Seja lay quiet and exhausted on her bed. Beula and Alaka stroked her body, her head and limbs. A few curious and caring guinea hens pecked around the bed and a golden retriever lay by the door anxiously watching Seja. Rowena was clearing the ground outside for earth-sharing and around the entire nest there was a rhythm of concern pulsing in and out as women over the ensconcement inquired about and sent enfoldings to Seja.

The sun was high now. 'No need for that glow lobe,' thought Alaka. She looked down at Seja, not yet fully conscious. Then there was a reaching out from the inert body, a mindstretch to Alaka. 'Welcome to the peaceful beauty of the Western Ensconcement,' it said.

Alaka smiled. Seja was going to be fine. She gave the deep curls an extra loving tug and then extinguished the glow lobe.

Clana and the Snakes

Clana had the entire morning free. Bintu who was her learntogether today was called to the Wanderground and the only other girl-child in the ensconcement lay abed with her own learntogether. Clana stood in a wide patch of low bushes, on hard ground tangled with briers and woods.

There opened under her only the tiniest of holes, no more than her smallest tooth in diameter. She knelt and scratched around the opening, amazed to see part of the red dirt fall away. It revealed a darkness as large as her fist. On both knees now, she dug. The winter sun on her back was unusually warm and encouraging.

Beyond her the forest crackled with its contrapuntal life sounds. Clana reached under a bare berry bush and dislodged a piece of shale to help her dig. The hole was even bigger now, and dropped from a vertical into a more horizontal blackness.

'I've found a digger's hole,' she thought. With that, she sat back on her turned-in feet and closed her eyes. Laying her digging rock carefully aside, she placed her hands on her bare thighs and began thinking, thinking of badgers, moles, groundhogs, rabbits, all of those slick-furry little animals, particularly those she could hold in her hand. She had hard-touched them often. She thought of all that she knew about them – how they darted and scooted, how they squeaked, how they nibbled at hard grain clusters. She tried hard to remember everything about underground creatures. Where she could not remember, she imagined. Soon she was only physically present to the sun and the forest, her soft-self off rollicking in a far meadow with leaping rabbits and field mice. She talked with them as they understood talk. Among other things not quite so important she told them that she would never without their full consent take life from any of them, that she knew them to be as much of her flesh as was her own body, that she yielded to their need of her even to her own dying if their touch with the mother required that. Those promises made, she reached to stroke them all. They nuzzled her with their wet noses and placed their tiny thumping hearts next to her neck and head. She smelled their muskness and their fur but not their blood. Blood smelling was very difficult, especially only in the soft-self. Slowly and with a caution she was just learning, she put them aside. Laying on them a last-hold, she came back to her sitting self. The hole was still there.

She felt ready to explore it now. 'Which of you will go?' she said to her hands. With fondness and amazement she held both her hands in front of her trying to make a difference between them. She often got lost in her hands, stroking and kneading them, so fascinating were they to her. They were equally skilled – perhaps the right hand more often practised in intricacies like needlework. She was still trying to break that habit, apparently residual from centuries of right-handed superiority. 'All will not be accomplished in one lifetime,' the sisters were fond of saying.

Looking now at both hands she could make no decision. Both were healthy, both a bit sunburned from too much time at the stream the day before. She was a lightskin, no doubt of that. She was thus in the minority in the ensconcement among so many dark women. Clana mused for a moment on her whiteness. That whiteness was a puzzle to her, for as far as she could make out, she looked not a bit like any one of her seven mothers, all so dark of skin and hair and eyes.

'Well,' she said to her hands, 'anyway, one of you wants to go down the hole. Which one?' Neither hand replied. Clana then pondered about sending both hands on the exploratory mission, but she dismissed the idea as impractical. Clearly she could reach further with one hand, and besides, if there were frightened animals inside, injury to one hand was better than to two.

Snakes! She had forgotten snakes! Perhaps the inhabitant of the hole was a snake! A hasty sigh and she sat back on her feet again, hands on her thighs. 'Snakes,' she thought. She had not hard-touched or even seen too many. She knew that there were some with a fatal poison here in this climate – even a family of water moccasins had been reported. But of the fast-killing brightly coloured snakes or their cousin cobras, there had been none. Still, it was wise to protect against all possibility. She began with small crawling snakes, the green and brown and grey ones, the baby ones and the brown ones, the striped ones and the speckled ones, the ones who scooted in the water and the ones who whished along the ground. She invited them over her arms and around her neck. They slithered over her warm body. In a quick movement of her mind, she unclothed herself so the small curves could slide over her back without encumbrance.

She then invited the diamondbacks, the stub-tailed cotton-mouths, and the orange-brown copperheads. She invited them by the hundreds to test her touch, to see her intent. In the hard world she had never seen a coral snake but she had seen stories of them. She drew on a low-hanging tree a pencil thin creature of red-yellow-black sections. It squirmed towards her, yawning and closing, yawning and closing. She motioned it to join the others – all intertwining together around her in a congenial mass.

The hissing was a conglomeration of varied intensities and lengths, mostly from the rattlers, she thought. They did claim a lot of the noise. She called the coral snake closer and asked for a dental examination. Obligingly it flung open its mouth so she could see the tiny mountain ranges of teeth. It was good that such a small animal had that deadly protection. 'Introduce me to the cobras,' she asked. And there they came, beautifully graceful greenish limbs suddenly not a tree at all but free winding clusters of longer larger snakes. Very slick and very evenly thin. 'You are different from the stories I saw of you . . .' but she was hushed by the slow expansion of one rising neck and then another. As if the excitement were contagious, ranks of cobras, gently and with the weaving motion she remembered from the stories, swayed before her, their necks flattened and their bodies nodding left and right in a classic hypnotic dance. Clana was happy. This was what she had recalled. They reminded her of something else, all these many kinds of cobras, reminded her of the many kinds of constrictors. She had left out the constrictors from her party. 'Yes!' she said, calling out the anacondas and the pythons and the boas, though the thought of their being in the tiny hole amused her.

She saw a collection of forms and an interwoven ritual. No longer did she will it. Instead, the slithering life around her made its own rules, moved in its own postures and patterns. She did not retreat. A sensuous drumming – bizarre and disconnected – as of a thousand mixed heartbeats, rose from the background. Grass snakes lined up with whipsnakes to form a mid-air grid of unending motion; big bodies became whole terrains for bouncing, dancing, smaller lines and curved masses. Clana watched, fascinated, the splendid loud performance that played across her softself. Other sounds came from nowhere, noises added at random that she did not recognise. No order. And underneath, the uneven beats of those drums.

As she watched and listened, she too began to move in sometimes clumsy, sometimes graceful steps with the serpent dance. Snakes climbed her body to make her movement their own. A misstep. Her foot landed on the back of a large grey snake. It writhed and hissed. She was quick to hold out her hand. The noise rose in volume, increased in tempo. The grey snake swirled in time around her outstretched arm and coiling about it swam up to her head. Instinctively she raised her other hand, her feet still pushing out the rhythms together with a teeming mass of undulating bodies. The grey snake wavered only a moment, then climbed in coil to her other arm, moving upwards on it towards her outstretched fingers.

She added her own keening voice to the hissing, sighing, purring, pounding, screeching, slickly swishing, rattling cacophony that surrounded her. The sound rose to a crescendo. Up and up it went until suddenly and without warning it broke off. All things froze into stone. And then she heard it. With the grey snake mounted high on her upraised hand she heard the sound from the top of the world: one clear and unadulterated tone, one single voice, one single instrument – she could not tell its source. She heard it in her bowels and in her brain and as it sounded she stood transfixed, the grey snake risen inches above her lifted arm, it, too, immobilised and hearing.

Clana on tiptoe and stretched to her topmost reach could not move. She had never touched such painful solitude. It held her rigid at the acme of a mighty intake of breath; it halted her blood; it stiffened her flesh; it impaled her on air and poured itself into the marrow of her bones. The note lasted forever. It lasted until the hearing itself was a silence.

The torrents came then, torrents of rain, washing over her from above in streams, pushing her arm down, her body down until she lay entwined with a thousand multicoloured, multiformed bodies all exhausted, all drained of any motion, all drenched by the rivers washing over them. She dared not move. She could not move. They lay there a long time.

She found her breath only much later. She opened her eyes to see the sun a little higher in the sky and her snake friends all fled. She had trouble remembering where she was. She felt the hole below her. She had rolled over onto it. Slowly she pushed herself to her knees. Her head swam. She was drained. She had not learned to protect herself yet from the exhaustion of such experiences. She could not stand. Breathing deeply and deliberately she revived herself. After a bit she was able to stand and look at the hole.

'We never really got to meet, hole. Maybe some other day.' Bending over, she stroked the sides with both hands and tried to replace around the edges some of the dirt she had scooped from it. Finally she left it loosely covered with leaves and branches. 'I never got to make my promise to the snakes,' she thought. But no matter. She had visited with them in a way that neither she nor the snakes would forget. Wiping her hands on her short pants she broke through the briers to the path and headed back to the ensconcement.

Sisterblood

Ono knew what Cassandra needed: packs of bloodearth. The mud was handy right from the stream, but where was she to get the blood? There was plenty of Cassandra's around but a sister's blood was needed. Ono had not seen any of her own for several years now and it was almost three days back to the Kochlias to the flow vessels. She looked over at Cassandra. Seventy pounds at least, she estimated, even if the dog could sustain a lightself for the journey. She soothed the long white hair. It was wet with the water she had used to clean the limp paws. Wet, as well, with Cassandra's sweat. She mindstretched gently to the hurt animal.

'How did you get two paws in it, Cassandra? How two?' She did not really expect an answer. She got none. Cassandra whimpered but declined to pant for Ono. Even with washed wounds and with warm care, pain was still her overwhelming reality. Her two throbbing front legs lay outstretched on Ono's shirt, both clearly fractured, both exposing raw tissue, both still bleeding. Cassandra's body was enfolded by Ono's heavy jacket. Ono did not press for an answer. She was simply grateful that the hound was eased now, lying quieter.

The hill woman was still shaken from the experience of finding the dog: there she was in the underbrush frantically pulling on the steel-jawed trap, hysterically chewing the flesh of her own front legs in order to free herself. Her howls should have brought every fringe farmer from beyond the mountains straight into the hills.

More than an hour ago Ono had been on watch in an ancient outland blind. Her spanner had picked up pain, a pain different from the forest's cycle of living and dying. This was an ugly pain. Almost immediately she had heard the cries as well. A hastily awakened Egathese had taken the watch without question so Ono could set out at a hard run to Cassandra. It had been all she could do to hold and calm the dog. Then with sticks and rocks she had pried the trap open to release her. What kind of mind, she wondered, could have designed such an instrument of torture? She looked over at the trap. It lay now at the other end of a wake cut through the leaves and brush. She had made that when she dragged Cassandra to the water. In its closed state the device looked serene, hardly worthy of the muscle and strain she had exerted to shake Cassandra free. How long it had been hidden there waiting for some prey, no one could tell. It did not seem rusted, but she knew it to be a hideous relic of another time. She would take it back to the Kochlias. It must be kept for bitter rememberings.

She turned again to the dog. With all of her conscious effort she scooped up ice blue coolness from the river air and packed it close around the panting body, particularly around the bleeding paws. 'I need help,' she thought. Satisfied that for the moment she could do no more, she extended to Egathese. She had to wait. The older woman was attending elsewhere. Ono frowned. She did not want to use an insisting call. Perhaps others in the Dangerland had heard Cassandra. She threw wide her own spanners, fan-fashion, in all directions. She found nothing unusual. She tried Egathese again, whispering the name softly as she cast out towards the distant blind.

'Egathese.'

'I'm here, Ono,' Egathese sent back. 'No trouble. All well. I was telling Rowena and Sue at the western post what happened. It's Cassandra, isn't it, that crazy dog?' Ono remembered Egathese's carjer, one of those personal bands of prejudice where hard things had to be worked out or at least understood. One of Egathese's carjers was her antipathy to dogs. Ono slipped into a mantle of tolerance, though underneath she wondered if Egathese were not all carjery, so many people and things did she dislike, so grumpy was she always. 'And I guess all that is my own carjery,' Ono thought to herself.

'Right.' Egathese had over-received her. 'Better deflect next time when you're open if you don't want me to know all your niggardly thoughts.'

Ono was suddenly flushed with anger. Without even knowing she did it, she told Egathese that she was a crotchety old woman, a bitch – apologies to Cassandra – and that it was a wonder anyone had ever loved her; that, as a matter of fact, she seriously doubted if anyone ever had. Egathese's laugh lifted up even more anger within her. Quickly she shaded from the old woman and came back to her hardself. She was furious. She sprang to her feet and tromped fitfully back and forth by Cassandra. She could not separate her anxiety over the dog from her rage at Egathese. Her stomach was in an uproar, tumbling up and down in a vacant torso. She picked up stones, hurled them into the creek, each with a burst of her own rough voice. She dropped hard to her knees and knelt by the water, slapping with both hands, splashing huge drops over herself and over a puzzled and pained white wolfhound. It had been a long time since she had felt so reckless, so out of phase and wasteful of her self-forces. She rose with a stomp that pushed a square metre of bank dirt into the stream.

'Take it easy,' she told herself. 'It's more than just Egathese. Have to come back to all this again.' She made herself breathe. With her eyes closed she let her extended arms describe opposing circles in the air before her. The anger began to subside until she was not quite at home but at least on more familiar territory.

'Sorry, Cassandra,' she shortstretched. 'So sorry. I really separated. Not nice to do to a hurt friend.' This time Cassandra responded with a love glow. Ono tased it loud and clear as it bounced from the dog's long nose over the path to her own shoulder. She captured it with a tilt of her head and nuzzled it soft and warm just below her ear. For the first time she felt real hope for Cassandra's recovery, real sorrow for her own unusual actions just now. They must have frightened the dog terribly. She sat down by the bundle of pain, then stretched out to her full length.

'We have to get you mended, Cassandra, or back to the ensconcement. Or both.' She was compelled from somewhere to close her eyes. As she did so, she was aware of her own hands and arms throbbing in rhythm with the dog's. Instinctively she licked her own wrist, imitating even as she did so the limp tentative little strokes of the tongue that Cassandra was applying to her paws. Their tongues were too harsh. Their wounds too tender. They gave up and lay back.

She must reach Egathese. Resolutely, with a sense-of-responsibility-for-mutual-concerns, which she assumed the older woman shared, Ono tapped outward. No answer. Another enfoldment. Still no answer. Fear passed briefly through her bones. Perhaps she had been unguarded too long and some traveller had got through. Perhaps Egathese was engaged in dealing with that. She tried once more. Still no opening. She knew her field was intersecting Egathese's. Was the old lady deliberately closing? Something stirred below her spleen. With a sigh, she slipped into a familiar practicing – familiar because during this last week in the outland with Egathese she had worked hard to understand the other woman, to bring herself to a listening place.

Now she called up again all that she knew of Egathese, everything from her domineering orders issued over the food tendings and her refusals to join evening ministrations to her proud insistence upon washing her own hair: the thin body quivering over the far-below tubs as she perilously bent her head into the falling rinse water; her failure to rub fast enough; her sheepish and exhausted request, at last, for someone to help her; Ono's own warm tears as she watched girl-child Clana mount the stool, kiss the cranky old cheek, and rinse the thin grey hair. Ono called it all back, called back much more. Then she wrapped Egathese in the softest of pale yellows and oranges, breathed on her the pinkest of warm carings, and tried again to rouse the woman with the name.

'Egathese.'

'Stop it,' flooded back to her. 'You're making me sick with that sticky mollycoddling. I don't want it, Ono. Can you understand that? Talk with me straight and clear. You are a hard woman yourself and not so young either. You do not need those sweet smellings any more than I do. I will move with you anytime you say and with any women you can name as fair-sisters for us. But stop pushing that mire of sweetness around me.'

Ono was not surprised. She had got this response before, and had even sat with Egathese once in sister-search. It was true. The old woman didn't respond to anything but stiff straightness. For her, meanings lay always in the line or maybe in the mass, but never in their interplay. Even her mindstretches seemed sometimes to probe rather than to enfold. Ono answered with seriousness.

'I ask then for sister-search, Egathese, when we go back to the ensconcement. You are carjerous for me.'

'Done.' The extensions were clear now, direct and efficient. 'How is the dog?'

'She's close to fallaway I think, though her spirits are good.' Ono held Cassandra as she extended to Egathese. 'She plunged, apparently, into an old animal trap and both front feet are mangled.'

'Both feet?'

Ono ignored the implied ridicule. 'Yes. She needs hardcure, packing in a sister's blood, and very soon, since she's losing much of her own. Pressure bandages are not working. I cannot carry her, I do not have the art of toting, and I do not know where to get sisterblood. What should I do, Egathese?'

'The bones are broken?'

'One forearm is shattered utterly so that whole pieces are missing. She may lose it above the joint. The other is small bones snapped clean below the bend. I have tried to set them. It's hard.' Her own hands burned again as she explained to Egathese. She moved deeper and deeper into them, watching them as they held the frightened hound, watching them burst open and spill themselves upon the silky hair, watching them hang crumpled and limp, watching them . . .

'Ono!'

She pulled away from the hands back to the exchange. 'I dropped away. I'm here.'

'Clearly,' said Egathese. 'You're by water?'

'Yes.'

'Are there fish leaves about?'

'I will pan for you.' Ono closed her eyes and dropped contact, moving to her hardself. When she looked again her seeing was for Egathese's reception as well. And there was more than seeing: there was understanding below what was seen. A long time on and under the injured dog. Slowly to the trap. Then the creek, the mud, the leaves, the sheltering trees, the patches of sky above the forest.

When Egathese signalled for recontact Ono resumed mindstretch.

'She does need hardcure,' Egathese verified. 'A knife?'

'No,' sent Ono. She felt something very close to disgust from Egathese. She resolved to ignore it for now.

'Can you mind-cut?' asked the older woman.

'My own flesh?'

'Is there someone else nearby to cut?' Egathese's impatience ridged the sarcasm. 'Of course your own flesh.'

'I don't think I can. I never have.'

'Where have you ever bled?'

'Nowhere that I can remember except . . .'

'Too long. Cannot manufacture eggs. Where else?'

'With my teeth . . .'

'How many?'

'Quite a few – the third molars were particularly gory.'

'That will have to do. Once open we can draw all we need. Prepare the leaves and the earth and then move to a loose position over them. Backself to the losing of the teeth. I will stay in stretch with you to aid the surge once you are open.'

'Will it work?'

'It may not. Is that a reason not to try?'

Ono clamped her lips between her teeth as if to close off her meaning there. Egathese overrode the rising anger. 'Prepare', she sent. 'I will have others cover the watch while we work. Touch me when you are ready.'

The breaking of the contact jarred Ono into her hardself. She was amazed to find herself crying. 'She's brittle and acrid, Cassandra,' she said aloud. More tears welled up. With a determined effort she stopped her breathing for a moment and paid very close attention to those tears. With a wrapping gesture of her hands she packaged them in a moss-covered seashell. 'Later,' she told them and set them aside on a shelf of afternoon light. Then she put her forehead to the dog's neck and tuned into the awareness there. On inhaling, pains, sharp pains, like millions of nerve endings dragging over rough salty floors; on exhaling, grinding numbness. Pain again, and again numbness, this time accompanied by an increasing weakness. She had to hurry.

She re-wove the cradle around the dog, this time in maroons and pinks, pulling in as well an occasional touch of mint. Cassandra liked it. Her mind smiled its thanks. Ono pushed the leaves from the ground to make a careful circle just by Cassandra's head. Moving behind the bulky figure she lay down in a curl around the dog, her head just above the cleared space. 'I can't mix here,' she sent to the dog. Cassandra responded only with a pale assent. Ono crawled to the other side of the circle on her knees. 'Here is better.'

With sure knowledge now she moved to the bank, worked loose the mud with strong fingers. It was dark and viscous, with very little sand in it. She scooped up a double handful and set it in her cleared circle. Another handful to the same place. A check into the dog. The life seemed to be draining from her. Ono hoped it was shock that made that seem so. 'Soon, Cassandra,' she sent. Another pale response.

She worked quickly with the mud, squeezing it into consistency with itself and ultimately forcing her fist into its mass to make a crude thick cup for the first catchings. She knelt on the brush by the circle and sat back on her inturned feet. With a residual enfolding pattern she enveloped Cassandra. She was about to extend to Egathese when another voice touched the edge of her mind. 'Leaves,' it said. 'Leaves!' Ono repeated aloud. Without breaking her posture she gathered and sorted about her neat stacks of the long spatulate leaves – only the yellow ones, for the green ones were too fresh and mostly still on the trees; the brown ones too brittle, too far along in the return to the earth. Only middle leaves could be used.

'Thank you,' she sent to the tall tree behind her. 'I was forgetting.'

'Again if you need me,' the tree replied.

Now she did extend to Egathese. 'We're ready.'

'Good. I will only ride with you while you backself. When you need my tension, indicate.'

Ono sent assent, an unnamed reluctance still gnawing her inner fringes. She was already breathing with Cassandra and her back channels were opening. She touched again what it was like to have in her mouth those old healthy but crooked molars. Suddenly she felt it all to be off kilter. 'Wait!' she sent to Egathese. She pulled up short. 'Not the teeth. Not the teeth.' The teeth obligingly disappeared. 'The nosebleed.'

'You had nosebleeds?'

41

'Often. As a child. At the drop of a hat, they used to say. I lost a lot, it seemed, every time.'

'Fine. Much thinner vessels and if you have a backvivid . . .'

'Oh, I do.'

'Then begin.'

Now she knew she could do it. She sat directly on the ground, her legs turned out to her sides. The shapes and movement were fitting together better this time, connecting at the proper joints and rotating or swinging as if they belonged there. She began her journey back to her childself. Even before she closed her eyes or caught the pattern of Cassandra's breathing, she was in the country schoolroom surrounded by children – some curious, some jeering, all of them watching the blood spill over her hand and onto her cotton dress.

'Her nose is bleeding again.'

'Just stand back and give her room.'

'It's all right. It doesn't hurt her.'

'My dress,' she thought, as usual more embarrassed than in physical pain. 'Again my dress. We'll have to wash it again. Try to let it go on the floor where it can be wiped up. Lean out.' The drops were rolling now over the desktop's carvings and scratchings, over the dirty words and down the hearts and flowers, over the smoothed corner of the wood, dripping now to the old oily floor, standing up there in round globules, round balls refusing to be absorbed into the grime and dirt, spheres of red unable to soak into the wood. Her blood. Her drops of life, bright and thick. How was it that this happened so often? An extra spurt now, an actual clot that hung from her nostril by a long ropy strand.

The teacher's voice: 'Ann, get her some wet toilet paper.'

The wet paper, always the wet cloth or paper. Always slapped onto the back of her neck. Always to stop the bleeding. 'It's my blood,' she thought. 'Why can't I bleed it? Why can't I do what I want with it?' The clinging clot released itself and fell to the floor. Aloud she said, 'No. It's all right. Don't bring any paper. Let it flow.'

At that, the dams seemed to break. A sheet of whining pain shot just behind her eyes. Twigs seemed to snap inside her sinuses. Pushing down came the rivers, hardly drops any longer but more like steady torrents from both nostrils. She leaned over further, her hands massaging the seat of her desk as she moved. Now between her legs she could see the drops drawing together on the floor, seeking each other. Blood kin. They made a big puddle. She kept adding to it, pouring down more blood. It grew up and up but never out. It grew until it burst its tension and broke into a wide rivulet that travelled beneath her desk and towards the window, the same path marbles and pencils took when they were dropped. She could not stop it now; nor did she wish to. She heard in the background her teacher's frantic voice. She did not care. 'I shall drown them all in my blood,' she thought, 'sweep them into an ocean of red. I shall bleed blood until *I* decide to stop!' She was feeling drunk with the power of those torrents.

It was a shock to hear Egathese from another world: 'Enough, Ono.'

Her head whirled. She leaned over and reached out her hands to the floor. She knew that for some reason she was to catch the blood and hold it. Then the floor was not the floor at all and its oily smell was flavours of dirt and forest leaves. Ono was bending over her hands, gradually aware that her body was wildly decorated with rivers of red. Her hands before her seemed not to be her hands at all, but disconnected entities mixing and kneading cool wet dirt into warm wet blood. She watched with fascination as those hands squeezed and moulded together, then rolled the mud over the diminishing trickles that cascaded down her breasts. The consistency was just right.

'You've got a sister's blood, Cassandra,' Egathese was sending to the dog. Ono came back then, completely to her hardself. Had she been mistaken or had Egathese spoken kindly to Cassandra? All an illusion, she decided. She breathed for the first time through her nose.

'Thank you, Egathese,' she sent. 'I can make the packs now.'

'Of course,' was Egathese's sign off. Ono made herself dismiss the curtness of that. She turned back to Cassandra with the mud. The rest was easy: moulding the thin tacky bloodearth around each limp limb until a cast was formed; laying on long leaves and then another covering of mud; more leaves, more mud. Cassandra had whimpered when her legs were moved but Ono could feel for herself the heat generating inside the packs. There was healing there. Cassandra seemed already drugged by the absence of pain.

She thrust her tongue towards Ono. Ono squatted by her and licked the black nose. Then both tongues met with loving taps. Cassandra rested her head. Ono stood beside her a moment, deciding what to do. With water the dog could lie there a day or two while help came from the ensconcement. That was probably best.

Her eyes fell upon the trap. She stepped to it and with effort picked it up. It was attached by a chain to the root of a tree. Ono forced open the metal snap and pulled the trap free. The tree sang out a strong 'Thank you!' It had not liked its role in the drama.

'Again if you need me,' Ono sent to it. She dragged the trap back to the sleeping Cassandra. If only Egathese would help her maybe they could . . .

'Ono.'

'Here, Egathese.'

'Blase can tote Cassandra easily. She has wrapped her mind around the heavy end of a redwood, it is said, and with a sister toted a country mile with no effort. She is on her way to you from the south-east border. You can hold her post for her with Earlyna. If you start now and go directly you should meet Blase's spanners within an hour. She will be reaching to meet you.'

Ono was astonished. What a complex system of relays Egathese must have engineered in order to arrange all that! She had taken so much trouble! Before she could say it in mindstretch Egathese was chanting:

Your trouble,
My trouble.
Our ease.

Ono sent back, still amazed:

My trouble,
Your trouble,
Our ease.

She stretched again: 'Thank you, Egathese.' There was no answer. Turning to Cassandra, Ono draped a pale green over her and decided not to wake her to redeem either jacket or shirt. She turned her blood-smeared body towards the approaching sister and

44

shouldered the trap. Then, from out of the air she picked up the seashell containing the tears, and set out on her journey towards Blase in the southeast.

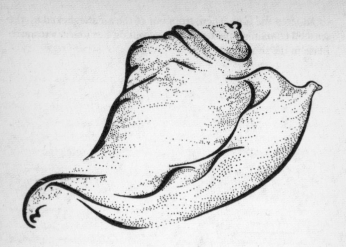

The Deep Cella

Fora had to feel her way to the next bend in the corridor. She had come in by a seldom used passage and had forgotten that the glow lobes were not open along these eastern shafts.

'It's okay, Lady,' she sent to the frantic claws on her shoulders. 'That's light ahead.' She felt only a little lift in the sparrow's tension. 'Listen!' Fora said. The sound of voices. Was it singing? Her relief coincided with the knowledge that her peripheral belt was being spanned and gently surrounded.

'Fora,' she responded, 'and my companion, the flyer, Lady. We are looking for the deep cella.'

'Li.'

'And Manaje.' Two different drifts. One continued, 'You're going towards it. Just keep on the down and you can't miss it. "All roads lead to the mother." '

Fora heard them so close that she felt overburdened. She shaded quickly and settled to her hardself, the more courteous mode of greeting, anyway. She spoke aloud.

'Thank you.' She reached the sharp bend to the right and saw at the same time two women with a large metal box between them. They had settled the box to the side and now were moving from the broad path towards her.

'You're visiting?' said Manaje, also aloud, and with an eyestroke for the still panicked Lady.

'Yes. We're from the Eastern Ensconcement.' It was polite now and faster to resume mindstretch. 'I'm representing a Pleiades. We're planning implantment and want to have it in the deep cella. Four of us who have seen implantments here are urging the rest of us towards this place.'

Both Manaje and Li smiled. 'Are you to be the flesh mother?' Manaje asked.

'Yes. I'm already so full of mugwort and thyme that I feel like I could do it right now all by myself.' All the women laughed. Fora saw something akin to disgust in Li's headshake. She pushed a short question around the look.

Li responded. 'It's children. They're not my favourite people. I need lots of distance from them still. I'm glad you're willing to take one on and I'll do my turns at the learnings but don't even hint that I be a sevensister much less a bearer . . .' In an instant Li's thoughts began to gather momentum. They proliferated and spun wider as if to dare the walls of the passageway to hold them back. A torrent of impatience and resentment began to pour out of Li. Fora felt Lady flutter at the unexpected energy and at the same moment she saw a soothing blue-white ice pushing out from Manaje to surround Li's tirade. Li's images gradually subsided and though she couldn't name what had happened Fora found herself joining the relieved laughter of the two women.

'There you go again,' Manaje's soothing blues were saying. 'It's a real carjer spot for Li,' she sent now to Fora.

Li nodded beneath some embarrassment. 'Anyway, I do honour your desire and that of your six sisters. I own my carjery. Actually the deep cella is a wondrous place, ancient and sober. I wish you well in the implantment, in the egg-merging, and in the bearing of new life.' Fora was touched. She swept a swirl of gratitude and acceptance towards the other woman, then brought from all sides a gentle closing of the matter, respectfully drawing shut the veil of temporary completion. She reached for the threads of another fabric. 'Do you live here in the Kochlias?' she sent.

'Only for a while yet. We're training.' This from Li, reoriented now and apparently aware of Fora's discomfort in the underground caverns. 'It isn't so bad. Your hardself misses the sun and the green sometimes.'

Manaje added, 'But if you're a good walker you can go up every day.'

Li looked at Manaje and back to Fora. 'And if you're a windrider you must go up every day, at least if you're addicted to it.' Manaje took the tease with a smile. Fora smiled with them both.

As she began to turn away, Fora shook her head. 'I would have to see the sky.'

'So would I, so would I!' All of the women caught this grim echo from Lady. Fora sent the bird a soft curl of care.

'If we have the implantment here I'll hope for your joining the touch,' Fora sent. She urged the wish with particular meaning towards Li.

'I would be glad,' both women sent back together. 'May you come again, Fora.'

'May you come again,' she responded.

'And again,' they said.

'And again,' she ended.

The two women looked at each other and then at the box they had left at the side of the broad passage. Fora gasped. The box rose a few inches off the ground and, guided by the two carriers, floated slowly up the passage between them. Very seldom had she witnessed toting. She was constantly amazed at the smoothness with which it always seemed to happen. Her own efforts to tote had so far resulted in a few shivering leaves and one broken plate. 'Practice,' she sent Lady. 'I need practice.' She cupped her hand beneath her shoulder to help Lady down to a ride on her fist. Lady refused.

'You don't have to come with me,' Fora said. 'I'll take you back to the broad sky.'

'If you keep me with you I want to stay. It's why I came, after all.' Lady seemed to settle on her shoulder peak.

'I will keep you with me,' assured Fora.

'As I do you with me, of course,' sent Lady.

They went faster down the path. It was well lighted now and as she walked Fora could look about her; beside her to the grey-brown rocks, below her to the wide earth-hardened path, above her to the occasional forests of stone columns that grew upside down on the ceiling; the more common smooth rounded places above her were also cold and wet looking. Every few yards a glow lobe hung motionless in mid-air, giving off a soft pink aura. She wondered again about the sustaining of them. 'I'll have to ask Krueva,' she thought.

'Krueva knows no more than you know,' said Lady.

Fora laughed. 'Oh, I know. We all know it all, Crazy Lady Sparrow. But Krueva would help me to release it.'

Lady managed a sparrow's equivalent of a grunt. They seemed to be pulled now, down the hard-packed dirt path beneath Fora's feet. Now and then sounds of work or laughter – perhaps sharp words – came from the passages that wound off to the right. Still the wide path rode steadily downwards, downwards and always slightly to the left, towards the heart, towards the centre.

Fora imagined herself marching in the cavalcade of her own sowing and implantment. A long line of women surging down the path, their arms and voices linked to each other, carrying with them the oils and the sweet scents, the fire, the water, the necessary green living plants. Beside them and before them, whatever small animals wished to come, whoever could make the long trek. She marched with their steps, beginning now to see specific sisters: Alaka of the long bones, her tall head weaving inches above the others; Ursula, her light skin and rare yellow hair, her broad thighs walking so strong now and hardly seeming able to make so soft a lap; Diana, the wide dark eyes, the deft body, the coarse wild black hair of her head mirrored in softer down over her entire body; big and steady Ijeme, small breasts and freckled, setting with uncanny lilting grace the easy rhythmic pace of those beside her; young Jacqua, mad Clea, girl children Clana and Gynia, Troja carrying Bru, Krueva the Enraged, Elsa – if she got back from her rotation in time; Germana, Pelagine, Rougee, and Olena whose dark skins had seen more winters than the rest; Artilidea, old and wise; Egathese, not only old but cranky; scores more, rank on rank, body on body, voice on voice. Entwined by her own arms were Tolatilita and Phtha, two of her seven sisters, and behind them

Yva marched, carrying in her cradled hand the precious egg-laden liquid. Yva of all the seven sisters was past egg-producing and as a reminder of her own part in the motherhood she had balanced on top of the small vial of living ova a large and wildly painted chicken's egg, aglow with her own name in gothic lettering. Yva was flanked by Lyssa and Rhoda and following them came the final Pleiad, Juda. Fora reached out in her mind to touch each one. Brightly they all swung down the curling passage, to the centre of the Kochlias, to the narrow low place at the bottom of the world.

Fora was lost in the splendid drama that passed before her eyes, that moved within her body. Her feet patted the path in their own free downward movement. Fora let them lead. She visited entirely within herself, inside, oblivious even to Lady. Lady, for her part, was pendulant, swinging back and forth from Fora's mind to the tunnel, sometimes joining in the joyous march, sometimes retreating to the hardself of Fora's shoulder. She gave her wings a tiny flex and tried to soothe her claustrophobia. 'Caution,' she thought to herself. 'You can't even get aloft in this dungeon.' She was cold. Even despite the glow of the lobes she felt darkness and tightness crowding in upon her. 'How can they stay here?' she mused. 'Their skins will get pale like white worms for lack of light. Their eyes will grow useless, their lungs will cave in.' She fluttered her wings to shake off the ugliness of the thoughts.

Fora stopped walking. Jerking her head and focusing her eyes, she left her softself inside and attended to Lady. 'Are you safe?' she shortstretched.

'Safe but cold,' sent back Lady. 'There seems no warmth in these rocks. Just tell me, Fora, why in the name of all who have lived do you want your implantment here? It would freeze the most fertile of wombs.' Lady had no sooner formed that meaning into message than she suddenly realised her missaying. The very point: a womb to enrich a womb. And it would get warmer. All the stories promised that.

Fora laughed. She moved forward again, this time gently holding Lady in her hands. The path seemed to turn less gradually now, to turn sharply to the left. Fora took notice of the small lime pillars that lined parts of the passage. They stood in tiny alcoves, as if planned, breaking the steady monotony of the tunnel. She passed her hand over her brow, surprised to find it wet.

'You should be warm soon,' she sent to Lady. Even beneath her light shirt and trousers she could feel the heat. Lady fluttered back to her shoulder.

'Are we almost there?' she sent.

'I don't know. They say it is warmer towards the centre . . .'

'You have a good bit to go yet.' The voice enfolded her. Fora opened in response. 'Li and Manaje again,' the enfoldment continued. 'We told today's keepers of your visit and they encouraged us to join you. Not hospitable, they said, to let you see the deep cella alone. We're coming behind you.'

Fora hesitated before sending her thanks.

'You want to be alone?' Li had picked up the pause.

'No,' Fora said. 'I thought for a moment I did but that was a passing wish.'

'We'll show you the cella and leave you to it alone when you say so.' Manaje this time.

'Come with me. We'll see. I'm getting hotter. Is it all right to take off my clothes?'

'Most do by the time they are as far down as you.'

Fora stopped by a small jutting edge to untie her boots and strip to her sweating skin. The heat seemed to seep through the path itself. 'Will I need shoes?'

'No,' Manaje sent. 'It seems hot at first. It never gets unbearable.'

Lady had taken flight. She was convinced now that she would not freeze. She fluttered about the passage desperately trying to discover the balance between her natural speed and the limitations of the corridor. Finally she flew straight ahead down the path, the only semi-freedom she could find, and was lost to Fora around the curve of the passage.

Fora left her clothes on the ledge and threw her long hair back behind her ears. It struck the middle of her back. Still walking towards the disappearing Lady, she deftly parted her hair and wound it into two knots on the back of her neck. She spanned the way before her, found Lady's channel and said, 'Wait for me.'

Being in Lady's self was always different. Now as she walked she cast herself wholly into the fluttering creature. She felt the small bird's residual fear of this closed-in space. Her own mind, bounding with each flap of the wings, felt obscenely imprisoned and sought only the increasingly warm air down and left, down and left, down, down, down.

Suddenly she was assaulted by space. The walls fell back and she was sailing out into a broad free area; then she lost contact with Lady entirely. She stopped in her tracks and held her head. She was trying to reset her spanners when Lady sent to her, 'It is a wonder! Almost like being up with the broad sky again. Hurry!'

Fora sensed Lady's excitement. She walked faster. The ground, she noticed, was more often bare rock now and less often dirt. Sending back to the women following her she said, 'Lady has reached the cella, I think.'

'Yes. You will too after a bit.'

Then for the second time that afternoon, Fora caught her breath. She had just emerged in her hardself, into the central chamber. The left wall of her corridor had dwindled away until now she stood stock still at the edge of a wide expanse, some sixty metres in diameter. To her right there was still the damp stone wall. Below her she could see the wide path again as it wound around the circle and down, growing narrower, around and down again, and again, each time in successively smaller orbits.

She tried to make out the usual tunnels leading off from the passage, off to the right and back into the earth. But there seemed to be none now. Only one way in from this point on. Only one way in and one way out. Unless, like Lady, she could fly.

Fora looked up. There was Lady, fluttering back and forth among low glow lobes, now beating her tiny wings up and up into an ever-widening, ever-darkening shaft. Fora strained in vain to see the top. She could not be sure that the blackness of those upper regions was a ceiling of any sort; rather, the funnel seemed to move up and outward into a forever shadow. She looked again at the spiralling path below her; it wound methodically into a circular area, to an ending, at last, of the downward path. She could not see it clearly, and it seemed hundreds of feet down, but she knew this was the deep chamber she had seen the stories about. For a moment an unnamed garment sheathed her mind, she became frightened. Li and Manaje read her fear.

'You won't fall. And there is nothing else to fear,' Manaje sent. 'But wait for us if you will. We're very near. In fact,' said a distant voice aloud, 'we're right behind you!'

Laughter and running footsteps struck her ear. She moved back seven or eight steps from the edge of the path to the wall. Even the wall was warm here. The thumping of feet became louder and the laughter more exhilarated. It came in bursts. Fora wondered briefly if it might not constitute some irreverence here at the centre of the Kochlias. Then she reflected on her thought. An obsolete response, that!

The reminder eased her physical tension and she was able to turn towards the upward tunnel, towards the merriment. Two running naked bodies were staggering down the path. Manaje was heading straight for her, both her hands awkwardly occupied as she ran in the steadying of her large breasts. She was followed by Li, limping silently but still laughing through a scowling face.

'Unfair!' she was shouting. 'Unfair because I tripped!'

Manaje reached out towards Fora, now flattened against the stone wall. 'Touch flesh, touch home!' she shrieked, swinging her arms around Fora's waist and dropping to kneel behind her. She panted and laughed as she sat flat out on the stony ground. Li slid into the space beside her, weak with laughter. They rocked back and forth catching their breaths only for a moment before Fora too sank down beside them, her own laughter involuntarily joining theirs.

'I'm out of shape,' shortstretched Manaje, wiping her wet neck, still chuckling.

'Maybe you're just behind in your windriding,' Li grinned. She looked at Fora and said aloud, 'With your hair that way you look like my learntogether. Like Yjanta. I've not seen her for years.'

'That's warm,' Fora said, 'your saying that.'

'Yes,' said Li. Then in mindstretch, 'Warm for sure! Let's go on. I haven't been this hot since the last time I was here and that's been well over a year. You do want to go to the centre, don't you?'

'Certainly,' said Fora. She pushed herself up and helped Manaje to her feet. Li was already leading them both at a sound pace down the path.

'Where's your sparrow friend?' Manaje was saying. To her delight, Lady swooped out of the dimness to circle her head. 'Rest on me, Lady,' Manaje sent. 'I'm a windrider, too.' As Fora reached into the bird's self she could read nothing but sheer joy. The sparrow seemed content to perch on Manaje's finger as the three of them wound deeper and deeper into the tunnel.

Fora stood finally in the small circle at the very end of the way. 'So this is it,' she said. 'The tight end of the conch.' Where she stood was no more than four metres in diameter, about twelve feet, she estimated. Just room enough for her and her sister-mothers to stretch out full length on the hard stone for the implantment rite.

She looked to where the way up began its incline, turned to see Li and Manaje sitting a bit above her on the path-turned-seat. She followed the widening circle of ledges around and up, around and up, until she could see it disappear into the completely covered passageway. 'The tight end of the conch,' she said again. 'The cella.' Her feet felt very hot, but not uncomfortably so.

They were all very quiet now, even Lady, perched on Manaje's shoulder. There seemed to be no sound and yet a presence. What an amazing thing it was, this room, this theatre, this hollowed-out-of-the-earth-hidden-in-the-earth-gracefully-winding-movement from far up into the heart of the mother. Fora began to wonder about the air. It was thick and hot.

'Can I see and feel the earthbreath? When they showed me the cella . . .'

'Surely.' Manaje and Li jumped down together. They knelt just beneath their seat and flanked an iron ring that was fastened into the upright greenish stone, the first artifact Fora had seen except for the glow lobes.

'How can it be so hot and so damp at the same time?' she was thinking. 'And is that the breathchannel?'

'Yes,' sent Li. 'We may have to tote the stone out. We don't usually open it except for ministrations or an implantment. Ready?' This last to Manaje. Manaje nodded and they both stood up. 'Take hold of the ring, Fora, and begin pulling,' she finished.

Fora sat straddling the ring and braced her feet against the seat. At first nothing budged. She knew better than to strain with all her might. Instead she concentrated upon the iron ring – placing upon it a steady pull, imagining its movement towards her. She could feel the attention of her two sisters, even of Lady, it seemed, on the rock. Something gave. The stone seemed to break free. To her astonishment Fora found herself dragging a metre-square rock from a black gaping hole. Before she could clear it, she was swept backwards by a gust of heat, almost painful in its intensity. It welled up from the earth's bowels, from far below her. It shot forward in a burst of freedom. Fora fell.

As she went down into near fallaway, her last memory was that of the hot flat stone on her wet shoulders. The room swirled. She was thrust into another time. The cella above her was crowded with women, sitting on the upward spiralling path, naked and gleaming bodies moving rhythmically to and fro to the sound of their own humming; to and fro then around and up, around and up, a never ending motion, never ceasing steady vocal rumbling, rising and keening with every breath that she swept into and out of her lungs.

She stepped aside and saw herself lying upon the floor of stone. Hot bodies surrounded her: Juda's head to her left at waist level, Tolatilita's to her right; Yva and Rhoda prone on each of her legs; Lyssa and Phtha hovering over her own head. They wiped her face, her body, with sharp-smelling leaves. The incantations swirled around and over her, words circling her head, her body, words sliding over her skin, drooping around her ribs and over her brow, under her fingernails and through the curling forest of the mountain slopes and plains; words leapt and pounded in the sockets of her spine; words bent and broke in the crevice of her brain. A thousand hands now moved on her flesh, a thousand eyes now peered at the window of her soul, a thousand lips caressed at the door of her deepest self.

'Fora!'

She swam upwards.

'Fora! Come up!' The voice was harsh.

She pulled her softself back to centre. She felt a flutter near her cheek. Lady was there. She opened her eyes.

'You were in fallaway?' It was Manaje's voice. The voice was anxious.

'No. But I fell into forwardsense. It's never been so vivid.'

'Or so dangerous,' Li added. 'Was it the earthbreath? What took you down? And so suddenly?'

'I don't know,' breathed Fora. Lady's tiny feet fidgeted on her flattened breast. She soothed the frightened bird with her finger, noting at the same time that the earthbreath had been duly repressed again. The stone was back in its place. She sat up. 'Thank you for your care. Without it . . .'

'You almost slipped away,' Manaje said.

Fora smiled. Lady fluttered about now, sometimes running, sometimes flying, always with the sharp movements of agitation. Fora stretched out her hand. The bird landed on it. 'We may not be able to have the implantment here after all,' she said. 'It's too deep a place for me, I think. The hilltop by the old mounds may do as well, unless the other mothers can convince me to return here.'

The two women nodded.

'But you must join me for it now. After this.'

'We'll come.' They both spoke.

Fora, breathing in long restorative cycles, stood up finally and stretched. The sweat was running from her head and shoulders, drenching her body. They stood, the three of them in a long embrace. Li pulled herself up to the first level and offered a hand to Fora. Fora took it and brought Manaje with her up the path. Lady untiringly escorted them up and out of the Kochlias.

They stood at the upper eastern caveway, now clothed again, welcoming the cool air.

'I take you with me,' said Fora.

'As I do you with me,' they answered.

She fairly ran over the rough ground that fell away from the cave's mouth. Much later, when she reached the timber line below she turned to wave. They waved back. Fora followed a wildly darting sparrow down the mountainside.

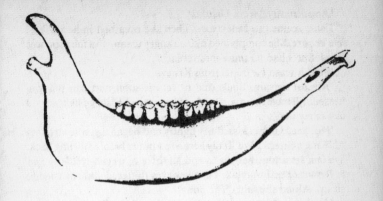

Krueva and the Pony

'We're bringing Ijeme home,' Krueva sent. 'She's not in deep fallaway or in retrosense. We don't know what is wrong. She is clearly exhausted. We may have to draw together for a gather-stretch – tomorrow after evening ministrations – and if we do, all the women must be notified. If you stretch to Evona before we return there, be particularly careful. Some have felt that she must be being watched.'

'No. She's not.' Ijeme's thought interrupted. Krueva had believed her to be totally unconscious. Ursula had picked up the thought too. Both women turned to the supine figure of Ijeme, Krueva from above where she stood at the edge of the trees, Ursula from her kneeling position as she held Ijeme's head.

Krueva outstretched again. 'I'll come again. We should be there the day after tomorrow afternoon.' She checked her monitor sweeps, found all well, and turned her attention back to Ijeme. Ursula was busy sending soothes through her body.

Krueva shortstretched. 'Ijeme. Can you talk?'

'I want to,' came back. Ijeme's sending was tense with effort. 'Evona is safe. She feared she was being watched but it was only one of their robos, a lockkeeper at her building, accidentally on her call circuit.'

'Accidentally?' from Ursula.

Ijeme seemed to fade away. Then she breathed in hard. 'Yes. We're sure. She complained like an angry tenant and the robo was fixed. She's had no more interference.'

'Sure it wasn't a trap?' from Krueva.

'Almost certain. She's due to return soon and can tell you herself. I'll have to leave now. I can't sustain. Shall I go light so you can carry me?'

'Not yet.' Ursula kissed her lightly and began a gentle stroking of Ijeme's cheeks. 'We'll stay here a few hours before starting back. We can set a together-shade and all three of us can rest.'

Ijeme seemed to relax. Then her eyes fluttered and she tried to sit up. Aloud she said, 'The pony!'

Ursula soothed her. 'We'll hold it. It will be all right.'

'It carried me well,' said Ijeme.

Ursula saw her body relax and fall into deep rest. She looked at Krueva. 'Shall I see to the pony? I think it must die.'

'I fear so, too,' sent Krueva. 'I will see to it.' She turned just in time to be struck by a strong sense of danger. Something, someone, approached. She warned Ursula with a hand-touch and then sent out spanners in all directions double-force before drawing them together towards what was clearly the threat. It came from behind them, not from the City. That at least was a comfort. 'Wild beasts I can handle,' she thought, 'even a score of them. But deliver me from one man.'

She stepped softly to the side of another tree. 'Cat,' she thought. 'Maybe coming for the pony.' She tried to smell, but in vain. She couldn't even make out the blood from the pony's wound. But that was undoubtedly what would draw a bobcat or a lynx. 'I'm going to shade with the pony,' she shortstretched to Ursula, 'and you'd best do so with Ijeme.' Ursula was already in shade.

Stealthily but quickly Krueva moved back to the edge of the open field. There lay the pony, its chest heaving. They had laid a rest upon it when they took Ijeme from its back; but now there seemed to be no rest for the throbbing body. Even without a moon Krueva could make out the deep wound on its flank, an ugly opening as long as the pony's own leg. It oozed red blood over the dingy white skin, a thick stream, seemingly endless. Ursula's temporary staunch had broken, and the little animal lay virtually in a pool of its own life force. Krueva touched the wound, and with a gasp discovered that the flesh gave way beneath her hand. It had separated from the bone and the pony's entire flank hung in place only by the skin. Krueva was struck with guilt. 'We were so busy with Ijeme,' she thought. Then again she felt the oncoming bobcat – almost heard it now with her first ears, so close it seemed. 'Hurry,' she thought.

Even as she knelt by the pony she was weaving about the two of them a wall of protection. Her breathing was fast and heavy by the time she drew herself up behind the animal. She stretched out on the ground over the low brush on her right side. She settled herself as gently as she could along the animal's backbone so that she could curl her head over the neck. She seemed to fit, to match. The rough mane was knotted and lumpy. She could not get her right arm under the pony's neck for the proper holding. Time was important, so she said, 'I will hold you better, pony. I will hold you and rock you. But in a moment. Can you breathe with me?'

There was no response from the heavy body. Krueva determined that it must be in the sleep near death. Without saying more she began to match her breathing with that of the stricken body beside her. In and out. In. And out. Up and hold. Down. Hold. Up. Hold. Down. Again she drew the curtain of protective shades about them both. Only for a moment did her hand leave the pony's neck to check the placement of her own knife. They were together now and the covering grew stronger. Even in its faintness and deep sleep the pony seemed to respond to Krueva's urgings. Together they built the dome against the cat. Together they bonded for protection against the approaching fear.

Krueva kept her eyes open. 'Where is it?' she asked herself. She had withdrawn partially from the cat's coming to concentrate on the shield and on the pony. She was still in light touch with Ursula and Ijeme, but she was having trouble holding her connections to three thought-vessels at once. Nowhere could she see the cat. Yet she knew it was near. She strained to see with her first eyes the forest's edge only a few yards away. Darkness. More darkness, it seemed, than before. Still pushing in and out with the pony, still light-holding Ursula and Ijeme, Krueva sent an enfoldment towards the cat. No contact. Had it gone? Around again.

There! She was brought up short by a hunger so intense that she physically shook. The cat was ravenous, and clearly come in search of the pony's flesh. It was in the open field now, very close. It seemed confused; its presence seemed to dart back and forth; it was trying to understand the dome of protection cast over the pony and the woman. Krueva felt the animal's frustration, its puzzlement.

'This is the tricky part,' she said to herself. 'Brave pony,' she addressed the warm heaving body beside her. 'Brave pony.' No answer. She tried with both arms to stroke the head. Still no response save the heavy pushing in and out. 'The cat can for sure hear that,' she muttered. 'Well, if not the pony then maybe the cat,' she reasoned, and gathering her courage she sent strong spanners out in the direction of the cavernous stomach.

'Bobcat!' she called. There was a connection. But this was bigger than a bobcat. The attention that flowed back into her suggested a mountain lion or at least a small cougar. 'It's not the time,' she thought, 'to wound an ego. Big cat!' she sent again. 'Hear me. Hear me.' In a wave of panic she realised that she did not remember the incantation for such an animal. She would have to do with only her strength.

'Big cat!' she said again. This time the full force of a stalking animal shook her. She grew frightened that the shade would not hold, that the cat would attack, that her sending voice would sound weak, that the cat would not hear her, that the cat would hear her. To her relief she felt Ursula's strength join with her own. 'Big cat!' they said together.

The presence halted. 'Who?' it sent. Loud and clear it asked, 'Who stops me?'

'We are the forest women, the women from the hills,' Ursula was answering. 'We have dealt you no harm and have pledged our lives to your protection save when you turn on us. Do you know us?'

'Know you well,' sent the cat. No quarter as yet. It was still hungry. Still intent. Perhaps even intent on a meal of women as well as of pony.

Krueva broke in. 'We parley with you for the pony.'

Silence.

'The animal still lives,' Krueva continued. 'We ask you to retire without its carcass.' Was that laughter from the cat? 'Our terms are these,' Krueva went on, with more boldness than she felt. 'We will talk with the pony and see to its wounds as best we can. If it is deemed good by the pony itself and by us that it return to the mother, then we will help it to go and leave the body so that in the round of life you may gain sustenance from it.' There was no answer. Krueva was brazen to add, 'It seems a healthy pony and one that no disease has infested. You would eat well of the warm flesh.'

The cat understood. 'It may not die. Unless I help it.'

'If it does not die and we make it whole, we offer this promise to you: that the first of any of our flock to choose a return to the mother will be your own. We will make the gift with due ministrations outside our ensconcement.'

There was an audible sound from what Krueva felt was a crouching cougar. Then as it seemed to understand what it risked losing, it released all its reality. '*Hunger*!!!' assailed Krueva's body, as from the brush almost upon her came a roar. She shaded within the shade, giving all her strength to the sustaining of the barrier between them.

'You cannot come closer, cat, anyway. You know that. Let me speak to the pony. It rides between life and death. Give me time.' Without waiting for an answer, Krueva passed the contact to Ursula. She felt her sister take over the channel to the hungry animal. She was safe enough to relax the shade a bit. Then she turned her strongest self to the wet warm flesh beside her. She did not have to go deep.

'I'm ready to go,' sent the pony.

Krueva tried again in vain to force her arm beneath the heavy hand. 'Carrier, we will work with your blood. We may be able to help you to life.' She tried to think of happier things, of gathering up instead of letting go. Letting go was always so hard. She tightened her arm around the body.

'No. I am ready. I've done all that was important for me to do. And I don't want to wear out my welcome.'

'In bringing Ijeme this far you gave us a great gift.'

'I have brought others before,' said the pony.

Krueva nodded. She wondered where in the City Ijeme could have come upon such an animal.

'I let her steal me,' answered the pony, 'outside the City. She was running and I called her to me. We rode well together. Until that

61

fence.' The pony moved its head to allow Krueva to place her arm under it. 'I cannot move or say more. I ask that you hold me for awhile.' It stretched its neck, fell back a bit on Krueva's arm then sent with calmer tones, 'I commend my body to my sister, the cat. May she feed well.'

Krueva was not surprised to find her own tears mixing with the sweat on the pony's neck. The laboured breathing was shorter now and louder. The big heart-pounding seemed amplified. This was the hastening of death, the hastening by the dying pony and the hastening by its companion. They lay there, the one clasped by the other, panting in unison to the final rushing of the blood. Krueva clung to the pony, sucked in the breath and released it in more and more violent bursts. She moved back and forth to the rhythm of the death-holding words. 'Easy,' she said. 'Long.'

> Easy. Long.
> It will not be so always.
> Leaning back.
> Leaning back.
> Leaning back upon the sea.
> Easy. Long.
> Easy. Long.
> She will bear you.
> She will bear you.
> Easy. Long.

The pony inhaled, then stopped at the top of its breath. Krueva held her own lungs full. Then a tremendous stretch. Back the head, down the legs, curving the spine, a long unending mighty stretch until Krueva felt she could not keep the stiffened body from bursting away from her. One last note of the heart and one last sigh of the breath going forth, going out, going down, not to return. The body relaxed. A huge shudder shook the heavy frame and then, silence. Silence and sweat. Silence and smells. Krueva still held the animal, in holding stillness, rocking and holding, rocking and holding, saying again and again the words of passing.

She tried to move her arm. It was pinned beneath a thick neck. No use. Dimly she recalled the presence of a real danger beyond. Her shade was still in place, but she had not been present for a long time, it seemed. Tentatively she stretched to Ursula. There was a moment before Ursula answered.

'All well. The cat knows and is waiting.' There was a long pause. 'Ijeme slept through it all. Though she's crying.' Another pause. Krueva joined Ursula's stretch to the cat. It was sitting calmly.

'Give us a long start to carry our friend,' Krueva said. 'Then you may have the pony.'

There was assent from the cat. Krueva asked Ursula for help in freeing her arm. She was stiff as she rose to her knees, stiff and bloody and vivid with earth and dying smells. She tried to see the cougar. No sign. She looked at the pony, touching its forelock. 'May you come again,' she said softly.

Lifting the shade entirely she rose to her own stretch. From her standing posture she could not see but could only feel the body beneath her. In one long stroke of her mind she last-held the pony and then started directly for the trees. She felt the cat not far from her path.

They would have to carry Ijeme. And there were important things to do. The whole ensconcement would be awaiting them. She found Ursula and Ijeme holding each other. Ijeme's sending had lost its tightness. 'I can walk for awhile,' she said.

With only one backward look to the pony and the cat, Krueva flanked Ijeme. The three women walked with surprising briskness through the darkened trees.

Ijeme's Story

'You'll have to say it all again, Ijeme, when we get back,' Krueva observed. 'Save your strength.'

'It helps me to say it. Words sharpen the edges tonight and make me understand better.' In the pre-dawn darkness her smile was invisible, but both her companions felt it. Ursula did not like the smile. Ijeme was hiding something.

They were speaking aloud, the three of them, at Ijeme's request. That was a discipline they frequently used for the refining of present images and the generation of new ones. Still it created a far less vulnerable state, even a less honest one, than their usual stretch-communication. They had stopped for rest and water on their all night journey through the hills. They were miles yet from the pass, miles from where they could begin to feel some safety.

Ursula had volunteered for spanner spread over the last few hours. She had been grateful to pick up no danger, no pursuit; only a few of their own outposts whose women expressed concern and even fear that a sister had returned early from her rotation. It was a constant possibility, of course, that one of their own for some reason – forced near to madness or discovered to be a hill woman – might return before time was up. That left a chink in their defensive armour, for the hill women formed a network in the City and depended upon each other for life there. Yet one chink was fairly easily filled. Already, Kua, Ijeme's replacement, was on her way to the City.

Ursula overrode her monitor for a full sweep check, affirmed the automatic settings, and turned her first ears to what Krueva and Ijeme were saying. There was a deeper tension between them, she thought, than she had ever seen; the use of words seemed to be intensifying the strain.

Ijeme was sitting on a rock. 'You're making too much of it all,' she said in a voice that Ursula mistrusted. 'You're talking about gatherstretch and increasing rotations. It's unnecessary . . .'

'Unnecessary!' Krueva was furious. She strode explosively back and forth between a clump of drying brush and the rock where Ijeme sat. 'Unnecessary! You break the City bond and escape homeward at the risk of your life, our survival, the life of a pony, and who knows what else, you refuse to explain anything, refuse to say why you're running away, and you . . .'

'I'm not running!' Ijeme was equally furious. The two women glared at each other. Ijeme seemed to rehearse her own words in her mind. Then she broke the locked stare, casting her eyes to her side. 'I was running,' she said more quietly. 'Of course I was running.' She seemed to speak only to herself. Then she looked back to Krueva. 'But I took all care in coming. I won't be missed for three days, if then.'

'You came without reason,' said Krueva, calmer now only because she did not wish her voice to carry. 'There can be no leaving your rotation unless you're beginning fallaway. You left feeling perfectly well.'

'Not exactly,' said Ijeme. She clasped her hands and looked down at her boots. Then she looked towards Ursula, as if seeking some understanding that Krueva could not give.

'That's an ominous statement,' Krueva said with impatience. She shoved her hands in the pockets of her jacket and waited. Seeing no other words forthcoming from Ijeme, she brought her hands out of her pockets and flung them wide to her sides. 'Ay-y-y!' She released the hoarse whisper and turned away from Ijeme entirely.

Ursula meanwhile was straining to see Ijeme's face. Her overwhelming impulse was to take this woman into her arms, to protect her from the anger that was flowing from Krueva. It was with effort that she held back and let Ijeme herself meet that anger. She contented herself with sending waves of care to her lover. From where she sat she couldn't make out Ijeme's eyes. She needed to see those eyes; she needed to know why Ijeme seemed so devious. Suddenly she felt she did understand something. She stepped to the rock, stooped, and placed her hands on the other woman's broad shoulders, then on her short hair, cropped to the style of the men. Gently she moved her hands to Ijeme's cheeks.

'Did someone discover you?' she asked.

Ijeme raised her head and looked at Ursula full in the eyes. Ursula searched the big face. There was a heavy scab on one cheek. Otherwise it was the same face she had always loved, roughened by weather and large-featured by inheritance. In its dissymmetry and its strength it could easily pass for a man's face. In fact, Ijeme's whole big frame was easily taken for a man's. That's why there had been such subtle expectations placed upon her – expectations that of all the hill women she would have least trouble passing. Ursula, just by holding the broad face in her hands, understood better. She was aware of Krueva at her back, of the need for them to be on their way, but she felt open with Ijeme now and did not wish to cut the flow. She asked again, 'Did they discover you?'

Ijeme shook her head. 'No.' She forsook words now. She said in shortstretch to Ursula, 'I have been protecting, protecting myself against what I've done.'

'Let me see,' said Ursula. She knew Ijeme would know what she meant by that, that *seeing* for Ursula meant understanding on all sense levels. She prepared herself for whatever might come, knowing that she was asking Ijeme to ask for help, a thing that was difficult for Ijeme under any circumstances.

'Let me in, Ijeme,' she pressed her head to the other woman's in order to secure the contact. As Ijeme opened to her, she was assaulted by a cacophony of feelings, tastes, colours, pictures, sounds, odours. Pain leapt in sharp blasts through her body. Streaks of rage, hurt, madness surged through her long bones. Fear screamed in her softself. And above, around, through it all, soaking every bit of motion, was guilt: self-punishment and incredible guilt. It drenched her. Her head bogged in it, then was clenched to its tight vise. It blazed through her skull and burst towards the top. Ursula inhaled deeply. Aloud she whispered, 'The beginning, Ijeme. Make a beginning. Come up on it easily.'

Ijeme relaxed. Ursula took the opportunity to shortstretch to Krueva. 'I've dropped the monitor,' she said.

'I have it,' came back. 'Go ahead.'

Ursula turned again to Ijeme. The woman was calmer now and was able to begin at the beginning, back in the City, in the mad alien place that Ursula had as yet visited only in her softself. The story unfolded through Ijeme's eyes and Ursula began to know on every level of her awareness how Ijeme had become terrified and why she felt guilty.

Ijeme let herself into her room with both keys and three successive hand combinations. The security necessities always tired her, yet neither she nor anyone else in the building dared do without them. Every man had at least three locks on his room – active from both inside and out. She swung open the door and said to the figure behind her, 'Come in'.

The woman scooted into the room, her every motion a contradiction of brazenness and insecurity. Ijeme reset all the locks and nodded to the upholstered chair. With the bed and a small refrigerator, the chair completed the room's furniture. The woman sat automatically.

Ijeme looked at her unbelievingly. She was a thing out of history to the hill woman: a thickly painted face, lacquer-stiffened hair, her body encased in a low-cut tight-fitting dress that terminated at mid-thigh; on her legs the thinnest of stockings, and the shoes –

were they shoes? – Ijeme could not believe they fit the same part of the anatomy that her own boots covered. How could she walk in these spindly things? And with the flimsy straps that fastened them to her ankles and feet? The dangles that hung from the woman's ears jangled in tune with her bracelets. She clutched a cloth-covered purse to her side.

Amazed as she was, Ijeme knew that she was in the presence of a woman – but not a woman as she knew women. This was the city edition, the man's edition, the only edition acceptable to men, streamlined to his exact specifications, her body guaranteed to be limited, dependent, and constantly available. Ijeme shuddered, then repeated to herself the words of an early lesson: 'What we are not, we each could be, and every woman is myself.' She tried not to feel pity, tried to hope that the woman's dress was a free choice. 'Though that's doubtful,' she thought as she looked at her visitor. She had felt that it would look good for her to have a woman in her room and this one had seemed particularly frightened as she had stood outside against the building, unescorted . . .

Vacant eyes stared at her as she went to the refrigerator and poured some dark liquid into a cup. She paused as she closed the door to look at her own clothes, her man's clothing: flat, comfortable boots, cotton socks, long work pants circled at the waist with a belt, a cotton work shirt. Underneath, her breasts were forced into flatness by the cloth binding she wore on the job or whenever she went out.

The woman watched her. 'Can she tell?' Ijeme thought. She risked a quick enfolding around the other's mind. Around and back. She was met as she knew she would be with a dull nothingness – no return enfoldment, no movement, no response. She felt immediately sorry that she had asked, even when the other woman had clearly not even known that she had done so.

Ijeme approached her with the cup. Did she cringe? 'Cola,' said Ijeme. The woman raised her eyes, took the cup. She drank all the sugary liquid in one tilt of her head. Ijeme looked again at her, judging her age to be forty-five or so, trying to be much younger. As she took back the cup she smiled. That was a mistake. The reaction that it caused made her sick. The hard painted face smiled back in what was a pitiful attempt to be tantalising. Ijeme turned quickly away. Not quickly enough. Before she knew what was happening she was backed against the refrigerator, the woman's body plastered against her own. Ijeme felt anxious hands flitting nervously all over her body. The woman was making throaty noises now. Her eyes closed, she was pressing herself against Ijeme's chest. Her hands were ubiquitous in their birdlike touch. They rubbed harder now over her arms and shoulders.

Ijeme broke into a sweat. Dropping the cup she seized both the hands. The painted face looked up at her, panting in seductive softness. Ijeme's stomach lurched. She struggled for a calm deep voice. 'Here,' she said, almost desperately. 'Let's sit in the air.' She moved to the room's only window, pulling the woman with her. Pressing the two lock mechanisms she was relieved to find that they both still worked. With her free hand she pushed up the ancient sash and drew the woman to it. 'We can sit out here,' she said. 'It will be cooler.' She pointed to the fire escape that led from above to far-below, down into the 'courtyard' framed by the buildings. In the dusk they could still see the alley that led out to the street. Other windows were open. Other sounds came from them. Some sounds were of women with men.

'No,' said her companion. 'No.' With surprising strength she jerked Ijeme towards the bed. Ijeme staggered, unable to keep her balance. As she pulled away, she realised to her horror that the woman was undressing. Already the dress was off, the breasts exposed. Ijme stooped to pick up the clothing, saying, 'No. That's not what . . .'

'Fuck,' said the woman as she flung herself on the bed. She was only partly covered by the old garter belt that held the high stockings. The shoes, spread wide apart on the bed, undulated with the rest of her body. 'Fuck. Fuck, fuck, fuck!' she said, shaking her arms towards Ijeme.

Imeje held her face in her hands. 'Centre,' she thought. 'Centre!' She tried desperately to find her own control. Nothing worked. She was entirely disconnected. With a groan she broke from the side of the bed towards the window. She did not make it. The creature was upon her again, this time from behind, on her back, the hands pushing, exploring, the throat heaving in some kind of unfeedable hunger.

Ijeme was frantic. She staggered and fell. She took the woman down with her. They sprawled on the floor rolling back and forth in an effort to control each other. Ijeme felt her cheek go raw with the digging of the long nails. Her shirt was tearing. The woman's mouth was active now, spreading her paint over Ijeme's face, making sucking, smacking sounds, biting her chin, her neck, her ears. Ijeme could not cope with her quickness. Desperately she tried to stop the hands that tore at her belt, searched towards her crotch. 'Raped,' she thought. 'I'm being raped by a woman!' The idea unnerved her even more. She twisted, turned, fought to catch the hands, to roll herself over to the top position. Turmoil flushed her brain. She felt hot and helpless. Where was her strength? What was happening?

Suddenly, the woman stopped. Ijeme froze. There was no movement. She realised with slow panic that the woman's hand was squarely on her pubic bone. It rested there in stunned silence, there on her rumpled trousers. The woman's face was close to hers. Her eyes met her own. Disbelief. Ijeme did not move. The woman's hand did. It slowly described a circle over the bottom part of her torso; it moved in between her legs; it came back to her pubic bone. Growing realisation crept into the woman's eyes. She leapt up, pulled at Ijeme's belt, scratched apart the fly of her pants, her eyes crazy now, her hands ripping, tearing away at the cloth.

Ijeme caught her hands, finally – but not before the secret was known. The woman said nothing. She jerked her hands free. Keeping her eyes fixed on Ijeme's she began to slither back towards the door. She reached for her clothes, her purse, then giving Ijeme a wide berth, she side-stepped towards the window. Her face curled in the ultimate look of contempt. Closing her eyes and clutching her possessions she screamed her parting words. 'Dyke! Dyke, dyke, dyke!' Turning, she rushed for the window, still screaming, 'A dyke, a dyke, a dyke!'

Ijeme found her speed somehow and leapt from the floor after her. She was not fast enough. The woman reached the fire escape, lunged toward its steps, still shrieking the infamy. Ijeme stopped, paralysed. The woman was falling. She had caught her heel between the thin metal strips and was falling. Her words became a full-fledged scream as she toppled downwards towards the next level. Ijeme watched with absurd fascination as the flailing body actually bounced from the railing on the next floor and went hurtling into the free space of the buildings' shaft. She could not see and did not hear her hit. She only heard the silence when it finally came. Back inside the room, she physically swirled around in incredulity, holding her head, searching for centre. She vomited. Twice. She clung to the foot of the bed, panting, trying to regain a sense of sanity.

Ursula had let it all come. She had not attempted to stop any of it. Even when Ijeme's sending became frantic she did not seek to soothe the other. She lived through all the touches and sights of Ijeme's pain with all of her own senses bared. She was shaken still with what she was knowing through her sister's head. No wonder: the pain, the guilt, and the terror. She understood, and at the same time began to ask who knew, how Ijeme had escaped, who heard the dying words?

Then she saw all that, too, how Ijeme had drawn herself together, signalled another of the hill women in the City that she was leaving, checked her room for any giveaway signs; how she swung down the fire escape, down the twenty floors to the darkness of the alley. Some men were gathered around a crumpled figure.

'Get her out of here. She's a mess.'

'Where'd she drop from?'

'I dunno. You find out.'

'I'm finding out nothing. Don't look to me like she belonged to nobody. Hey, buddy. She belong to you?'

Ijeme's voice, 'No, I heard the noise . . .'

'Yeah, me too,' another voice. 'What a screecher.'

'Well, she was too old to bear so it's no loss. Get her I.D. there. Help me clean it up, Joe.'

The fast walking through the streets, the security checks, the bars, the groups of men, then breaking alone for the lower parts, the river and the swim in the black water, the running, the moments of stretchtouch with sisters closer to the Wanderground; then the lapse into fallaway, the awakening, again the running, the fear, the exhaustion at dawn, and the pony, the brave pony who strayed deliberately near to calm her and to carry her for nearly two days through the fields and woods to the deeper forest's edge.

Ursula knew it all now. She was shaking with Ijeme's sobs. She held her and rocked, soothing the face, the shoulders. Held her and rocked.

Ijeme spoke. 'I'll need more cleaning. It's not all out.'

Ursula held and rocked.

'I killed,' said Ijeme.

Ursula held and rocked.

'I killed a woman,' said Ijeme.

Ursula held and rocked. Held and rocked.

Krueva had not tuned to the story. She heard Ijeme's words now. She was suddenly sad for her own earlier impatience. To affirm herself, to make real her usefulness, she began the necessary clearing of the ground, the scraping away of its sticks and leaves. She found the earth cool but not cold. When she'd swept it clear, she motioned to Ursula. The two of them led a limp Ijeme to the circle. Unbidden, Ijeme stretched herself spreadeagle on her stomach, her hands rubbing the earth, her whole body moving up and down. Ursula and Krueva flanked her, holding her, holding each other, holding the cool earth. Krueva's last act before the rite was to check her spanners once again. Then, the three lying against the earth and against each other began their movements.

'Breathe with me, Ursula.'

'Breathe with me, Ijeme.'

'Breathe with me, Krueva.'

They dropped their soft-selves to diaphragm level and began. They drew in the earth, these three, into themselves, into each other.

They came back only later to the forest.

'Fully given and well-taken,' said Ijeme.

'From eternity,' said Krueva.

'For eternity,' said Ursula.

'Deep.'

'Deep.'

'Deep.'

All three voices: 'Red waters. Deep and soon.'

It was time to start for the low pass. As they walked, Ursula took up the spanner spread again. Behind them the grey sky was showing the first rays of light. 'It's as if our earthtouch has hauled up the sun,' she thought with a laugh. She covered the earth again where they had lain together and set off after her sisters.

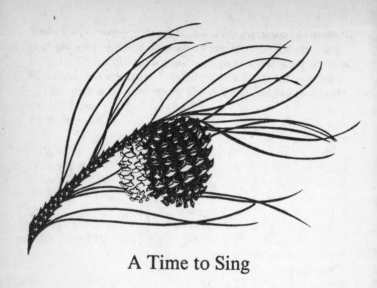

A Time to Sing

'She cannot be reached.'

'Try again!'

'I tell you, Troja, she cannot be reached. She's clearly elected not to receive any enfoldment. We've been trying for hours.' Blase's impatience punctuated the response.

'Then invade, Blase, invade! We can't wait any . . .' Troja's message trailed off into thin nothingness. There was a long stretchsilence. An incomplete grammatical structure hung over the miles between them, meaning without movement. Troja sent first. 'Blase?'

'Here.'

'I didn't mean . . .'

'I know.' Blase was near the top of a tall pine just at the place where its genuine foliage began. It seemed years since she had lofted there to try for clearer ranging towards the south. Now she shifted from the bucket of light that had been sustaining her to her hardbelt. Troja's violence had shaken her. She needed all her energy to address it.

'I will sing the Kore story,' Troja was sending now.

'Will you wait until ministrations?'

'No. You may not be available tonight and it was with you that I tore the cloth. I'll sing it now if you'll hear.'

'I'll hear.'

Troja sounded less frantic. 'I am with others at the moment,' she sent, 'here at the water rocks. It's like spring. Let me tell Jacqua and Britta to help the small ones while I sing.' She passed off and away.

Blase shifted slightly against the lash loop that held her stiff-legged to the narrowing tree trunk. She felt more centred now. Below her and to the left Earlyna was on watch at the bald rock. Blase sent a care curl to swirl around those dark brown shoulders in the sunshine. Earlyna looked up, smiled and waved.

'Troja's going to sing,' Blase sent. 'I don't dare sing with her here but I'd like to have Huntsblood with me to listen and to hold. Do you know where he is?'

Earlyna sent two simultaneous messages, all the while broad-sweeping in a half-circle: with a flash of colour and movement she showed Blase that all three cats were exploring nearby; with a question mark bending of a woman's name she asked about Troja's attempts to reach Rula-ji.

'Rula-ji is closed to mindstretch,' Blase reported, 'and Troja is anxious. More than anxious. She intended man's crime.'

Consternation from Earlyna. 'That's why she sings?'

'Yes.' Blase passed off for a moment. 'I just tried Rula-ji again. Still no response. Could she have been discovered?'

'Well by all that's precious don't suggest that to Troja. They haven't loved together long and first bonds are very taut. Is she ready to sing?'

'Not yet. She's with small ones at the bathings. Perhaps singing will take her mind from Rula-ji.'

Earlyna nodded. 'Tell Troja I kiss her breast.' A pause. 'Huntsblood is open. By the fallen limb there, below the ledge.'

Blase stretched down to the big grey cat, surrounded him with a warm invitation. Huntsblood let her in. With a mild shock Blase remembered how traumatic it always was to connect with Huntsblood. The trenchant overwash of feline cunning engulfed her. She seemed to meld immediately and intimately with the cat, and for a moment lost herself entirely in a powerful swirl of

75

history. Catself was the repository of the past. Then she felt herself crouched in a tense expectancy, staring unblinkingly and with narrowed eyes at a very particular harmless leaf. Some neighbours to her rectal muscles contracted in a slow sweep of the tail she did not have. She felt herself in danger of toppling from her high perch. With an effort she sucked herself apart from Huntsblood, staying only in light touch with the cat's sending/hearing. It wasn't easy to get away. Catself was strong.

'Troja at the ensconcement is about to sing the Kore story,' she sent. 'She slipped into man's crime. Intended an invasion. You said you wanted to hear a singing next time.'

'May I sing?' sent Huntsblood.
'Not out loud. We are too near the edge of the Dangerland.'
'Then I'd rather wait for this field creature.'
'As you wish.'

Blase was about to search north for Troja when Huntsblood came again. 'No one would think a cat voice strange. Let me sing, Blase.' There was a calculated pause before Huntsblood added, 'I'll monitor your dreams for a full night.' Blase hesitated. That was a tempting bargain. The cats rarely offered to dreamwatch. Blase wrapped the request in all its implications and sent it down to Earlyna with a what-do-you-think.

'Take him up on it. It's well worth it and big cats crying are common hereabouts. No notice will be taken.' Both women could feel Huntsblood's smug smile.

Blase laughed aloud. 'All right, fascinating feline. Boost up to me and you can sing with Troja.'

Huntsblood rose from his crouch and sent to Blase, 'Tote me.'
'You can boost, Huntsblood. Get footloose first, like a leap.'

'I haven't practised enough yet,' said the cat, but before he could argue further, Troja pressed Blase again. Without further preparation Blase enfolded the cat in cradlelift and swept him off the ground. Huntsblood rose directly into the air towards the treetop, his four legs absurdly stiff below him and his face motionless in the attempt to seem accustomed to this undignified mode of travel. Blase brought him straight and swift to her own breasts.

'Velvet claws,' she cautioned as Huntsblood balanced on her

chest. She bucketed both the cat and herself for security and turned all her attention northwards.

'I tried Rula-ji again,' she sent to Troja. 'Still no answer.'

'It's as well. I'll learn some patience from this maybe. What concerns me now is intending the invasion.'

'Can you show us where you are so we'll have some homesense?'

'Of course. Is Earlyna with you?'

'She's on watch and sends greeting. Huntsblood's going to sing aloud with you from here.'

Troja cast a greeting to the cat. 'Jacqua and three of the small ones want to be close to me as I sing. And to sing with me, right?' With a turn she was enfolding into the message field the many-hued excited rhythms of young, very slack and, as yet, unstretched sensibilities. Troja's extension expanded until Blase and Huntsblood held a wide view of familiar hills and meadows. Troja was slowly panning.

It was one of those rare winter days at the water rocks: bright hot sun through clear space, making every line stand out, every drop of water hang mid-air as a speck of light. From wherever Troja focused, a sharp image rolled over the wilderness to the treetop hill woman and her cat companion. Blase and Huntsblood saw the meadow and the winter wild flowers first – white, yellow, blue dots stretching toward the creek bank. Then a tableau: a huddle of tiny naked bodies standing, squatting, lying motionless, intent on watching some river creature. The shoulders of the girl-child Britta rose above the rest. Troja was panning clockwise now, to dark pine trees spruce and fir, and lower oaks, all guarding a deep noon shade beneath them. Then the smooth meadow fell down and down until it scooped a hundred grazing goats into a fold of its wide expanse. She could not see them, but Blase knew that on the further plateau there would be women in the rye fields – Fora, Krueva, wild Clea who had loved so well, perhaps even old Pelagine – cutting and gleaning or binding straw for nest thatchings. All she could see were trees and blue sky, then more trees, behind which she knew was the hill of the ancient mounds; beyond that was the grove of soft grasses, its air thick with moonlit memories. Huntsblood's head sagged onto her neck. Blase felt a nudge of homesickness. 'Where two or more are gathered, that is home,' Huntsblood reminded them both. She stroked the cat.

Troja was sweeping behind them now to the more scraggly part of the forest, rising still upward to the stream's source. Beyond the stream were the nests of the ensconcement.

There was another burst of colour as Troja's gaze came back down the green meadow through the early poppies, closer now to the noises of the small group with her. A foot, now a leg, now a whole brown grinning girl-body – Jacqua struggling to hold up Ziska, dark wet-faced baby, to the roving camera that was Troja's eyes; two less pudgy small ones crawled corner-to-corner on a broad blanket at Troja's feet. One pulled herself along only by her arms – Bru, whose legs had not moved from birth; beautiful Bru, whose smile wiped away centuries of pain. The other, Blase did not know. She was marvelling at the sheen on the child's straight black hair when Troja drew the panning to a close.

'Thank you, Troja,' she sent after a mutual sigh with Huntsblood. 'I feel more whole to see your day there. Who is playing with Bru?'

'A city child that Elsa brought back. She was among those condemned to the needle but she responded to Elsa's mindstretch. There is a long story to sing about their escape. We call her Brightness until she chooses her name.' The child's warmth reached over the miles. Together with that of Bru and Ziska her pure energy was almost overwhelming.

'I would like to sing now, Blase,' Troja sent.

'Good. We're ready here. We are Huntsblood and Blase.'

'And a ponderosa pine.' The voices seemed to come from everywhere. Huntsblood inspected the canopy of green branches over his head. Blase tightened the hard belt loop so as to brace herself closer to the tree. She soothed with her hands the plates of pocked yellow armour that clothed the slender trunk. 'And a ponderosa pine,' she repeated.

The three opened themselves to the pulses moving from the north. Troja was beginning her free rhythms, slapping gently in a searching pattern up and down her body. Palms and fingers on her thighs, fists and fingers on her chest, lightly tap the cheeks, the calves, and now the open ground. Slowly tapping, slowly rapping, accent where the bass notes sound. But any steady rhythm soon was broken, not allowed. There were no small noises now from the children, but rather, a cacophony of each one's own special

78

thumpings on each separate instrument. Even Ziska could be heard, a gleeful slobber sound accompanying every fat hand clap.

Tiny slaps on feet and stomachs, now and again on Troja's back, each one weaving accent magic on her own bare body's slopes. To it all there was no order, and a repetition rare, never a completed cadence, only syncopated chaos. Wild percussion yearned for centre, reached for patterns to be shared, beat in isolated motion seeking one to guide them all.

Blase and the cat and the ponderosa pine listened without moving. The din pushed their minds together against the upland air. Then the tempo hastened. The chaos increased to *con moto* pace. There began to be some sequence, some obvious configurations; a finger snapping beat played again, then let go, only to be recaptured. Suddenly each drummer seemed to hear the other, but heard as well a different thing. They knew in one instant where the centre lay. Troja's measured pounding strode into focus while that of the others subsided into intricate support. She was not yet near the accents of Kore's story, but then she had not yet added her voice, either. Gently, with bare suggestions, Troja shifted the beat to another subtle plane. As she slowed the poundings and directed the rhythms, she began her humming – a steady single tone. A chorus joined her in thirds and sixths – simple things at first for ones so young in singing. Then came the climbings, the far-stretching intervals, the many ancient melodies from a hundred secret homes. With rising lightness the tunes addressed each other, spilling over baby teeth to a duel and a reconciliation.

Now the pine tree joined in the singing. Far away from the voices she rustled her needles and swayed her passengers under the downpour of sounds. Huntsblood was in ecstasy. His head was erect, his eyes closed, his voice an amazing soft obligato. His paws pumped on Blase's breasts in alternate half-time pressures. Blase heard her own heart fall into line with the stresses. 'A dancing heart!' she thought as a minor theme slid by her cheek.

The chorus filled the air, one none had ever heard before or would ever hear again, the blending of those particular voices above those particular rhythms, with those particular variations, each with the other. Blase did not want the story to begin. There was too much new and brilliant in the singing together; she had trouble letting it go. She recognised Bru's clear voice and of course the subdued but still stronger singing of Troja. Even so, it was all one, and when she sensed the shift into the tonalities of Kore's narrative, Blase was somehow sad.

Troja was orchestrating now, gathering notes and intensities from all those around her, integrating qualities, deftly arranging pitches, moving stresses back and forth until something emerged from the random singing; a meaning structure formed like a crystal dew. Troja viewed it softly, approached it indirectly, and then as it beckoned her she drew her voice alongside to blend with it. Firmly seated then upon the well-worn form, she began the chanted telling of an ancient tale.

Troja sang of Kore, daughter-lover of her mother and of how their loving threatened gods and men. How Hek, gentle manchild, sought the love of Kore, swearing his trust to the mother of the maid. Knowing woman-love sufficed her, Kore nay-said the offer, and Hek turned discouraged from his earnest wish. But Dis, his mighty kinsman, Lord of the Underworld, scorned such a courtship and his nephew's weakling ways, saying half-men petitioned, full men demanded; and that Hek must possess the girl against her will. 'Why do you ask?' he raged. 'Take her if you want her! Women yield to force. They desire it so!' Yet Hek refused the challenge saying, 'Oft will I ask her, but never can I take her if she does not choose to go.'

'Never can I take her if she does not choose to go.' The refrain, led by Jacqua, was otherwise a near infant talk: many vowels, most of them not appropriate vowels, yet all were singing, even Ziska.

Dis then was outraged,
Angered in his loins,
Vowed to punish such worthless kin.
Smote he his nephew
With worst of his curses,
'Make now the outer form
Fit the truth within:
Be forever woman, impotent she-man!
Hek no more your true name
Be now Hecate!'
Thus the shroud of manhood
Fell from Hek that day.

'Never may I enter where the way is not open, never can I take her if she does not choose to go,' sang Jacqua and the others loud and clear.

Then Troja sang of Dis' vow to take fair Kore for his own. How, swollen with power, he swept up the daughter, took her down to rule as the Queen of Dark. How, cruel in jest, he brought with them Hecate, that she might observe how he ravished the virgin. How in her sadness Hecate dwelt there, serving as handmaid the imprisoned queen.

> *Yet Kore flourished not below*
> *Bore no sons for Dis to know.*
> *Forced to yielding in his bed,*
> *Still she crept through all the dead*
> *To hold her lover Hecate*
> *Who never entered, only knocked.*
> *Hecate, who whispered,*
> *'Never can I bring her*
> *If she does not choose to come.'*

'Never can I bring her if she does not choose to come.'
Troja sang the ending, how the goddess claimed her daughter, at least for the summer, autumn, and the spring. How with each turning of earth into flower Hecate dwelt by Kore's side.

> *Giving love and fealty to the mother-lover,*
> *Giving love and fealty to the lover-daughter,*
> *Finding the love and fealty from the daughter-mother,*
> *They knew in their bodies that the gods were doomed.*

'For though we be entered where the way was not opened, never will they bring us if we do not choose to come. And never may we enter where the way is not opened, never may I bring her if she does not choose to come. Never may she enter where the way is not opened, never may she bring me if I do not choose to come.'

The singing faded softly into rhythms. The rhythms seemed to resonate for a long parting time. At last they lapsed entirely. Blase couldn't see the group but knew that they were locked in silence, holding and rocking on the hillside's deep meadow grass and sun. Huntsblood felt the holding, too.

When Earlyna looked again toward the treetop, there were two figures, one far larger than the other, but both locked in the sweeping embrace of a gently swaying pine.

Pelagine Stretches

Except for the declining drone of night creatures and the constant wakefulness of the morning watch, the whole Eastern Ensconcement lay in a deep sleep. It slept on, through the grey light of a beginning day. When she opened her eyes, Pelagine saw the winter sun already heaving over the south-eastern hills. It fell through the opening in her nest and landed by her head in gentle, insistent waves, as if to remind her that old women should be up before sunrise. She felt fine. Perhaps there would be longer hours of her hardself today – longer hours, some of the younger women would say, for her to be demanding of them.

'Demanding,' she grumbled. 'Don't ask for help out of my nest. Take my turn at the soap cauldron. Demanding. Demanding, demanding, demanding. Demand some respect. Haven't been where I've been; got a lot to teach them.' She shook her head. What was happening? She had lapsed again. So hard to escape the patterns, even when you've been away from them over seventy years. They come back, apparently, towards the end, those patterns. Back to trip you and trap you. Back to make you remember who you were.

'No wonder they can't stand my hardself,' she mused. 'Time to go for sure.' Pelagine was nearing her death. She had known it since the solstice less than a week ago, and had chosen the spring as the appropriate dying season for one so old, for one who lived in so many other forms as well – or at least so it seemed in her dreams. To release this old body was more than appropriate now. It hankered to be dust again, to relax the tension that holding itself together had required all these scores of years. To let go and scatter. To let go and drift. To let go and be at ease again with the family of dust. And to die just a shade short of being overdue, just this side of the full awakening of the earth's blood – that was good. She felt she could get her ducks in a row by spring and perhaps her moving down and away might correspond with Helge's bringing forth. But spring was three months off.

'Are you up yet, Pelagine, old woman?' The greeting was a familiar enfoldment: it came down a sunbeam, bounced off the floorboard and lit upon a peripheral ring of her consciousness.

'Not for impudent children,' she sent back, via the same sunbeam. It was Jacqua, the girl-woman, already bustling around and agitating the day. 'Besides,' she sent, 'haven't done my stretches.'

'I'll do ministrations,' Jacqua responded promptly.

'Not today. I'll do my own.'

'I'll bring you breakfast, and news! Ijeme came back from the City last night and needs you . . .'

'No! Pesky child!' Pelagine fairly burst the mindstretch channels with her anger. 'Bring me nothing. None of your news, none of your charity. I've climbed out of this tree every day since the Eastern Ensconcement. I'll climb out of it today and I'll climb out of it tomorrow. Furthermore, I'll climb out of it the next day. I'll climb out of this tree for eighty more days. I'll do it by myself and without even your stretch-aid. Let me be.'

No response.

Good. That ought to hold her, Pelagine thought. She swished her buttocks back and forth to rearrange the mass of beans beneath her. The cloth bag was in need of several patches. Through the thinnest parts she could almost see the broad beans. They ground against each other as she moved, shaping themselves to her form with comforting crunching sounds.

'Oh, Hannah!' she sighed aloud. Pulling both her arms from beneath the wool-packed coverlet, she thrust them upward, then above her head. She closed her eyes. The pain was excruciatingly beautiful. 'Aleta!' she whispered, at the tiptoe of her stretch. She let out her breath to the rhythm of a long ago memory.

She eased her arms and felt a woman's head rest between her palms. It laughed and kissed her fingers as she pushed and stroked its straight brown hair. Pelagine, still with her eyes closed, reached to find the wide strong body already slipping beneath the coverlet gently to meet her own. They held each other with mild fierceness, intense tenderness. They rolled together back and forth, exchanging breastfalls, over the wide rattling bean-filled bed. They played. And worked. And sighed. Pelagine wrapped her legs about her partner's in a gift of leave-touch, then said good-bye and lay remembering.

'Hard,' she mused. 'It's been hard work.' She lay snug, still warmly covered from the chill. Hard work learning new ways, hard work learning new skills. Practice. Lots of practice. Hard work building nests and barns and keeps. Building a whole ensconcement, in fact, with only a few women at first. Understanding the out-of-doors – things about wood and fire, rivers and dirt, wind and weather. Learning to listen to what the land wants you to do and still keeping your ears open while you do it. Body work. The kind that makes your muscles move and hurt and toughen so they can move better and hurt more and get tougher still.

She felt herself into her whole body. Time for her torque stretches. First to the right with her bent legs while her head and shoulders resisted to the left. Straighten. Hold. Then the other way. Ah. She held and held. She moved to yet another stretch place. After each pull-release she pushed herself to new positions. With her hands she spoke to her stomach. It contracted for her and dropped back to ease and comfort. Then to her spleen. She gave them love and thanks. She continued. Wherever there was a taut organ or limb – and they seemed to be everywhere, always needing to be stretched all over again – she pushed it tauter just to the threshold of pain, until it seemed that it would burst or break, until sometimes the pain did come. Then she had a choice: to invite the pain closer or to hold it off a while. She varied her choices, sometimes calling forth the hurt and easing into greater calm, sometimes retreating right away into lesser ease, before the pain could gather force. She grinned. None of them ever understood the way she socialised with pain. 'Dangerous,' they said. 'Dangerous my hind foot full of blue salve.' She grinned again. She knew her pain. It knew her.

Time for the legs and upper stretches. She sighed. The sun sighed with her, scouring her eyelids with yellows and oranges; then she let her eyes drift towards her forehead, swathing them in maroons and deep blues. In several quick motions she bent her knees up to her chest, whipped off the coverlet, rolled her torso into the air towards her head, pulled the coverlet beneath her, and landed again upon it, her knees still close pressed.

The effort exhausted her. She panted once or twice, noting the grey puffs that sailed from her lips. Then she began the greeting of her feet and legs. Such white legs. They got little sun any more, but the flesh was still firm. Slowly, with calm attention, she massaged first one foot then the other, one calf and then the other, pressing each, pulling each, soothing each, thanking each. She sat up, caught her heels in her hands. In a mighty push that made her knees burn she straightened her legs. Her back leapt in sympathetic pain. She did not ease it yet.

'I can take more,' she thought, feeling the junctures of her spine go tense. 'Come and hurt,' she invited. 'Come and hurt more.' The pain obliged. She let it climb, and still she held, legs, arms, back, head, stretched to the utmost, pushing, straining, a perfect precarious balance. The sneeze that formed behind her cheeks and nose condensed into tears. She let them wash her temples.

'More,' she whispered, stretching wide and back. She drew another breath and sat impaled on thin unmoving air.

Nothing stirred. The sunbeams had curled around her optic nerves, painting the inside of her skull a glaring orange-red. She would stay this way forever, she knew, here at the apogee of pain.

All that she had ever been began to swirl before her in chaotic competition. She ordered her mind. Chaos responded by falling into linear motion. A procession began. They passed before her, all of them, at first in textures, smells, and rhythms, then in swift visual sequence. The women. The women of her life. Each one who had touched her days and left a wake across her history.

'Ah,' she thought. 'I'm going deep today.' As if to preview some main feature, she clothed herself again in strange garments, held her lovers only in darkened circumstances, lived again the violence of subtle secret threats, and always checked her collar for tell-tale lipstick smudges. She was reaching far back now, for an old memory, changing whole years into milliseconds, quickening the backward-sweeping montage, pausing only where she touched moments which in themselves embraced eternities.

'And what bright enchanting scene from my chequered past will be my visiting place today?' Always a certain excitement accompanied her deep recalls; she loved the rediscovery of details that only immersion there would yield.

The backward momentum was slowing. It would cease at some unannounced place in her history and from there begin a forward re-play of her life. Or, eschewing chronology, it might lead her outward or under, around or above in a flow of association ordered in no way by time but by other mysterious connections which only occasionally she could identify as colour, sound, movement or so frail a link as smell or taste.

Pelagine recognised with apprehension the approach to her last day in the City, a good while before the purges, when things were only beginning to get bad. She had had another name then.

Kate could see Vivian among the women at the punch-out, pushing towards the door. She looked haunted and nervous today, not her usual feisty self. Kate could tell she was stalling to allow her to catch up, stalling to make seem as natural as possible their falling in together to walk across the lot. Kate elbowed ahead of others, mostly women, trying not to seem in a hurry. She reached her card just as the clock rang Vivian out for the day. Two more dings and she too was out of the door. Vivian had paused in the flow of homebound human traffic and was rummaging in her purse. As Kate came up to her the shorter woman snapped open a small plastic container.

'Jesus,' she was saying for Kate's benefit as she simultaneously moved forward and began pulling the custom-made plugs from her ears. Vivian did long stints in The Loom Room, twelve hundred square metres of whirring, clacking machines, the ugly and loud behind-the-scenes operations that assured the world of Benton's Cottons in Stunning Prints and Pastels. 'But watch out, spies and counterspies,' Vivian was fond of saying, 'because I can read lips with the best of you.' To Kate who handled the Stunning Prints and Pastels themselves, even the pay Vivian pulled down wasn't worth the risk of going deaf.

Kate waited until the other woman had her plugs snapped into the plastic and back into her bag. Vivian irritated her sometimes with that quick nervous energy. She seemed often to be nothing but a bundle of rapid-fire responses to her environment, a series of totally unpremeditated movements. Morever, she had the habit of talking about what she was doing while she was doing it. Kate herself went in for more smoothness and less strain. 'Quiet,' they had called her back home and everywhere she'd gone. She shifted her weight from right earthshoe to left earthshoe. Quiet on the outside, she thought, but inside pissed, impatient, intolerant. They started forward. Vivian seemed assured that they would not be overheard now. Kate still waited for the other woman to speak.

'I'm going, Kate.'

They walked in silence towards the car stop as slowly as they sensed was safe. Others hurried by them, brushing them occasionally, pulling on jackets or coats against a brisk afternoon wind.

'Hi, sweetheart!' An arm was around her shoulders and Kate was pulled off balance. She automatically repressed the urge to squirm and looked instead into the face of one of the floormen. It was a genuine hug. He wasn't testing her.

'Hi, Al,' she returned in relief. She didn't have to play with Al. He laid a kiss on her cheek.

'We'll have all the walls down Monday,' he sent back as he strode off towards downtown.

'You've got to help me with Alice,' Vivian was saying now. 'She won't come with us. She says it's all just temporary. Things will get normal again she says. Says it's crazy for me to go.'

Kate was still digesting Vivian's first words. She was going. That made her face again her own indecision. As for Alice, crap. She didn't trust her, had never trusted her, couldn't understand Vivian's attraction to her beyond the obvious sexual one. Alice was on the way up and made no secret of it. A climber, a schemer, one who seemed to get a little too much genuine pleasure out of the games with men. She would make it. She had the looks, the style, and the desire. Kate had seen the lady operate, had even crossed her a time or two, enough to know that she was ruthless. But under it all, Kate had to admit, Alice had some fierce loyalty to Vivian. That's why over these few years of their acquaintance Kate had kept her opinion to herself; she had given Alice every chance. Ironically, Alice did seem to trust Kate.

Kate was trying now to make her glance around the lot seem casual. She wanted to stop, to talk right to Vivian. But she knew, everyone knew, that no place was really safe to talk except maybe the middle of a cornfield and even then you'd better do it in pig-latin or in fancy code.

'Sure you want to go, Viv?'

'No stopping me. They're onto me already, me and my sick-leave, me and my big mouth. It's either get out of here or they put me back in the looney bin. Nothing will get me there again, Kate. Nothing.' She deliberately pulled her voice down. 'There's four of us going. Now. While there's still time.' She paused. 'Will you come?'

'I don't know,' Kate felt dizzy. They were approaching the car stop now. No bus, no car, was in sight.

'Walk to the next corner,' Vivian said, speeding up so Kate would have to follow. 'Hey, you okay?' Vivian stopped, put her arm around Kate. Kate shook it off with some violence.

'Stop,' she muttered. And louder, 'I'm fine. Just fine. Maybe catching cold, that's all. Dizzy in the head.' As Vivian released her she straightened. They let the light catch them before the crossing. Then as traffic stopped again they hung back, letting more eager pedestrians pass. A lanky man, bearded and hip-looking glanced back at them, seemed to reconsider some far-fetched idea, and moved on ahead of them.

'Kate, they're true. The stories are true. About how they're hunting women. Swear to god. Sue and Sandy saw them pick one up. Put her in the wagon. And her doing nothing. Not a hooker. Doing nothing. I hear another story every day and oh, I got to tell you this, Kate, I got to tell you.' Vivian was looking everywhere but at her. She spoke almost without moving her lips, as if she expected Kate to supply the missing consonants. In spite of her rattled head Kate made herself listen closely.

Vivian was continuing. 'The men. All of them was laughing about it yesterday. You know that singer, Gwen Aquarius, the libber? Well you know they took her down to the Hall. They booked her for defacing public property. Because of that midnight mural, you know, on the H.E.W. building. And with attempted murder because she shot the policeman. Well, they could have locked her up for life but they let her go the guy was saying. And this is true now, because she's trying to sue the state: they let her go Kate, but they cut out her tongue. They said that ought to be plenty punishment because they found out she was a lesbian. They got such a laugh out of that. Them and their smut. I couldn't laugh, Kate. I said some things I shouldn't have.'

'Jesus God,' Kate breathed. Something moved in a deep part of her body. She walked upright only with great effort. She wanted to pound down the walls of the brick building beside her. 'When do they leave? When do you leave, I mean?'

'Tonight.' Vivian's voice took on the yammering quality that signalled the presence of others. 'Oh, Katy, it's going to be a blast. We'll go up in Sue's Datsun and stay overnight at her aunt's until the guys come in on their bikes. We'll have the whole weekend . . .'

Kate wasn't hearing her. She saw a bus out of the corner of her eye. 'Listen. Here's mine. I've got a party early in the evening. It's a testing party so I've got to show. But I'll get plenty sick. My date will bring me home by nine and I'll be at your place by ten. Don't let them – don't leave before ten. Okay?' She risked a search of Vivian's face, even in the midst of people crowding on the bus.

Vivian was nodding, 'And you'll talk to Alice?'

'I'll talk to her.' Kate leapt on the bus, revealed her pass and let the lurch throw her to the spot she saw by the horizontal rail. As she grabbed the bar she automatically took her billfold from her hip pocket and held it in her hand.

She was going. She knew it now as surely as she felt the bodies pressing in on her from all sides. She was going to leave the city. Back to the country. Back to the boonies. She smiled in spite of her growing anxiety. She flashed on the countryside where she had grown up, flashed on the small town girl running away to the far-off city, looking like nothing she'd ever seen on TV and in some part of herself not wanting to look like it. Her daddy crazy with the d.t.'s, crazy with guilt and resentment at her dead mum, her bitter aunts promising him he would roast in hell. She hadn't even heard him when he ranted about what happened to young girls in the city. She had her bags packed, her high school diploma not yet framed but already flattened in the top compartment of her suitcase, and a letter to-whom-it-might-concern from Mrs Keys at the Lazybreeze Motel in town saying she was a dependable girl, a top-notch worker and that any firm would be smart to hire her.

The years here. The finding of her own kind. On the job she'd been able to dress up her plainness well enough to pass for pretty. Then the minute she got home out of the dresses and into the jeans, or into classy clothes for a night out. Those first years with Edie, the seemingly endless round of crises – jealousies, secrets, tale-bearings – and the better years with Patty, but always the game; for all but the close circle, it was always the game. Patty's leaving. Her depression. The isolation. Only recently her working out of it. Protecting herself. No more falling in love. No more Patty. No more of that.

She strained down to see what street the bus was at. She knew better than to lose herself in her reveries; too often it had meant long walks back to her stop. Sixteen more blocks. Sixteen more blocks that she wouldn't be seeing after tonight. She rested her foot on a seat brace. When had she first dared to wear pants to work? Neat pants, but with pockets. Nobody had cracked. There were lots of women doing it. But now the new rule. No more pants on the ladies. All girls got to be in skirts and hose. Like the old days. Next month that would be effective.

Kate shifted hands on the rail and pulled her jacket closer. Was it really the new dress regulation that made her want to leave the city? 'That and the walls,' she murmured aloud. Next week all the partitions were being removed. The walls had allowed workers to function in groups and had offered a suggestion of rooms. Now all the girls were to be in one big space. Kate wondered about that. It gave her the same spooky feeling she got when they took her picture every time she went to the bank or the supermarket – her picture and her thumbprint.

The tightening up was now accelerating. She read about off-beat political groups that either dispersed or were Brought To Justice. Some bars known to be gay went out of business. Women's

Sunday softball had been discontinued after some ugly incidents with vigilante Christian groups who patrolled the parks with clubs looking for queers. Since private citizens had to be protected, the police force was doubled and you saw prowling cop cars twice as often. Since women need even more protection, a ten o'clock curfew would go into effect at the beginning of the year. More and more protection, more and more isolation. Shorter rest periods on the job so you couldn't socialise. The return of styles to restrictive clothes. The way clerks looked at you now when you tried on shirts in the men's department. Alice was wrong. It was getting steadily worse. The other morning in the mirror Kate's reflection had told her for the thousandth time: the city is no place for you. Better to leave than to be inspected every day by some Geiger counter that detected unfeminine behaviour. Better to leave than to convince yourself that you wanted to totter around on spike heels. Better to leave than to have to meet secretly like Vivian's group does.

Cut and run. Could she do it? What would they do? Where would they go? What made the country any safer than the cities? Was it true there were women living together there without men? How did they do it?

Her questions hit the pavement with her as she piled off at her stop. Bob and Martha were not back at the flat yet. She pulled a chair up to the kitchen window and began making a memory of the kids playing in the street three stories below. Deliberately she observed the light, the texture of colours, the angles of movement. She was leaving this. She wasn't coming back.

Leslie, the eight year old from next door had dropped out of the kickball game and seemed to be looking up at the window. Kate would almost swear the child was talking to her. She seemed to say, 'I'll be there too.' Kate shook her head. The message seemed to insist. 'I'll be there too, Kate!'

'You do what you gotta do,' she thought.

Below her, Leslie smiled and waved. 'Yes,' Kate heard through the traffic din, through the closed window, and over the distance of three stories. 'Yes,' she said to herself.

She packed without making it apparent that she was leaving for more than a weekend. She bathed, dressed, ate, left a note for Bob and Martha, and then stowed her soft bag behind the garbage cans where only she would find it later.

She was a mild success at the party, managing nicely to listen to several men – they thought she was a real winner – compliment the hostess, fake a sick headache and lean wearily on her escort's strong arm as he helped her to his car. He wanted to come up and see that she was all right, and further to force his intentions, but Kate gave him no chance. She stood leaning back on the foyer door until she heard him zoom down the street and career around the corner.

Still in her femme-drag she caught a cross-town bus, her soft bag in tow. With the skill and boredom of long practice she evaded the stares of men who clearly wanted to take care of a single girl. One of them followed her after she got off the bus, a big red-faced man who paced himself at exactly her speed, however she varied her stride, and stayed precisly seven metres behind her. Kate was infuriated as always.

'It's time to change my life,' she told herself. In a movement born of rage and daring she stopped dead in her tracks and whirled as she threw off her medium heeled shoes. In her stockinged feet she advanced upon the startled man. She said nothing, only thought: 'I'm tired of you following me. I'm fed to the gills of you thinking you got all the power. You got none. None! It's draining right out of you, right out of the soles of your feet. Watch it there running into the gutter! You got no power anymore. You are nothing but a marshmallow man!' At that point she stood squarely in front of him. He paled. He turned. He ran. Kate almost fainted. Then, after redeeming her shoes she too turned and ran – straight to Viv's apartment house. By the time Vivian let her in she was so flushed and exhilarated she was ready to lead battalions of women against the United States Army.

Alice and Vivian brought her back to reality. Both women had been crying. Alice was dressed for drama, Kate observed, and seemed if anything to be even more sexually attractive than the last time Kate had seen her. Her lacquered nails constantly worried her earrings. She stood by the bar in black lounging pyjamas. The top was of some soft metallic fabric. She was smoking. The full ashtray said she had been smoking a lot.

Vivian, much the same build and colouring as Alice, nevertheless was a contrast in clothing and movement. She was still in her work clothes, slacks and blouse. She had a scotch bottle in one hand and in the other a glass that she kept refilling. Her small figure cast a large shadow as she paced up and down the tiny living room.

'You talk to her,' she said as Kate put down her bag and coat. With that, she went into the bedroom and closed the door.

'Are you going?' Alice offered Kate a cigarette.

'Yes.' Kate refused the cigarette. She felt awkward, standing there in her simple-girl attire. She longed to strip off her party dress and get into comfortable cords and a shirt. Kate, the girl with the unremarkable figure. Kate, the shapeless, gawky one. She was alien to the whole world. She did what she always did when she felt this way: she moved. She slid onto the sofa, ran her hands through her shoulder-length hair, and crossed her legs like she had on pants. That helped.

'Vivian figured you would. You're both fools.' Alice turned to the window.

'Seductive,' Kate grunted to herself. 'Why won't you come, Alice?' she said aloud.

'That's an open-and-shut case. I won't come because I'm in too good a place here. And it's getting better. I didn't bust my ass all these years just so I could throw it all over and play stalwart pioneer in the country. Another year and I'll be able to call the shots in my division. We'll move out of this dump and I'll fix Viv so she'll never have to work again. That's why I'm not going. And if I have anything to say about it, Viv's not going either.'

Kate said nothing. She was wrestling with a complex rush of emotions. In the first place she could identify her sheer jealousy of women like Alice. It was kind of rancour that she, Kate, could never move with Alice's assurance, could never wear clothes like that, make them seem so alive, somehow, so much like a part of the body that carried them. Very close to all that envy was the unadulterated sexual desire that Alice provoked in her. Apart from both these feelings was Kate's long history of distaste and distrust for this woman. She wanted to seize her and shake her. She wanted to seize her and subdue her.

Instead she said, 'Why do you want her here, Alice? What do you get from Vivian that you don't get from your men?' There. It was out.

Alice snapped at her like a whip. Kate felt physically seared by the rage in those eyes. Then Alice gathered herself, masked the

94

anger. 'I should have expected that from you. You've never liked me.'

'You didn't answer my question.'

Alice was across the room in an instant and in Kate's face the next. Her hands were on Kate's shoulders. 'I'll tell you why I want her here, you cheap imitation of a baby butch. Because I love her. Love. That may be a word lacking in your vocabulary. It's spelled L-O—'

The buzzer.

Both women froze. Vivian came out of the bedroom.

'Too early for Sue,' she said. 'Maybe trouble. I'm not here.'

Alice was pushing the voice relay. 'Who is it?'

There was silence; then a man spoke. 'Looking for Miss Moratti,' it said. 'Miss Vivian Moratti.'

'She's not here,' Alice replied.

'Are you her sister?'

'What's that to you?' Alice flared, then, recovering herself, 'Who are you?'

'We're from the Benton Mills Personnel Office. We understand Miss Moratti had a little trouble at work yesterday and we want to talk with her about it.'

'You're liable to get a big promotion if you go on working nights like this.' Alice was walking that thin line between go-to-hell and come-to-bed. Kate marvelled. She thought she heard the man chuckle.

'Can you tell me what time Miss Moratti will return?'

'She's out with her boyfriend and she may not be back tonight.'

'Oh. I don't suppose you know her boyfriend's name?'

'No I don't and you better believe I wouldn't tell a stranger if I did. Goodnight.' Just the right proportion of righteous indignation, haughty self-control, pleasant rebuff, and implicit familiarity. Alice kept the switch open a moment but there was no further remark. Vivian crossed to the window trying to see the walk below.

'That's it,' she muttered. Then back to Alice and Kate. 'They're trying to make a psych charge. I need adjustment to my co-workers.'

'Why they looking for you at night, Viv?' Alice tried to turn Vivian towards her.

'I told you. Because I been shooting off my mouth.' She was

pacing again. 'They got Lucy at her house last week at night. Lucy. Lucy's not even queer. Just does her own thing. Like trying to organise women in the cutting department. That was a mistake. They let it out that she had a nervous breakdown, that she was laid off until she rested. We won't see Lucy again.' Vivian was at the window once more. 'I tell you, I'm not paranoid. I know what I know. I buck them. They don't like it. They move me out – a little concern about my health, a little needle in my arm and I'm off in dreamland. You won't see Vivian again.' She paused. 'He's driving off. They may believe your story and track down good old Roy. I hope to hell he's out shooting craps so they won't find him until morning.'

Kate sensed a shift in mood. Vivian was looking at Alice now. Alice seemed stricken, as if she suddenly understood Vivian's panic. They weren't saying anything. Kate felt like an unwilling Peeping Tom. She picked up two glasses and took them into the kitchen. When she got to the sink she leaned on it and shook her head. What was she doing anyway? What did they think they were doing? If it was true what Viv said then there was no escape. They had all the machines they needed. How could five women resist even the highway patrol? If they wanted Viv they could get her. Couldn't they? And do what to her? Tinker with her brain a little. Make her want to be a whore or a housewife. Or just keep her doped up. Doped up and docile. And convinced that a whore or a wife was all she could be. She'd live if she cooperated. So would they all.

Kate felt another shift inside herself. That was the third or fourth time today. She knew all over again they had to get out. She began to see in her head some plans for how that would happen. When she went back into the living room Alice was standing in front of the fake fireplace. She was holding a sobbing Vivian.

'Maybe they're right.' Vivian was pushing the words into Alice's shoulder. 'Maybe I have wigged out. Maybe I ought to stay and get better . . .' She broke into a new set of low-level shrieks.

Alice shook her. 'Vivian!' She shook her again. Then with a harshness that shocked Kate she slapped Vivian hard. Several times. 'Shut up!' She slapped her again. Vivian looked at her, silent and frightened. 'You're going to go,' Alice said. 'You're right. And you are going to go. Now.' She turned to Kate. 'Is Sue coming here?'

'In half an hour.'

'Not soon enough. You two go there. Right now. Get out of town as quick as you can.' Alice took a tissue from her pocket, shoved it into Vivian's hand. 'You're going to make it.'

Vivian was still in shock. She started to protest. 'But you're not coming?'

'No, babe. Not this trip. I'll stick around and be sure you make it first. When I find out you're not eaten by bears I'll come and join you.'

Vivian was incredulous. 'You will?'

'Sure.'

Vivian threw herself into a clinging rocking embrace of the other woman. Kate met Alice's eyes over Vivian's shoulder.

'Liar,' Kate's eyes said.

'I know,' said Alice's. Then she broke the clinch. 'Now get your shit together.' She was about to go towards the bedroom when the buzzer sounded again. There was another frozen moment; all three women were galvanised.

Kate forced herself to move to the intercom. 'I'll take it.'

Alice stopped her hand. 'Let me.' She pushed the button. 'Yes?'

A man's voice. The same man. 'Miss Moratti?'

She motioned for Kate and Vivian to hurry, then went into high gear herself. 'Why, who wants to know?'

'Is this the lady I was speaking to earlier? Or is this Miss Moratti, Miss Vivian Moratti?'

'Well I may be both. But I'm not accustomed to conversing with strange men. Suppose you tell me who you are and what you want.' Another gesture to Kate and Vivian.

'I want to see Miss Vivian Moratti. About a work-related matter. My name is Harvey Lowder.'

'Are you all by yourself, Mr Lowder?'

'Well, no. My partner . . .'

Alice interrupted him. 'Mr Lowder would you hang on for just a second? There's something on my stove.' She released the button and covered the mouthpiece for good measure. To Kate and Vivian she said, 'Get out. I'll invite them up. You'll pass them on the stairs. They'll have no idea who you are or which apartment you came from. Now go.'

Kate looked at her.

And Alice looked at Kate.

Then Kate moved quickly, throwing on her coat, holding out Vivian's jacket. 'You heard her. Let's get going.'

Vivian flung her arms around Alice. 'I'll be in touch with you, like I said. And you'll come. Promise you'll come?'

'Sure love, I'll come. Now get.' She received Vivian's quick kiss and watched her go out of the door.

Kate wanted desperately to say something. She couldn't find the words. Instead she said, 'How long can you stall them?'

Alice's eyes met hers without even a flicker. 'Oh, you know me, Kate. I'll stall them all night.'

They might have stayed there much longer, searching each other's eyes for understanding. Alice broke the movement by turning to the intercom. Kate dragged both the bags out of the door and began her plunge down the first flight of steps to where a dazed Vivian waited for her. As she closed the door she had heard Alice's voice.

'Mr Lowder? I'm sorry to keep you waiting. But that little emergency gave me a chance to check the liquor cabinet. Would you and your partner be interested in talking about this over a drink?'

They were on the bottom stairs when they passed the men. Kate hoped she and Vivian sounded gala and giddy. Lowder and the other man gave them no more than a glance. The look on their faces suggested that there would be plenty of time for the women to clear the city before the Benton Mills Personnel Office picked up Viv's trail again.

There, stretched silent at the top of the world, Pelagine relived it all, to the closing of the apartment door behind her and Vivian. The full remembering now was over. The forward-moving memories were speeding up, tumbling towards her from the past. The driving out of the City, Sue's aunt, their separation from each other – all flowed by her again in more and more rapid cycles. Another scene hung for an instant as if to expand itself: Vivian's capture. Then it changed its mind and raced on by. Pelagine was glad. She could not have relived that horror again today.

Her life was only flashes now, flickering through her head,

whirring at top momentum until she felt the present coming on. The montage slowed. The scenes ticked by, one-by-one, each closer to today, each calmer. Still Pelagine held her stretch. The girl-woman Jacqua passed as she had been just yesterday, offering a holding for the long night. 'I have to talk with Jacqua.' The thought brought her the last step back to her hardself, to the thin and stiffened naked body, arms and legs outflung, buttocks-balanced, transfixed there in a puddle of sunlight in the centre of a treehouse on a chilly winter morning.

With the practice of over four-score years, Pelagine began her retreat from memory, her retreat from pain. She eased the glottal dam that had held in her breath, began the push of air from below her heart, and slowly lowered her feet to the coverlet, bending them sole-to-sole into her crotch. The coming down was glorious. She sank back spread-eagled on the beansack, still exhaling, still rehearsing, still expanding. She became liquid, seeping into every corner of the room and oozing out of the cracks. She dripped to the forest floor and flowed through dry leaves over soft moss and hardened stones. She covered the earth. She flooded the universe. Again nothing moved. There she lay without even a heartbeat, splayed out all over the world. There she lay at the floor of her air, in absolute comfort and repose. 'I could do it now,' she thought, 'if I wanted'. Simply refuse to take in breath. Simply stay here at the bottom of the great release. Why become taut again? Why contract the muscles, stir the blood, activate the personal brain? Why be again?

'Because it's not yet time to go.' She did not ask who said it. She began the slow climb back up the funnel. She breathed now, but very shallowly. Her eyes still closed, she sent tongues to work. They began with her face, the lovers' tongues and lips, smoothing her cheeks and ears, drawing even her short white hair into slick damp planes. They soothed the still thick down on her neck, her shoulders. Simultaneously at front and back they washed over her torso, easing her spine, smoothing her wrinkled breasts, making her buttocks warm, her stomach cool. They rode down her arms and thighs to tickle her elbows and knees. In a delicate trailing off into air they stroked the fingers and toes, and drew the fibres out into the distance, kilometres away. They left her, again motionless, again at the bottom of the world.

'You others,' she smiled. She brought air back into her frame and lay lightly breathing in the warming sun.

'I love you, old Pelagine,'

'I know you do, Jacqua. Come tonight and hold me?'

'Ijeme . . .'

'Ah, yes, Ijeme. She's been to the City.'

Jacqua's enfoldment told the old woman something of Ijeme's story. 'She asks to hold you tonight, Pelagine.'

'I reckon we do have some things to share, some holding and rocking to do together. She can come early tonight.'

'And in a few days before I go to the Kochlias, I'll be at your door, old woman. Shall we hold one another?'

'Of course. Come again, Jacqua.'

'Come again, Pelagine.'

The old woman laughed aloud. 'And again,' she responded.

They said no more that day.

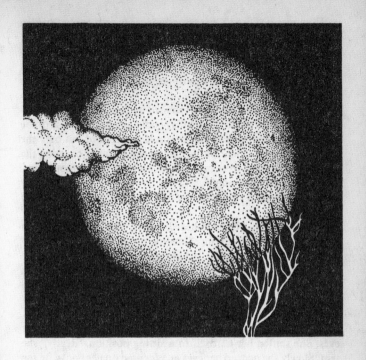

Diana and the Moon

The white moon waxed just a shade short of full, laying even the valleys open in pale blue light. Everything paused in silence, in anticipation of some special greeting. Diana was squatting on the lower part of the ridge basking her face in the full-risen glow. She was panting. As she rested her head on her folded arms her buttocks hesitated a few centimetres from the rocky soil. She backpulsed towards the ensconcement – cold miles behind her now – with her spanner still widespread.

'I'm ranging clear,' she sent. 'I rode wind all the way. All the way in about an hour.'

'How was it, Diana?' Li was asking. Her own name tumbled towards her with a comfortable soft-touch of recognition.

'Just as you said it would be. I cried most of the up time. Beautiful. Frightening. Alone. I remembered you and Manaje as I went over the Kochlias. It was ringed in blue tonight.'

'It often is. Were you cold?'

'I don't remember being so. I shaded by the old patterns as you said and scudded the last few hills. Too much to see and do to be cold.' She moved back to her hardself and looked out over the forest below her. There was a mist in the distance covering the place where the tall trees began their walk up the far mountains. She scrutinised the moon.

'We may have to wait one more day,' she sent, 'though I want to try tonight.'

'It was waxing when we heard before,' Li responded. 'And anyway, no harm in offering. Can you mark the stars?'

'They've yielded entirely. It's like day here.'

'No matter. We are gathered four-into-one and waiting here. There are two more at the Eastern Ensconcement and Seja alone in the west. Manaje and Wanza span cover while we are open. May I see the bald hill?'

Diana loosed her mindstretch into laxspread and closed her eyes. She shifted her hardself to a sitting position. 'Ready,' she sent. Slowly she opened her eyes and focused on her boots; on the wide area stretching out from them; on the edge of the ridge and the deep drop beyond its rim. Then with a careful panning, she turned to her left and let her eyes fall on the three charred trees at the north-east corner of the clearing. Bleak and leafless, they stood together against the sky, rallied in mutual indignation. A set of equally black stumps masked their lower trunks. Diana continued to pan.

Li broke in. 'Enough. You are on the right bluff. The angry trees are unmistakable.'

Diana lifted back into mindstretch. 'I'll rest until it is low enough to flood.'

'Here, too,' Li closed.

Diana slid a circle monitor into place, checked its parameters, spanned one final time and locked in the monitor at low threshold. She stood and stretched. Turning to the angry trees, she took up her panning again. Around to the north the hill rose steeply behind her. The trees began again not far beyond the rise and marched in grand succession to the top of the ridge just above her. She walked to her left now over hard dirt towards the western edge of the bluff. Her eyes and feet sought flat comfortable ground. Here and there a hardy bush thrived, but there was no grass. Only a rocky shelf, only the solid side of a mountaintop cloven and bared by a long-departed machine.

Diana stretched supine on the hardness. Level it was. Comfortable it could never be. With a glance at the sky she plotted the probable course of the moon, shifted a bit so the soles of her feet addressed the south-southwest. 'That ought to do, huh?' she murmured aloud. Pushing against the small loosely packed rocks at her side she mustered a surge of warmth from below her ribs and passed her watchfulness to her lonth while she slipped into suspended rest.

She waited there a very long while as fireflies might reckon time; by the calculation of the trees only a few moments. She was gossiping with Brownsblood back at the ensconcement, the stealthy, patient cat of the children's bath, when her monitor stirred. In an uncharacteristic move, she opened her eyes before attending the warning. She was just in time to see a heavy wing slice across the moon. A condor sailed over the western vale. Diana checked her spanners. There was another one. Widely dipping, both of them, in opposite directions. She found no others. In a burst of civility she extended to them, tapping gently first towards the moonslicer, then the companion. No response. Diana shrugged, sat up. She watched the broad birds swoop into the far valley, weaving and rising, circling and dropping. They shrank into dust motes on her spanner.

The moon was just past its zenith now. Lifting her hands Diana washed them in the pallid rays. She stretched and yawned. 'Not yet time,' she thought. She decided to prepare anyway. She pulled herself to a kneeling position and began removing her jacket, her woollen shirt; then standing, the heavy trousers, socks and boots. Her outmoving breath scooted grey over the clear cold air. Diana was not cold. 'Too much body hair,' she smiled. There was absolutely no sound save the rustle of her clothes as she laid them by her rocky bed. She faced the moon with her bare body.

'I greet you,' she said to the bright face. Her arms reached out as if to embrace the whiteness. She placed herself in the grainy light that stretched between herself and the moon. Her head vibrated. She felt joy rising from the earth beneath her, rising to meet the moon through her. Suddenly, without warning even from her shallow self, she felt her voice shouting, her arms disengaging, her legs pumping, her body leaping across the clearing and falling sideways on its hands, wheeling to its feet and over to its hands again. Round and round in a circle of high breaths, expulsions, and high breaths again until she was dizzy with exhilaration and her own deep-sounding laughter. In a final forward somersault she sprawled supine on the hard rough rock, laughing almost without control. She felt bruised and scratched.

'A lunatic,' she whispered between gasps. 'I love, I love a lunatic!' She hugged herself with all her frenzied strength. She folded her knees into foetal position and rolled over to her side. She laughed. She laughed more. She laughed until only an insistent tapping on her northern spanfield sobered her.

'Are you all right?' Li's call carried more than a touch of the frantic. Diana swept the hurry from her brain and tried to soothe herself. From deep inside herself she invited calm kindnesses to visit her whole body. There was no response. She tried again. This time a dry heave of exhaustion answered her.

'I need earth,' she sent to Li. Her head felt fuzzy.

'Of course,' Li answered. Diana lay flat on her stomach, her arms and legs outstretched on the wintry ground.

'Breathe with me, Li.'

'Breathe with me, Diana.'

With her ebbing strength, Diana felt her way into Li's high waist. They came together to the earth, there on the bare bluff in the stark pale moonlight in the middle of a gentle winter. They drew in the cold air without caution and sent it without challenge through the marrow of their bones to their flesh, then to the earth that was also their flesh. They rose and fell together. They surged upwards with the pull of their lover the moon and downwards home-deep to the bowels of their mother the earth. They did not rest until whole civilisations had flourished and passed on. They did not depart until some faraway Saturnid moth broke through darkness and pushed out to its greeting of the world.

'Fully given and well taken.' A long pause; then, 'Soon, Li.'
'Or deep, Diana.'
'Soon.'
'And deep.'
'Red waters.'
'Deep.'
They spoke together: 'Deep. Soon.'

It was a while before Diana lifted her head. She felt rested. With easy swimming stretches she shifted to a sitting position. The moon was well into decline now. Diana looked at it with wonder. 'You touch my madness,' she said aloud. Li was rubbing the outer surfaces of her words. Diana let her in.

'I did not shade myself,' she said.

'You tried to meet the moon alone,' answered Li.

'She loosed the knots and sent me back. Back to before I tensed with knowledge, to where I was slack and innocent. I am her servant.'

'No more so than she is ours. We have to greet her together, that's all. Do you want to wait another day for the listening?'

Diana looked around her. She massaged her feet and legs, her back, her stomach. 'No,' she extended. 'I am ready and I wish to try it now.'

'No exhaustion?'

'No. I am in my body fine. But I could not approach her alone again.'

'None of us could. One is too small a vessel to carry her. Ursula and Manaje are on watch. We're ready when you are.'

Diana stretched a nod. She stroked her leg and back muscles into patience and then deliberately with short breaths alone pumped her body into a standing position. 'Now,' she said to the long-strong tissue. Obediently the muscles bunched and eased as her legs carried her to her pallet by her clothes. She settled into the ground, made a pillow of her trousers and jacket, and sighted down the middle of her bare body to the far mountaintops. The bright lowering moon struck her stomach at an acute angle. As its heaviness weighed upon her torso, her hips undulated in a familiar vulnerability. A touch of the frenzy came upon her again.

'We're here, too,' Li broke in to her. Diana eased.

To her right and towards the west in her line of vision was a clump of scrub brush. She did not know its name but she felt she wanted it for a marker. She sailed a soft scoop of thick green towards its ragged top, asking for recognition, for participation in the coming openness. The bush awakened and uncovered itself to her. They knew each other instantly by an exchange of old forgotten rhythms. Diana plunged all the way to its roots in thanksgiving. The bush, for its part, channelled its life liquids from its forks and branches into the forks and branches of Diana's own blood's path. Diana had to break the flowing, else they could have been together there a very long time.

'Be with me,' she sent.

'Be with me,' the bush answered. They acknowledged and held at nodding distance.

To her left there was no land guide, only white bright air. The far hills were too low. Would the body of that cirrus cloud do? She stretched to it, covering its edges with a soft petition. With all her attention she lay open to the elongated wisp. Nothing came. It was not as if the cloud were refusing her, only as if she were dispersing it with her very enfolding. Unexpectedly it answered. She had not expected such a message. She had to listen with her unintentional ear, give to the cloud only secondary or peripheral attention, and in fact pretend no attention at all to the cloud. When she did that, there was the cloud's gentle whispering at the back door of her mind. Diana laughed. It was not easy to speak so indirectly and the conversation was more a line than the usual seeping, but they understood each other. The wind was not pushy tonight and the cloud intended to be there a good while. It was glad to be a marker. Diana introduced the bush; cloud and plant greeted each other somewhere near the top of her skull, just within the shades of her moon-shadowed hair.

'I have my anglepoints,' she stretched to Li. 'And the moon already draws me. We're almost ready.'

'Here, too. We have all felt the rays now. If your body tires during the listening, call us to it. We may not know.'

'It won't tire. It pulls and surges already. I think the tension alone will sustain it.' Even as she spoke Diana felt herself drawn upwards against the earth's pull. She struggled to stay grounded.

Her eyes were closed; it was as yet too uncentring to look upon the moon. She spread her hands beside her to check her place, shifted her torso against the rock, felt the dirt beneath her calves and knees. She was in no way footloose or likely to ride wind. She was very much attached to the ground. And yet the periodic tugging on her body was a physical force. She was slipping into the grip of a hungry suction. 'It's time,' she sent. She looked to her markers, raising her arms towards them with her hands out-stretched. They connected. She began steadily taking in long breaths, exhaling through her mouth, through her fingertips and toes. Her breathing moved into rhythm with the pulls upon her body. She forced open her eyes, the better to see a lover full in the face and she gasped at the intimacy there. A searing whiteness was wrapped in bright metallic tendrils, starshot and rain washed. They fell in an ecstasy of silence across her open body, they plunged into the earth and bent within it to encircle her shoulders, her spine, her legs. She was drowning in light, drummed by pellets of quickening silver, swept and pushed back, pulled and released, drawn and expelled. Her breath, when at last it let go, escaped in a long cascading cry. It was not her cry only. Other voices joined and in the silent valleys, pools of darkness reached to sweep the sound within themselves, to nest it there and give it gentle hearing.

Diana was breathing again and moving now into full listening posture. Without breaking the rhythm of the oceanic sway, she flattened her arms to the ground beside her and slowly raised her legs until her feet blocked the centre of the moon. They stood in black silhouette against the broad pale sky. To assure their readiness, she swirled through a last deep check with the others. They were present.

She was aware now of a rising wind in the distance, a sound akin to the tuning of an orchestra. Her feet were painfully yet restfully drawn upwards to the hidden moon; her body followed in an upsweep that paused and did not return, though her hands still grasped the earth beneath them. The wind went in a glissando now through the closer trees. With infinite slowness and care she began to move her ankles apart, to see between them the bright face beyond. Her muscles pushed wider and wider until the thin white field broadened to refill the sky; her eyes were again dazzled. She spread each foot slowly outward towards its marker. One touched the line and locked into the bush top to her right. Its partner moved to cover the cloud.

She was transfixed. Her eyes closed with the warm kiss of cold light and she smiled in an expectant contentment. She could listen now, her whole body attuned, her whole body the ear, the channel of meaning. The wind subsided into silence.

They were not long in coming, those unfamiliar women's voices. They fell from the moon in a deluge of strange beautiful sounds. Diana could not extract any sense from them. Only the rhythms became understandable, and the rhythms mentioned excitement, delight, and disbelief. The rhythms said, 'Again we meet! Who are you?'

Diana was aware now of Li and Seja and the others from the ensconcements, all present within her and spanning upward with her in bright deployment, mutual enfolding all open and receiving, all hearing and understanding. The scent of oceans swept through her – and fresh fruits and smells she could not name, smells of stickinesses, others of hardnesses and of roughnesses. She felt rather than saw thick forests, warm air, and white sand under blue water. It seemed in some distant part of her to be her home of some other time.

The rejoicing was upon them all. Shapes began to form. She saw them with the eyes that her viscera had become – dark brown women, wild black hair, white teeth smiling in the joy of the together listening and knowing. They lay holding together, some eight of them, each open and turned towards a pale rising light. Strange colourful birds clucked and squawked among them, climbing over their bodies, occasionally joining the listening. The sounds of the women were no longer a cacophony but a practised enfoldment now of their own, sent forth to the moon, their high lover and draped through her over the women of the hills.

Diana scarcely breathed. She understood that the messages were passing through her, understood even some of the messages themselves: that these faraway women had no need to hide, that the melting mountain had taken many of them, that only a few hundred of them had survived and some of the gentles with them. She knew in her tiniest cell how these women spent their days, of the tasks they had set for themselves in the girdling of the globe, of the healing mineral springs in their mountains, of the passing into food of each of them for the others. They shared secrets about the moon that strode the sky between them: how she lifted up the tides and set them down again, how she drank from mothers' milk to whiten her face, how even when she seemed darkened and shy still she sought the caresses, the passings through and over her, of her earth daughters. For their part in their listening, the hill women shared the textures of their lives, the boundaries of their fears, and the importance of the work they took to be their own.

There was a tightening of the bonds that hug the earth. The closing was near. They sang without words the meanings of words, the islanders first:

Digging high. Painful sight.
Never trading love for might.
We are here.

The hill women answered:

Climbing deep. Our children bend.
Nor close the womb at either end.
We are here.

Together they sang over the ages and miles:

We are here.
We are there.

The hill women said:

Our fire
our rest,
our open deed
remembered well.
We claim it now.
Deep and soon.

We claim it now, they were answered.

Soon and deep.

And we, you.

And we, you.

Then together:

Deep.
Soon.

The bush and the cloud waited until the moon had passed beyond the horizon. Then they gently joined in a warm shade to cover the sleeping Diana. Even the condors did not rouse her when they flapped out of the valley with the dawn, and the trees knew that their anger was not at her.

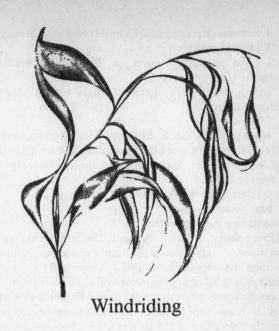

Windriding

'The gentles say they must meet with us. A matter both wide and deep, they say.' Evona matched the rhythm of the words with her own short footsteps. The gravel-dirt road scratched her boot soles. She had left the City hours before her scheduled departure.

Quawa was far into the mountains north of her. She was surprised. 'The gentles?' she sent. 'In the City?'

Evona pulled herself up short. 'No, no!' she stretched. 'I told you, Quawa, no. They are not from the City.' She stood now mid-road under the dark trees, pushing her senses towards the other woman. 'They come from east of the City – '

'Evona, I'm not enwrapped, not hearing. Are you still? In your hardself, I mean?'

'Yes.'

'I'm not understanding yet. Can you stretch to Tulu or Blase?'

'They are not open.'

'How long before you reach the Chameleon Glade?'

Evona considered. 'Several hours if I could scud. More by foot.'

'Why not scud?'

'I haven't scudded in over a year. Remember where I've been Quawa –'

'Of course, I didn't intend to weight you. It returns with practice, though . . .'

'I know.'

'However, then. Get to the Glade. From there you'll surely be able to join with Tulu or Blase for sending. Meanwhile I will reach the others in the Eastern Ensconcement. We may need a gatherstretch.'

'I'll send again before dawn.'

'May you come soon.'

'And may you receive me.'

Evona shifted the heavy backpack. The further to the north-east she hiked, the more abandoned the road seemed. With sudden decision she stopped. Looking about she caught a break in the roadside brush. She pressed into it with a lurch and dropped to her knees. Twisting again towards the road she leaned back against the resilient branches of a felled tree. With an effort she drew her arms and shoulders free of the padded leather straps until the pack rested entirely against the brush. Unhindered, her arms swung up and out in gratitude.

She swept the vicinity full circle with her near-reach. Only the night sounds. She spread a monitor for an all-around sweep then was up on her feet again. She closed her eyes and began a murmuring. Before her, in keeping with her incantation, her fingers moved swiftly in ladder-climbing movement: right thumb on left forefinger, left thumb on right middle finger, right thumb on left ring finger, and so on and on in perpetual motion back and forth, climbing back and forth.

We do not new-born spin the web
we do not span the path at birth
but practise, practise, night and day,
the tiny bridges first.

Straight and still she stood on the dark roadside, only her hands in rapid motion, only her lips repeating over and over again,

'Practise, practise, night and day . . .' Her movement gradually stopped. The murmurs ceased. Evona drew in and held a deep breath. Then exhaled. Another. Held. Exhaled. The breaths came more quickly, released more suddenly. Evona's arms spread to her sides. Again the intake. The hold. The release. Then as she sensed a readiness, a long long breath, a hold, and a bend at the waist. At the same moment her knees moved and her feet lifted from the dirt; she clasped her arms about her legs and ducked her head, a slow-motion folding into a foetal position. She closed her eyes tighter, concentrated upon the air which bore her – caressing it inside her lungs, rolling it outside her body. She knew herself to be suspended now, just a few centimetres above the ground, a ball barely hovering in space. She bobbed a moment and lifted to the right, to the left, even spun now a little until her weight centred. Then she settled, back up, gradually rocking to a gentle floating on the air. She found herself repeating:

The wind she lifts my laughter
the wind she lifts my cares,
and bearing both my pain and joy
she thus my body bears.

It seemed an eternity that she stayed there. Then with her exhalation, as deftly as she had folded in, she dropped her feet to the ground and stood again outstretched. Inside herself she was exhilarated. Then the whole process once again: inhale, suspend, release and back to the ground. Each time longer, each time a more steady suspending. Then as she hovered she dared to spread her attention, to reach out with her mind to check her monitor. She swept a full round, alert to danger. There was none. And most miraculously, she stayed suspended. Not even a quiver. Almost smugly she drew back and tested an alteration of her hardself. Very slowly she extended her arm, let it drop until the fingers brushed the gravel, the dust of the road. Still she hovered. She dared her other arm, letting it sweep gently across the dirt.

She drew on her memory now – movements and swayings from her first learnings of windriding. Manaje was with her again, standing firm on the ground beside her. Manaje, assuring her; Manaje, guiding her with her hardself. 'Now stretch out full length,' she heard the other woman say. Panic seized her. 'I will hold you, Evona. I will hold you in my hardself. There is nothing to fear. Stretch out.'

Evona remembered sharply the press of Manaje's arms across the front of her shoulders, beneath her legs. Slowly, relying on that touch she stretched out prone and parallel to the road. 'Don't leave me!' she flung out to the memory of Manaje.

'I won't leave you,' Manaje answered.

Then Evona felt the strong presence rocking her, swaying her in the air – first by arms then by hands then by the very slightest of fingerbrushings – moving her back and forth, left and right. Then Manaje was turning her, turning her over, supine, like a sleeping body resting there a metre from the ground.

Her eyes still closed she felt balanced just above Manaje's fingertips. Her arms hung to her sides. 'I must release breath,' she sent to the memory of Manaje.

'Go ahead,' was the answer.

Slowly, carefully, she released the air, reaching with her very skin and clothing to keep the contact with Manaje's fingers on her legs and shoulders. So barely touched; yet still she hung above the earth. Gingerly she drew in another breath. 'Release me now, Manaje. I remember.' And it was gone. The light connection disappeared. Evona lay stretched on thin air there above the fallen tree and her battered pack.

She dared to float and breathe. With careful intent, she bent her consciousness to her lower abdomen and transferred to her lonth there her suspension and her breathing. Satisfied that her lonth would indeed take over these functions, she returned to her full body. 'Practise,' she thought. 'Practise each step.' She stretched her arms above her head and envisioned how she looked from the outside, how an observer would see her. Then, holding that image in her bones, she felt herself into her limbs and filled up her skin completely, stretching it outward to its fullest. Her softsensing was coming easily now. She pictured and felt and heard how she wanted to move: her supine body drifting back and forth across the road in a widening circle. As she hovered and breathed, softsensing her desires, she began to push her arms gently to her sides; then up again, above her head; then down again. Cool air swept by her cheek. Was that her softsense? She opened her eyes to a dark roof of trees moving past her. That was not softsense. She drew down harder on both arms now, less hard on the right so as to make the circle. Again she stroked. And again. She was gliding across the road now, face up and stretched full length. Extra hard again on the left arm, there, to avoid the scrub brush. Around and around she went, breathing evenly now, fully aware, fully moving. Then reversing her route back the other way. Then face down and parallel, moving both arms and legs against the air. She dared even more as her confidence grew. She dared to sit, to stand perpendicular, trusting the air to hold her upright self. She moved her arms and legs in sweeping walking-running-scissors motions, up and down, climbing by the trees until she was manoeuvring more than thrice her height above the road.

Remembering more and more, risking more and more, Evona drew gradually into her centre. She shortened her arm stroke, the movement of her pumping legs. She transferred more and more control to her lonth, freeing herself more and more for newer performances. Her body slowed: she became less active. Her body slowed: she became more active in her lonth. Together with her breathings and efforts to stay aloft the lonth, the low centre of her self, was absorbing now her movements and her softsensings, absorbing one-by-one the changes that she was making in her flight. She could feel them all now, not in her immobile limbs but there in her womb: the breathing, the hovering, the arms and legs in concert, back and forth, still subject to her will but sustained now within her deepest place of self-holding.

Finally she laid her arms to her side and drew her ankles together. She was using no conscious physical movement whatsoever. Her lonth moved her immobile body, made it sweep and slide, coast and skim. She was fully lonthing now, letting that lower part of herself control both her suspension and the guidance of her upright body fully four metres above the earth.

'I do remember!' she gasped aloud. With her astonishment she faltered, dropping a metre towards the gravelled road. She caught herself by a swift intentional spread-eagle and a dip of her head, very much in her hardself. She righted her body and set herself the twin task of staying aloft and repeating with climbing movements the litany of the spider. 'Practise, practise, night and day . . .'

How long over the quiet road she sped and braked, drifted and dived, Evona did not know. As she rehearsed paradigms of movements and their variations, she was aware that she was waiting for something. She could not name it until it happened and when it happened she named it aloud: 'Footloose!' The change had come – the shift from being earthbound to being windborne. Until now her effort had been to get aloft and to stay there. Now the magic time had come; from this moment on it would be no strain to stay aloft; instead any effort would be to keep from going higher. It was no longer a fight against gravity but a fight to regain it.

Relief flooded her, relief she hadn't known she sought. She knew now that she could make the Chameleon Glade. Doggedly she addressed herself to the matter of being footloose. Physically she fought the buoyancy, pushing herself downwards, making herself heavy. She envisioned and felt large weights upon her shoulders and limbs, weights to keep her from flying off to the stars. Then she turned again her concentration to her womb, there to transfer her new knowledge to her lonth: 'hold down, don't push up.' She pressed into her centreself all the work of her muscles; she gave it to her softsensing, the weights themselves, handing them over one by one and feeling them taken from her, absorbed into the function of the lonth. Her knowledge of being footloose was now in control, taken over by a deep level of her being. 'Once you know something,' she smiled in remembrance, 'it becomes immaterial'.

She scudded easily now, just above the ground just above the treetops, just above whatever lay below. With a new exhilaration she dived and swooped some more, upright and prone, sitting and kneeling. Once in a new position, she moved her body only slightly, allowing the lonth clear control. She looped above the trees in wider and wider arcs. She relearned the handling of pitch – a throwing up and downwards of her legs; she rehearsed the secrets of direction – the pointing always with the third eye, or more accurately, with the widow's peak just at the central meeting of the hair and forehead; she experimented with the skills of yawing – a matter of shoulder position; she addressed with more and more precision the banks and turns, the drag and thrust – pushing always to her lonth the motions that could be involuntary, keeping always in her awareness and in her flesh and bones the necessary changes, the newer postures or inclinations. Always in the transfer from voluntary to involuntary she entertained the subtle suspicion that after all, there was no difference between them, not really . . .

Rising high above the trees she rode the full wind in the cloud-darkened sky. As she spun and drifted, Evona reset her monitor to capture vertical interference as well as the horizontal. That meant a doubling of her mindsweeps, an additional involuntary function. She flushed, as often she had done before in other situations to realise how vast her capabilities seemed to be. Her near-ecstasy was not so much now from the joy of riding the high wind as from the awareness of a thousand operations functioning together with such precision within her body. She felt herself to be an infinitely complex organism elaborating in its turn each complexity. 'To know the many in the one,' she remembered, 'is as rare as it is possible.'

Evona almost forgot the City with all its tension; even her sisters to the north seemed like a dream. As she swept starwards in one burst of joy, she recalled that there was something she had to do – carry some message . . . She literally came down a few metres. Her backpack. She mustn't return without the information from the City. Reluctantly she pivoted and dived full speed towards the road, the place of the broken bushes. As she evened with the tops of the yellow pines she doubled into the elementary foetal sphere and slowed her speed by half. It was only moments before she drifted down to the backpack's resting spot and moored herself a metre or so above it.

Here was a problem she had not anticipated: how to mount the heavy pack upon her back without sitting on solid ground. It seemed too cumbersome a task for one so recently transformed by grace and beauty. For a moment she was struck with the comedy of it all: how, flailing in mid-air, she would cut an ungainly figure wrestling with the pack. She didn't wish to ground herself and begin again; footloose seemed too hard to achieve. So she hovered still, a suspended sitting figure puzzling down at this extra burden.

Time was wasting. She would never make the Glade by dawn at this rate. Then she opened herself to the here-and-now existence of the pack itself and immediately a solution flashed before her: she could *tote* the pack. Or could she? She had not toted since her childhood and then only small articles. Could she tote it alone? Perhaps. She had lifted herself hadn't she? She could suspend it a metre at the proper height and then slip into it without effort. Something shifted below her. The pack. Had it actually stirred? Had her softsensing of its movement been that strong? Evona sharpened her attention and rapidly enfolded the pack. It shifted visibly. She then moved swiftly in her hardself, twisting her shoulders down and towards the pack so she could no longer see it. She extended her legs in a right angle to her torso. As she did so, she poured a cascade of attention on her envisioning of the pack, asking it to rise and join her. Obligingly the pack rose in her mind. She stretched her arms behind her, reaching for the straps, hoping for their reality. They were there! She slipped her arms through the loops and drew the bundle snugly to her back. It seemed to have no weight, yet she could feel its presence; its rough canvas reassured her hands. She buckled the hip band.

'Okay, Manaje, what now?' she sent humourously. 'Will it come with me if I rise to ride wind? Or do I have to tote it while I climb? Or do I just hang here and analyse?' She decided on action. Quickly she consigned the toting to her lonth and with the confidence of a veteran windrider, cast off her hover-mooring and rose with the pack far above the trees.

A pass or two over the road to get her bearings; a mere skyful of awe at the blanket below her – a quiet darkened forest on gentle hill pillows; a vow to be in another life a bird who makes maps; and over her shoulder a look of distaste and fear for the City to the south-southwest. She visited her lonth deep inside her and set her monitors for spherical clearance. Assured that all was well, she sang to herself as she rode the high wind over the deepening valleys in the north-east.

The wind she lifts my laughter
the wind she lifts my cares,
and bearing both my joy and pain
she thus my body bears.

A Man in the City

From the smallness of her rafter room Betha spanned over the entire house. A card game in the basement, under the pipes near the tall man's room. Five of them there amid tobacco fumes. No one in the other basement rooms. No one at ground floor except the two cats. Betha mindstretched to each simultaneously. One blocked. The other opened.

'Micksblood. Betha here.'

'I know,' the cat returned, some trace of exasperation in the stretch. 'Watch out for the tall one. He sometimes feels it when you enfold him.'

'Perhaps he's a gentle.'

'Not a chance.' Micksblood flashed her the pain of a large boot thrust into sleeping catribs. He tongued the ribs, remembering, 'They're all gone except for those in the furnace room. The big lashers are both working a split shift tonight.'

'Good. I'm meeting Aaron and perhaps another gentle at a bar, the Thumbscrew. Some crack in the seal is going on that they will tell me about. If you can get to the ladder door I'll leave tuna cake there. Enough for Athena too.'

'She's off her feed. Says she may decide to die. I'll give her some tuna cake if she'll have it. Will you touch a sister?'

'Mito has just arrived on her rotation. She will stay in brushtouch with me. Nothing of high notice but she will know of any danger. She's at Warren Distribution. The warehouse near E-flat from this centre. Warn her gently if you approach her. She's night-guarding for them and is training to be jumpy.'

'And I will night guard for us here.'

'Do,' Betha sent. 'Something is out of joint. We need to find it quickly. Can't be too watchful.'

'A shade that shields you, Betha.'

'And one to you, Micksblood.' Betha closed off from the cat, reaching at the same time with her hardself into the wall compartment cooler. She moulded the nearly dry tuna cake into the patty and in a flash of creativity shaped it into a fish. 'Tuna,' she smiled to herself, 'I doubt that Micksblood's ever seen a real fish. But he ought to love you instinctively. May you have loved living as Micksblood loves eating. May your going have been when you were ready and at your will.' With that she checked her reflection in the glass of the darkened closet door, unscrewed the bare bulb in her ceiling, picked up her jacket and backed down the ladder that nudged through her floor. In the blackness at the bottom she fumbled with the two bolts and the single padlock before the slit of a door opened onto the narrow second floor hallway. She snapped the padlock into place from outside, turned the bolt lock with a key and set the tuna cake at the bottom of the door casement.

Down the stairs, past two more locks, and she was out in the street. A row of temporary housing stretched between her and the buildings on the other side, along the centre of the block and where cars used to go. Long dumpy huts of plyboard and masonite, they ranged in the semi-darkness for blocks in each direction. Betha could see lights coming from the joinings and speculated on how long the squatters would be allowed to stay this time. Squatter-cleans took place spasmodically – a matter simply of moving everyone out of the huts and into the streets while the City disinfected or sometimes tore down the old ones.

She remembered living in one of the flimsy structures when she first arrived for her rotation – further east in the district. There had been a mandala-shaped bloodstain on the wall by the door. *KILL*!

had been painted over the blood. The fragile structure had seemed cold and damp and her spirits more so. But it had been hers alone. One blessing of the rotation was that the city men cherished privacy with almost religious fervour. Except at the breeding homes where all the children were at first kept together, every person, even the women, had to have a place to themselves. Betha had been glad for that. Even so, in the six square metres of space she had felt pushed in upon by the residents on either side and by the hordes that seemed to walk the city streets all through the night. However sacred it was, privacy meant only not being seen; she could be heard, smelt, and even felt as the wall between her and her neighbour – also sitting against his side of their shared wall – would give back and forth with their unwilling duet. She got to know when to lean heavy, when to lean light, and to identify her neighbour's mood by the way his body touched the partition. The huts only parodied privacy; its illusion was testified to by the absolute absence of locks. People in the huts expected to be robbed or killed. Often they were.

Betha sighed the memory out of presence, giving a moment's attention to her present room at the top of the house. She had waited long months to occupy that room. Ijeme had told her that the bureaucrat who helped her to get it was rumoured to be a gentle. Betha did not know. She only knew she was grateful.

She took note now of the grey sky, the darkened street. As she set out towards the bar strip Mito's mindstretch surrounded her.

'All well,' she responded. 'Moving up on a tag check. Come again.' Before she walked into the field of the magnetic eye she double shielded against all stretch-contact and pulled sturdily into her hardself. Carefully – always carefully, as if to protect the breasts that would give away her disguise – she drew from beneath it the metal tag on its chain. 'Bill Bellario,' it read by the imprint of her thumb. 'Mason appren. Level 4. ALL IMM. Drk cauc. 1.70 m. 292643 Orient St. 62-921-67-4908.' Standing close to the check box, she thrust the small metal strip into the slot. A click. She replaced the tag and proceeded.

Still she held off mindstretch. No one knew precisely how long the central computer took to register a pedestrian or to find that pedestrian irregular. Always she felt that at any moment lights would flash, whistles would blow, sirens would bleep, and she would be encased in a cloud of immobilising gas. Instinctively she held her breath, and transferred her bodily activity to her lonth so she could concentrate on danger awareness. Almost mechanically she continued to walk at her strong but casual gait while her shade opened all its external sensors, alert to any unusual movement. There was nothing. Relieved, she rapidly calculated that she could evade tag checks for several blocks. Gradually she pulled into herself again, still alert, still operating out of the routine of the lonth, but now able to risk brief touch with Mito.

'Stay light with me, sister,' she sent.

Mito was open. 'I don't know the gentle you will meet. Aaron, you said.'

'You knew his lover. He was one of those burned at the last public instruction.'

'I remember.' There was a short-stretch silence. 'I'll hover lightly. Go well in shade.' Mito withdrew without waiting for response.

Betha was coming now to a more well-lighted portion of the City. She met others, always men, or women who were being physically supported by men. Near one corner where the housing gave way to an auto-driven street a woman walked stiffly in the company of a rentscort. Betha had learned to recognise the usually bored look on such a man's face, the dead giveaway he'd been hired to walk with the woman.

At first when she was high with the success of having passed as a man Betha had thought seriously of working at one of those agencies. The pay was good, she would be constantly with women, and as long as ordinances required every female to be accompanied by at least one man the job would be steady. Unfortunately the men who got those jobs tended to be much larger than Betha; she had ultimately decided not to risk trying.

Now as she gave the couple a wide berth she dared a full look at the woman. What the escort was in vertical muscle, she was in horizontal softness. Fat, they would call her here. Calling up exactly the proper degree of civil inattention as she passed, Betha lowered her eyes. There she marvelled for the thousandth time at the pace that a city woman could manage on her spike heels. But of course; that was part of the excuse for the escort. Betha ached in her midsection as she glanced at the helpless fingers clinging to the manly arm. She tried to imagine the women at the ensconcement dressed in such a way, clinging in such a way – Diana, Alaka, Earlyna, Ijeme, she herself. The pictures were not funny. 'What we are not we each could be,' she murmured in recall of early lessons, 'and every woman is myself.'

Betha was thus depressed as she hit the bar strip. The neon got brighter every time she came here. More tubing, more blinking, more beckoning, more green-pinkly-lit enterprising doors. A slim figure brushed her arm in passing. Betha cringed. Sure enough, he was looking back at her. Immediately she straightened her shoulders, swept her steps into a wider swagger. It was difficult not to move like a boy, difficult to move like a-man-looking-for-a-woman.

Two more tag checks, one at a crossing – there were occasional cars, all of them with panelled siding or boarded-up windows and always with the blackened windshield – and another check at the door of the Thumbscrew. The bar itself was behind the large foyer. The foreroom was crowded with standing and sitting men all locked into the video screen to her right. As she pressed over tables and extended feet she dared a stretch to Mito.

'Here,' came the faint but steady reply. Betha withdrew quickly, revived even by that brief touching. The bar seemed even tinier than the foyer. Betha tried to look thoroughly but without anxiety for Aaron. Men were boasting, women were listening, barmaids were hustling, but there was no sign yet of the gentle. She accustomed her eyes to the dimness, her lungs to the smoke, and her nose to the smells. It wasn't easy. Some instinct for survival projected a movement plan into her mind. She knew what to do.

She hitched her trousers and strode to the centre of the bar. With apparent ease she clasped a man of about her own height on the shoulder. 'Move it over, buddy.' With only the mildest of pressure she urged him closer to his companion and without removing her gregarious hand she quickly squeezed into and enlarged the handspan of space between him and a burly man to the other side.

'So far, so good,' she thought. Turning from side to full front she claimed her complete space. She was able now to bring both hands to the bar. 'Watered scotch,' she told the woman who was in non-stop movement behind the counter. The glass was before her in an instant and just as quickly the woman's hand swept away the two rec stamps Betha extended to her.

Betha took a long moment to centre, to check her shield. The pressure of the bodies to either side of her was not comforting. She drew in her shade until it was skintight around her hardself. Mito was still in hover.

'No Aaron?' The question was not in words.

'I don't see him yet,' Betha returned.

'Hey, Bill. I got a table.' The voice was Aaron's at her side, suddenly, pushing up over the late rock music, over thinly disguised cries of pain that passed as laughter, over the din of double-edged sex games. Aaron was in full business suit, his cravat threatening now to release itself from his loosened vest. He'd clipped his beard since this morning and his hair now reached precisely the point below the ear that city fashion recommended. Betha followed him to a remote part of the room, reaching out all the while to surround him with her warmth. Before he sat down he said as if to the wall yet for her hearing, 'This corner is safe. But there's a dangerous set of ears at the bar. By the way,' he continued, full front now, 'thank you for that.' He sank into a chair that was bigger than the table it attended.

'You're welcome,' Betha said, astonished and pleased to realise that he could respond to an enfolding of care, particularly in these circumstances. He was not a woman, after all, and there seemed only the thinnest possibility of mindstretch between them. Somehow men – even gentles – found it difficult or impossible really to share power. 'Meaningful communication is the meeting of two vessels, equally vulnerable, equally receptive, and equally desirous of hearing. In the listening is all real speaking.' The words came back from over the years, from the remember rooms at the Kochlias. 'Tui,' she thought, 'the lake on the lake, female on female.'

Yet Aaron did respond to enfoldings. 'What makes him a man?' she pondered. She had asked that question in one form or another all her life, but particularly since she began training for her rotation and particularly since she had been living in the City. About most men here she could give a quick easy answer. About the gentles she could not; her absolutes began to get fuzzy around the edges when she tried to make them apply to a man like Aaron. Even beneath his cultivated hard exterior she could feel his understanding of the essential fundamental knowledge: women and men cannot yet, may not ever, love one another without violence; they are no longer of the same species. He had been one of her few dependable contacts here. For him she felt something of the same loyalty she felt for Mito, Evona, Ijeme – other women who formed her network in the City. 'Yet not the same at all,' she had to admit, looking now in what she hoped was a comradely way over the small table. 'But I would trust him with much that is dear to me.'

'Howzzit down at the brick works, Billy Boy?' Aaron was just a shade too loud, she thought as he poured his own drink from a full bottle. Their public relationship had long since been established as one of mentor and promising-young-man. Both characters in the scenario had agreed tacitly to that – and to the difficulty it would involve: avoiding any appearance of a queer relationship. All told it had worked well, Aaron even managing on their last meeting to get caught in the act as one of his co-workers approached of recommending slit houses.

'It'll do until I get in school,' she said.

Two men and a woman squeezed by them heading for the door. Aaron said as they passed between him and the bar, 'Evona is carrying a half-truth back to the ensconcement.' Exposed again to the bar he said, 'Apprentices are always impatient. You learn more now than you ever will in a school.'

Betha could see another couple coming towards them. She timed her sentence to include,' The gentles want to meet with us; that is the message she carries.' The couple had passed.

'Precisely,' Aaron said without masking. He sprawled in his chair now and looked the room over, 'The place has changed.' He was loud and easy in the statement.

Betha, forgetting for a moment the drama of the game, reached out her hand to assure him she had understood. She was shocked by his immediate response. 'I remember years ago,' he was saying, 'when it was one of the elite places in town.' Then without changing pace or facial expression he spoke in a warning voice deliberate and harsh, but without moving his lips. 'Do not touch me with affection.' As if he had not just rebuffed her he continued in his jovial fashion, 'It's too crowded now for comfort.'

Betha was about to signal some apology when a commotion at

the bar interrupted her. A thin wiry man, business suit clad, was standing directly in front of one of the bar customers. There was an altercation fast becoming a fight. Every eye in the place looked at the two shouting men. Aaron and Betha looked, too, but as she craned to see Betha heard her companion saying in full voice next to her ear. 'That's Tom. At last. Now listen carefully. The gentle that the women must meet has been hurt. He cannot go to them. They must go to him. The courthouse. In Earlytown. Eastern window on north ground floor will open. Same time. Dare to repeat to me, Betha.'

His use of her name startled her but her recuperation was quick. It included Mito.

'I'm here,' the other woman stretched back to her.

Aloud, under the noise of the fight and simultaneously in rapidstretch to Mito, Betha repeated: 'We must go to the gentle as he is hurt. The courthouse. Earlytown. Eastern window on north ground floor will open. Same time.'

'Good,' he muttered, still intent on the fight.

'Got it,' came from Mito. 'Shade yourself, Betha.'

'I do.' She withdrew from Mito and concentrated on observing the scuffle. It was waning now, and people were settling again in their seats. The two combatants were being held apart by others while the voice of the tall man – Tom – still rose in indignation.

Betha turned to Aaron, not daring to risk an enfoldment. 'Well, that's my excitement for the night. See you at the block meeting.' They did not reach out to each other except in understanding.

'See you, Bill,' Aaron said.

As Betha raised her hand in good-bye she took a keen look at the man Tom had picked a fight with at the bar. He seemed no more dangerous than others. Yet she now knew him to be a special enemy. The bar was calm again. Without haste she moved past the video watchers and onto the street. It was raining. Good. An excuse to hurry. She and Mito would have to risk a stretch to the Wanderground. Evona might already have reached the ensconcement; if so, the watchposts must relay the corrected message.

The marquee of an all-night palace flashed letters a metre high: 'WOMEN, WOMEN, WOMEN! WOMENWOMENWOMEN!'

'Yeah,' Betha thought as she turned the corner of the darker street that led to her rafter room. 'Women.'

The Gatherstretch

'Gatherstretch. Tonight after ministrations.'

Zephyr was in her nest grace-making when the message came from Pbila. She responded immediately. 'What cause?'

'The gentles want to meet with us.'

Zephyr absorbed the message. 'Shall I reach others?'

'No. I'm free and will continue to stay as centre-reach here. Needing you I'll come back to you.'

'Come again if so,' Zephyr sent.

'Always.' Pbila's touch dropped away.

The gentles, Zephyr thought. They had never met with the gentles, at least not so formally. Zephyr shook off the interruption, setting aside thoughts of the gatherstretch so she could return to her grace-making. That setting aside was not for her a simple process but a conscious discipline. Zephyr's natural bent called her to remain with anything that caught her attention until something else reached out and snagged her. Thus, if she let her natural flow control her, she'd be forever shifting from one thing to whatever else might come along. Or, untouched by any outside demand, she might dwell for hours in the intricate pattern of a fungus growth – totally captivated by it, totally wrapped in its complexity. Either way, she rarely felt in control of her life; more frequently she felt she was a slave – albeit a happy slave – to her environment.

'A matter took me,' she often apologised when she came late to an appointment. The hill women, understanding and honouring Zephyr's struggle, made their mindstretches to her brief, except when both they and Zephyr had a clear wish to visit. Usually, too, except when she was badly needed, they assured her that their message was strictly informative and not meant to call upon her to *do* anything. Even so, Zephyr waged a constant battle with herself; to complete what must be done – task number one, and, task number two – to dwell no longer with its doing.

Now. Back to the grace-making. She had been centreing upon Seja today, paying close attention to an envisioning of the other woman, noting in her mind every detail of her memory of Seja, dwelling with care upon Seja's temperament, upon her behaviour, upon her intentions. She closed her eyes and turned her awareness to each aspect of her sister. She felt herself fill with appreciation. She let the feeling overflow like clear water from a cup. She made a wide stream of the water and let it run over Seja's head, drenching her with respect and care. When she came upon the parts of Seja that she could not like – her boundless high energy, for instance – she addressed them directly, attempting to establish contact with those parts, however unpleasant they were to her. To them she said simply, 'I see you and I don't choose to praise you. As you are a part of Seja I offer you, too, the care I send to her.'

All the while she worked she was careful not to enfold Seja, not to ask for her attention. It was not a mindstretch that she sought but instead the creation of a gift for the other woman, a gift of love and strength that Seja could reach for in a crisis. Seja had been having a number of crises lately, Zephyr mused, and could use a little grace.

This was the grace-making, the creation of extra attention and love, either towards one woman or towards a number of them. Zephyr did not understand what *grace* meant; it was now an archaic word which some equated with good fortune. It was not always a purely pleasant concept, she had heard, and yet it spoke well the principle that was a part of all their sustenance: if each woman offers attention beyond what is needed, then caring energy will always be available to each of us. The trick, she knew, was to offer the attention only when it came from her own fullness, never from duty or obligation. 'If I do not give from my overflow, then what I give is poison,' she reminded herself.

There was some closure now on her attention to Seja. She last-held her image of the other woman, leaving final warmths and soothes over her whole body. Then with her readiness on tiptoe for another task, she opened her eyes. They fell upon a pile of broken and damaged clay pots. 'Got to get those out of here,' she thought, as she moved immediately toward the pots and began dragging them to the door of her nest. Herva and Gynia and Su would be here for ministrations and could join her for the gatherstretch. It would be nice to have a little more room. She'd meant for months to address herself to the stacks of pots, boxes, boards, crates, papers, and unidentified paraphernalia which constantly occupied a large portion of any nest she lived in. The stacks would enlarge, space would grow limited, things would be more closely crammed together and then inevitably she would have to take extreme measures – like hauling it all out-of-doors to be exposed to the weather.

Outside her nest the prospect was similar. Covering the premises were layers and stacks of unused, overused or unusable articles and materials, most of which had at one time or another enjoyed the priority space inside her nest. Prominent among them now that she viewed them with an eye to placing the pots were: the pile of smooth stones, each carted with good intent from the river for the chimney she had not yet got around to; odd forms of driftwood, some large and some medium or small, scattered like sea dust over the entire yard; a hand-carved box of tools, open but gradually being covered with the gentle growth of ground roses; a long bannister railing which leaned reluctantly on the hood of the ancient auto for whose uniqueness Zephyr had chosen her nest site; finally the broken potter's wheel that peeped out from behind brown sacks of walnuts and tiers of abalone shells. Surrounding it all was the infinite variety of all the items Zephyr kept collecting and could not throw away.

As she contemplated the scene with some desperation, she wiped her brow with her handless arm. Then she resolutely hauled out one box of the pots to the pile of stones, leaning them back against the side of the hill towards the sun. It occurred to her as it frequently did that she ought to learn toting skills – she in particular who had one less hand than her sisters with which to move things in her hardself and who, among all her sisters, seemed always to be rescuing things and groups of things from some otherwise wasted fate.

'Someday,' she determined.

That ritual word of hers was suddenly surrounded by an enfoldment. When she responded she found Pbila again.

'I need your help in reaching the Outposts, Zephyr.'

'Good,' Zephyr replied.

'Mostly assurances,' Pbila went on. 'Earlyna, Chthona, and Egathese have probably roused all those along the fringes of the Wanderground. We simply double-check those on watch to see that the news has travelled. We reach Blase, Koe, Rhylla, Ono, and Christa. Then Arlino and Pru. Ready?'

Though they had never touched channels in first-reach before, Zephyr found that she joined easily with Pbila, a comfortable fit with no loose ends or thin edges. She was grateful for Pbila's strong field, for her openness and her steadiness. As they drew together, Pbila's comfort in its turn reached Zephyr so that the first-reach was a fortunate coupling. They stretched the combined offering of their vitality and their spirit to women far over mountains and valleys, to women at the very edges of all safety. Every hill woman would want to know of the gatherstretch. Probably all would want to join.

In winter, darkness came suddenly upon the Western Ensconcement. Zephyr had drawn a special torpor around the nest for the evening, wrapping it in layers of lamb's wool and a bright spring sunshine. She and her visitors had let the wood fire burn low.

Though it was not yet her bedtime, three year old Gynia had fallen asleep in Zephyr's lap and was now snug in the loft. Even the excitement of gatherstretch couldn't keep her awake. 'She must have had a rough day,' Zephyr observed as she descended the ladder.

Su was smoking what old Artilidea called 'that foul pipe'. 'She did,' Su shortstretched. 'She and Shuto waited all afternoon for the bear. It never came. She's more disappointed than tired.'

Herva was filling Zephyr's tea cup. 'We'd better start,' she stretched. 'I'll need to touch both of you. I always become terrified.'

'So do I,' Zephyr said. 'It's got to be trouble.'

'Big trouble,' Su joined. 'Come, Zephyr.' Su was pointing to the mat beside her and moving pillows about so the three of them could sit comfortably and at the same time remain in physical contact with each other. When finally they settled, Herva was leaning against the centre post with her feet and legs entwined with those of the women on the mat. Amid some giggles that were more nervous than lighthearted, the three began to move their centres together, breathing separately at first and then, with some effort, in unison. At last, as they linked their energy sources, eyes closed, they breathed effortlessly together.

Zephyr felt herself vaulted in slow motion towards a new awareness, not simply of Herva and Su, though the first-joinings there had been overwhelming at the outset. She was further aware that most of the women from the western hills were coming together. Probably only those on watch would stay away this evening, she calculated. She stood now in the pathway of a tremendous sweep of power. She was both in its channel and anchored by it. She could not locate the source of the sweep; it came from inside herself, from Su and Herva, from a hundred gathering vessels, from everywhere. 'The power of women,' she said to herself.

'The power of women,' the echo came from all directions. One-by-one, two-by-two, three-by-three, ten-by-ten, the women from the Western Ensconcement channel-linked, gathering together in another presence which was itself created by their coming together. Already Zephyr felt her own curiosity and her apprehension intensify. Yet as each group joined she felt more deeply grounded, more vital, more steady, more nearly at home. She waited with ease for the movement that would bring together those gathered here with those gathered from the Eastern Ensconcement. Then there would be the final movement of joining with the women from the Outposts and the Kochlias. It was the same pattern on a far larger scale that the Long Dozen experienced nightly.

The Long Dozen. The women who had called this gatherstretch. Who were they this term? She made herself remember: Doceturva, Beula, Chelyssa, Three-Fold from here, from the Western Ensconcement; Troja, Orino, Batya, Three-Fold from the Eastern Ensconcement; Nova, Li, Annatoo, Three-Fold from the Kochlias; Earlyna, Egathese, Chthona, Three-Fold from the Outposts. The Long Dozen – long because there was always another created – came together across the hills every evening of their term. They brought to each other for sharing or decision all the woman-matters, from threats of external danger to work rotations or the discovery of a covey of quail at a meadow's edge. From her own time of serving as one of the Three-Fold Zephyr knew the extent of the happiness and the depth of the pain that went with being one of the Twelve. In her head she could hear the gathering chant, just as she had heard it each evening a few years ago:

There will come:
Three from disquieted Dangerland's edge,
Three who at work will first see the sun's rise,
Three who at work will last see the sun's set.
Three whose long labours see no sun at all
Rise from the shadows, from deep earth to call
To the west,
To the east,
To the far Dangerland,
Saying
It is the eventide, it is the coming time.
Meet now the three on three on three on three.
Meet now the three on three on three on three.

Were the Long Dozen already together, Zephyr wondered, or did each Three-Fold come to a gatherstretch with its quarter? She did not know. There had been no gatherstretch during her time with the Dozen. There had been some since, though. The last one had been during the spring when waters threatened the grain fields. Apparently the matter of the gentles was calling forth far more women than the floods had.

With growing astonishment Zephyr felt the gathering rhythms lengthen, the tempo slow to a heavy lazy rate, as more and more groups joined the Quarter-Fold. If this was happening in each of the other quarters then the gatherstretch would be the largest ever. Fear struck her. What if it were too big? What if the combined energy were too great? What vast consequence could occur if hundreds of women inhaled together and then released their spirit into the biosphere beyond themselves? She shook. That prospect, she knew, could be a reality some day. All the women were preparing for that – those learning in the Kochlias, those hiding in the City, those patrolling the borders of the Wanderground, those sustaining life in the ensconcements and smaller breakaways, even those living in the deserts thousands of miles to the south and those gathered in communities all over the continent of whom the hill women had only small knowledge – all of them were preparing for the time when it would be possible to gather their power, to direct it, and to confront whatever murderous violence threatened the earth. Many hoped it would not be necessary, that the violence would continue to be contained in the cities, but all held in common the knowledge that even if unnecessary, such an energy-gathering must be made possible. Now was not that time, Zephyr knew. 'We are far from ready for that,' she reminded herself. 'We don't know enough yet and we haven't practised long enough. We don't care enough yet and we're still the victims of our own violence.'

Then why was the movement so vast this evening? Like a handclasp she felt Herva asking the same question. As if to underscore the question the movement shifted. There was another texture, another taste, another tempo abroad now in the common knowing of the women. Zephyr felt turned upside down. Her head swam in a sea without centre. In the distance a cry began, tiny as a pinpoint but expanding as it came forwards, drawn along a long corridor of silence. The voices of women burst from isolation into joy. The cry filled the corridor, it fell upon Zephyr's whole history and carried her forward with it into tomorrow's tomorrow. She felt her own voice joining the cry. She gave herself up to it, hung suspended in its swell of volume and pitch. Gradually her head righted itself.

'A fortunate joining.' She felt rather than heard the greeting of the women from the Eastern Ensconcement. Her own response with that of all the western women reached to touch a presence beyond the low mountains and over the cool river. Enfolding that presence she touched her own centre. 'At home,' she smiled. It was like slipping into old forgotten boots, like curling into sleep after loving, like settling spoons into each other or fitting together every piece of a broken cup so that there is no sign of a break. At home.

Zephyr was not ready for the final movement into the Full-Fold when it came. She began to perceive all over her body dangerously increasing vibrations. The image of a coiling snake filled her mind: a shortening, a tightening of rhythms, a hastening of the tempo as if in preparation for some outward thrust. But the outward motion never came. Instead, the tightening continued, increasing its inward-moving direction and growing hotter and lighter with each movement. None of the hill women was ready for what was happening. Zephyr encountered now all around her a startled and rampant fear rushing through every one, a deepening vortex of terror encircling the common centre of the power that they had sought.

It was moving too fast now, moving swiftly inwards and out of control. The final joining, the coming together of all the quarters, was too vast for its speed. The gatherstretch was teetering on the brink of implosion.

Then without warning and in the midst of the frenzy a chanting of words began. It came from nowhere, from everywhere:

Slow sisters,
Slow sisters,
Help us move slow.
Slow sisters,
Slow sisters,
Give us your pace.

Zephyr heard her own voice join the chant. As it did so she brought her attention to her slow sisters, to all the women and girl-children she knew who walked slowly – with a cane, with a crutch, with a limp – or who walked not at all, the women who discovered wonders that moderate walkers rarely saw and that runners overlooked entirely. Zephyr addressed them now. 'Your pace must be ours,' she said. 'Show us.'

Over the rhythm of the chant the roaring madness flashed forth for an instant with a renewed force; Zephyr was certain in that moment that they would all be whipped to the centre, sucked in, seared by their own speed, and doomed to spin forever in some internal cavern of paleness-and-white-light where none would know another or that another knew her not.

Then the motion broke. As if some raging buzzing motor had suddenly ceased, a silence smote the air and hung there with relief until the chant emerged again, this time soft and slow, this time with gratitude, this time bringing with it a measured manageable pace for the linking of the power of the women. The colours cooled. The wind eased. The chant became more joyous. Somehow the slow sisters had worked their magic – or, attending to the ease and patience of slow sisters, all the women had worked the magic.

The joining was at last complete. The vast presencing of all the women to each other shifted and turned and adjusted until comfort settled on them all. The presence was finally seated in herself. With a keen awareness of the peril they had just escaped, women from every quarter began to draw themselves now into careful attention. Every quarter drew itself to that same attention. Zephyr struggled before she could bring herself to the business at hand. She had found a vision in the deep returning rhythms of that final joining – or was it a memory? – a vision of a green world filled with laughter far beyond the stars. She made herself be present. The listening had begun.

Drawing her own presence to the centre of the gatherstetch, Li, from the Kochlias Three-Fold, brought the question before them. Li did not address an audience but instead herself became a hearer as she wove back and forth in her memory between narrative and reflection, description and evaluation, attempting to throw open to all the women the information that had come to the Long Dozen and the work in thinking that the Dozen had done with the knowledge: how Evona from the City carried a request from the gentles that the hill women meet them less than one week hence; how the place of the meeting had been changed; how certain recent apprehensions among the hill women seemed to correlate with the fear of the gentles, fear that changes in the City would soon affect the hill women.

As Li laid open to the presencing of them all the considerations of the Twelve, the sense of curiosity and concern was gradually disturbed by an irritation. The disturbance rose into the presencing from a number of vessels. It was an opposition, a mixing of fire and water. Even before the discomfort was offered up in any formal fashion Zephyr knew its nature: to some of the women it did not matter that the gentles were men sworn to isolate themselves from women; if they were men then there was no reason for concourse with them. Zephyr was impatient. Such an old story. Such ignorance, she felt. The hill women needed the gentles. Women from rotation could say how much. Why always these purists, why always the moralists? She called herself up short. She relaxed her impatience. Far more than she herself wanted to hear, she wanted the dissenting women to be heard. She sighed, then she moved her own presence towards the centre of the gatherstretch.

'I name an opposition that lies with us,' she sent. 'It's the belief that we must have nothing to do with men. Will you own it now, you who believe it?'

'I own it.' 'And I.' 'And I.' 'I own it.' 'It is mine.' Immediate responses came from individual women in all quarters. They came with varying degrees of intensity. As Zephyr and the others waited in silence more women joined the owning until altogether more than fifty women declared their opposition to any negotiation with men.

Zephyr offered her presence once more. 'Thank you for owning.'

'Thank you, Zephyr, for naming it.' Wal-kara, one of the dissenters sent.

Zephyr continued. 'Before we address the dissent I want to hear from women who feel a special danger in these days and I want Evona to share with us her understanding of the gentles' request.' From all around her, even from those disagreeing, Zephyr felt the same desire.

The sharing began – small tales and long tales of separate matters, each not so grave in itself but which when taken together lent an ominous tone to the last few months. Troja catalogued her vain attempts to reach Rula-ji who had intended to stay in close touch on her travel to the desert. Rowena reported stories from the Dangerland and even the Wanderground of useless killings, particularly of deer and particularly the further beheading of does. Alaka repeated the observations of the birds that angry men were abroad again outside the City. Women who scanned the heavens and those who read raindrops or the bottoms of tea cups – any who on any occasion had discovered some danger sign – listed and described the omens. There were more of them than anyone found comfortable.

Ijeme's story, known to those of the Eastern Ensconcement, brought questions. Was the woman who fell to her death testing Ijeme? What changes had she, Ijeme, detected in city routine? There was, as well, a moment of standing-with and affirming Ijeme's grief and her feelings of helplessness. Seja's telling of Margaret's rape caused most consternation; Margaret herself was still being cared for in the caves of the mothers, her madness still often upon her, her silence still virtually complete.

Evona was carefully heard. She told of the closer watches on everyone in the City, of even more security measures, of the growing scarcity there of some goods – particularly luxuries like tobacco – of the increased danger there for the women trying to pass as men. She assured them that Ijeme's escape was not known; she felt that Ijeme's experience was isolated, not necessarily connected to other growing pressures. She recounted the urgency of Fabian, the gentle, who had reached her at her work in the City, how they spoke in an elaborate code, prefacing every message word with some ancient religious symbol. Fabian had been for a long while an established contact for hill women just coming into rotation. She trusted him. She trusted the anguish as well as the urgency that she saw in him.

Rumours were, he had said, that some men had discovered that they could be potent again outside the City, even if only for very short periods of time. There was an undercurrent of speculation among the groups of city men. Most would give no serious overt attention to the information, implying by their lack of concern that though they'd never been outside the City to try it they were sure they'd have no trouble being cocksure there or anywhere else they so desired. Others, more daring, were venturing into the countryside for short jaunts, sometimes taking their women with them to test out the rumours, sometimes hunting for solitary women – like Margaret – who were surviving in the country or in a ghost town. No one could say for sure whether or not the rumours of country potency were true; if they were then it was clearly a matter of rare occasions that it was so; otherwise men would have been flooding out of the cities to recapture the whole earth again.

So far none of the gentles outside the City could confirm the rumours but, as Evona reminded them, that was no real test. The country gentles had long since found it a relief not to be sexually active – that's why they were able to be in the country – and probably could not perform sexually even in the heavy energy of the City.

Machines outside the City, continued Evona, were working no better than usual. Breakdowns were still consistent – planes faltered after less than an hour's flight, trains and autos ground to a stop after short bursts of speed, sails and oars were still the only means of progress over water. Natural-grown food was still a luxury, the chemical substitutes still the standard. Communication with any other surviving city was limited to runners. Horses and mules and other beasts-of-burden still refused male riders or drivers.

Evona knew very little more. In answer to questions: yes, she felt the meeting with the gentles was essential; no, she could not explain the change of the meeting place but she had trusted the combined mindstretch of Betha and Mito who had made the correction: yes, she would be willing to be one of those who would meet with the gentles if there were a clear wish to do that. The questions came less frequently, then fell away entirely.

There was a long but very full silence in the gatherstretch. No one moved to centre, yet all listened to each other, to themselves. It was a time of assimilating, of understanding the news. Zephyr was aware of raw emotions surrounding her, predominantly outrage and fear. She felt the hot responses of many of the women, herself included. They were having visions of manslaying, of man-mangling, fantasies of swooping down upon the City and crushing tall buildings with their feet, uprooting miles of pavement with their bare hands. The pictures were bloody and vicious.

Some women were sad and then angry and then despairing. Some were nauseous. In a few a high pitched terror resonated and amplified itself. Others drew on it, added their own to it. For a few moments they let the fear seize them all. Then, having faced it, they found no more fear to yield to. Silence descended again.

Still opening herself entirely to the presencing, Zephyr discovered more sophisticated variations now on the rage and the fear: grim determination, resignation, lingering incredulity, impatience, wry cynicism. It seemed an eternity that the chaos of emotions rolled and tossed over the presencing of the women.

Then the silence began to part. Someone would speak. Earlyna moved to centre. 'Do we have a clear wish? Shall we meet with the gentles?' For a moment Zephyr dared to hope that a clear wish was upon them. Then the rumblings began again. 'Why do we need the gentles? Let us prepare our own battles.' 'Why not withdraw from the City entirely? Let us wait here and gather our power. By the time they attack we will be ready.' 'Let us wipe the City out now. One directed gatherstretch . . .'

Evona's presencing strode to centre in a reassurance. 'The gentles have some plan –' She was not heard to her finish. Wordless angry objections replaced her centre presence. It was Earlyna who threw herself open and vulnerable into the growing heat.

'I ask for the Regard of Tui!' her opening said.

Silence. Miraculous silence. The remembering of who they were. Tui. A moment for the hope of agreement. A moment for the readiness to struggle, a moment for re-commitment to care, whatever the eventual outcome would be. Gradually the presencing grew strong again. Some unity, some bonding on a fundamental level struck an ultimate sense in every gather-stretching woman. It went as deep as their female nature and spread as wide as their infinitely varied temperaments. All leaned together towards the image of woman-on-woman, women-on-women, towards the sameness and towards the differences that mark any two or any two thousand women. All moved towards the gentle holding of two calm lakes, each one of the other.

Earlyna asked for the First Acknowledgement: 'Can we, on both sides of the matter, yield?' 'The hardest question of all,' Zephyr thought. She looked hard at her conviction. Would she be willing to refuse the gentles? Yes. If it came to that. And that was all that was required of her – not that she yield, but that she be willing to yield. Every woman in the gatherstretch was examining herself for that willingness. It took a long time. It took particularly long for Wal-kara and others who dissented to find that willingness to go along with a meeting with the gentles. Finally the acknowledgement came: every woman open, every woman willing.

It was Li who asked for the Second Acknowledgement. 'I am called to remind us that at any moment we can cease to be one body. No woman has to follow the will of any other. Always we must know that we can separate, even splinter or disperse one-by-one, for a little while or forever. We rest our unity on that possibility. Do we acknowledge this?' 'No,' thought Zephyr, 'I was wrong. This one's the hardest question of all.' Breaking away, separation, the lack of clear wish in the gatherstretch: it was all threatening, even sickening to her. Yet she knew it was vital. So did all others. The acknowledgement came.

In its ending the Regard of Tui broke into words:

I embrace the possibility: I may yield.
I may not. Yet I may.
I embrace the possibility: We may not be together always.
We may not. Yet we may.

I may not. Yet I may.
We may not. Yet we may.

It was Li who opened the way for the return. 'I need a catalogue of reasons from those who now wish to refuse the gentles.'

The long arguments began. First women poured out to the open gathering their mistrust of men, their loss of hope for their ever being truly human or life-loving, their fear that woman energy might again be drained as it had been for millennia before the Revolt of the Earth, their sense that the gentles were not needed, their anger and apprehension, their pride and hatred, their sadness and care. They were heard.

Then came the arguments for the meeting. Women spoke the loyalty of the gentles, the need for the continuing rotations of women to the City, the urgency of the present, the inadequacy of alternatives. They too were heard.

The to-ing and fro-ing went deep into the night, far into the morning hours. At one moment Zephyr felt certain that fifty women would withdraw from the rest, withdraw and have no more to do with any quarter. She knew from the remember rooms that that had happened on at least two occasions in the past. It could happen again.

'They need us. We don't need them.' Wal-kara's impassioned extending was urging. 'Let them die if they cannot sustain themselves. We do not have to nurture them any longer. What else has our hill history meant if not that?'

The anger was hot; accusations and counter-accusations raged. A bone-deep weariness spread among the women. It seemed that no clear wish could be reached. It was then that Tulu came to the centre. There was a hush, a renewed interest, for Tulu had lived many years with the gentles before joining the hill women. She of them all understood the ways of those unmanly men. Her message lay open to the gathered women:

'I shall be going to Earlytown at the appointed time. I shall meet with whatever gentles are there. I shall speak only for myself. I shall return to my quarter and share – in gatherstretch or with whichever sisters wish to know – whatever I then understand the gentles to want from us. Only I, Tulu, will be bound by my words with them. They will understand that. I will welcome the company of any woman who wishes to come with me.' Tulu ceased. No one responded. No objection was raised. Zephyr sensed that little more could be said.

Wal-kara brought herself to the centre. 'Go well, Tulu. I won't try to stop you. Remember, you don't speak for me.'

'I don't speak for you or for any of us. I speak only for myself.'

Wal-kara continued. 'I ask for still another gatherstretch when Tulu returns.'

Li addressed the whole presence. 'Is that a clear wish, that we gatherstretch again?'

It was a clear wish.

Zephyr could hardly believe it was ending. Where was the characteristic lift, the usual surge of warmth and love which would carry her back into her daily routine? There was no closure, lots of rough edges. Things hung suspended and without proper form. She felt battered, angry, disappointed, and deprived of something she had been promised – or had promised herself. Were they going to move away from gatherstretch feeling this unsettled, this dissatisfied?

Old Artilidea came to centre. Her presencing lay open for any who would join. 'There was once an infant,' she was saying, 'not yet used to the world or to the hurts and aches that the world could inflict. One day, after a particularly hard attempt to function with those outside herself, she felt bruised and bloody, cut to the bone in parts of her tiny body. She needed holding. Stroking. Easy and long. Easy and long.'

Zephyr took the vision inside herself. She folded herself into a round ball. She began to cry.

'We bend ourselves around her to protect her, to stroke her,' Artilidea's message went on.

Zephyr stroked the tiny child.

'We feel her bend around us. She holds us, protects us,' said Artilidea.

Zephyr snuggled into the warm arms, was the warm arms.

The mindreach of hundreds of women, sad and sore, battered and disappointed, hung in the air above the northern mountains where, just a ridge or two beyond, the coast hills meet the sea. They created the presence which held them, held and rocked, held and stroked, held and soothed.

'Take your rest. Take your rest. Take your rest.'

Gynia came down from the loft and crawled upon the mat among three sleeping women, all nestled close, all holding one another. She curled up among them and atop them, a breast for a pillow and a shoulder for a blanket. They sprawled together in outrageous tangles, soaking up warmth and comfort.

'Like a kitten pile,' Gynia thought as she found her dreams again.

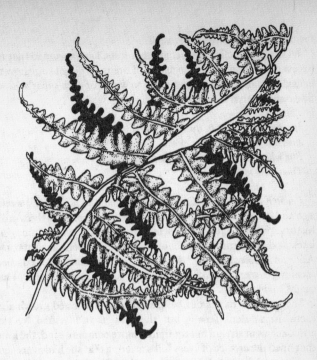

On the Way to the Kochlias

The up and down of the hills was hard going. Clana was tired. She calculated that in order to keep up, her short legs had to pump exactly twice as fast as Alaka's or Voki's longer ones. They had been travelling all day, with frequent rests for her sake. Alaka and Voki had offered to show her how to go light; that way, they said, they could carry her like a feather. Clana had refused that offer, knowing that it meant a state of only semi-awareness. This was her first time to come to the Kochlias and she was not about to spend her trip half-awake and being carried by her sisters. Her excitement had, in fact, made her a good traveller. It rose almost uncontrollably above her fatigue. The prospect of the Kochlias – its remember rooms, its learning places, its workers, its mysteries – sustained her and kept her moving at a good pace just a few metres behind the other two.

As she began climbing yet another hill Clana reasoned that an excess of excitement and an excess of tiredness ought somehow to cancel each other, ought somehow to work for each other's good. She remembered the rhyme:

It's passing sweet to quench a thirst
And not create another need.
But when two vessels fill each other
Then that is sweet indeed.

Quench. A new word. Seja had explained it to her several weeks ago and then had promptly grown all preoccupied with the word's history. When Clana saw her last that day she was rummaging back and forth through a set of old books muttering, 'Amazing. Ah!' and occasionally, 'No!' The rhyme, Clana mused, had meaning a-plenty. 'Like bushes and people,' she thought. 'That ought to work.'

She held her hands out before her and envisioned growing in them an opulent fern – not the kind that lavished by the ensconcement stream but the lighter more common kind, the kind that lined the crevice of every hill's meeting that she had ever seen.

'Oh fern,' she said, 'will you pretend you live on tiredness? And I will live on being excited?' The fern immediately agreed and thus, pushing up the steady rise, Clana established a rhythm to her gait, a regularity to her breathing. As she trudged, she inhaled the rich energy that was the fern's exhalation and gave back to the plant with each of her own out-breathings her tiredness; that tiredness was the stuff of the fern's life. She could actually see the plant soaking up her fatigue, quenching its thirst.

'It works!' she thought. *In* with excitement, *out* with weariness; *in* with the energy, *out* with the fatigue. Clana stepped faster and wider. Her head lifted. She felt buoyed up on the rhythm of her breath. The fern, too, perked up, waving its fronds in brisker, happier motions.

The two figures ahead of her on the hillside heard her coming. They turned to see a speeding girl-child, arms extended, bounce up behind them and swiftly overtake them.

'Hey!' shortstretched Voki to Clana's figure, far ahead of her now. 'You were so tired! Where you got your energy?'

'From the fern,' sent back Clana as she whipped through the tall weeds towards the crest of the hill. Voki and Alaka stopped and looked at each other.

'She can teach us a lot,' Alaka laughed. 'Come on, or we'll lose her.'

They quickened their own pace, both long-striding women as they were. Even so, it was an effort to catch up on Clana. When they found her she was galvanised on the brow of the hill, her mouth open wide, her arms no longer before her. She was transfixed by some scene that Voki and Alaka could not yet see. Even as they watched her the child dropped suddenly to her knees and scrambled behind a clump of bushes. Her fear and puzzlement reached out to the other two women.

'Hurry,' Voki shortstretched to Alaka.

'But take care,' Alaka was sending back. Simultaneously she pushed towards Clana a wave of calm and reassurance.

Voki led the way. Cautiously she bent low, climbing through weeds and over tall grass clumps, signalling Alaka to stay behind for a moment. Alaka, even amidst her sudden fear, took note of Voki's lank form, how it had nothing of the awkwardness about it which usually accompanies the spurt of adolescent growth; how, even bent, it loped noiselessly, smoothly up the hillside.

A country she had never seen flashed through Alaka's mind: a low and hot savannah with waving grasses being pushed aside by the slow deliberate pace of a pride of lions. Crouched in the grass on a rise was a figure, respectful and wary, at home with the heat, the grasses, the lions. The figure rose to a standing position. It laughed aloud. It was Voki, her hands on her hips and mindstretching now to Clana.

'It's all right. All right. They are our women.' Voki was sending an open channel both to the child and to Alaka.

Alaka relaxed her caution. She sent a check sweep wide in a full circle and caught to the east what must have been the cause of Clana's fright. At the same moment she topped the hill to stand by Voki. She saw with her first eyes a skyful of floating bodies. She counted fifteen women, all in foetal position, all with their backs up to the sky, all suspended at varying heights in the air over the downside of the hill and over the short valley beyond. Alaka laughed too. She turned to the bushes where Clana still crouched.

'They're learning to ride wind. It's the beginners from the Kochlias.'

Clana, not yet fully reassured, crept to Alaka's side. 'Beginners,' she muttered, still agog at the fifteen bundles of woman-flesh. They were apparently unaware of the three observers; they were apparently giving all concentration to the task of clasping their arms about their legs and keeping their heads down.

'How do they stay up?' Clana asked.

'Don't ask me,' Voki returned. 'I never got into it.'

'They use their breath,' Alaka answered.

'And the lonth.' The message enfolded their mindstretches. There was another presence. Alaka opened.

'Who?'

'Manaje, from the Kochlias. Alaka?'

'Alaka, Voki, Clana, coming to the remember rooms,' Alaka sent. 'Greetings Manaje. I'm told to tell you that Terpsichore brought forth seven kittens. One solid black which will be for your special care if you choose each other.'

Manaje's delight encircled them. 'I'll visit soon. I'm told to tell you, Alaka, that Tulu will be with you in the remember rooms tomorrow. She asks to see all the gentle-memories again in preparation for her meeting with them. Evona will be there, too. Voki, I remember and greet you. Clana I do not know.'

Clana, aware of all that was transpiring, felt the need to identify herself but she did not quite know how.

'This is Clana, a small woman to whom ferns give their strength.' Voki's introduction smiled towards Manaje.

Clana blushed. 'I'm coming to remember,' she added.

'A welcome to you, Clana. I am Manaje, happiest when I am windriding. We'll be practising for several weeks. You can watch us later if you like.'

Clana was grateful for the mindstretch sustained among them all. 'Can I ride wind?'

'Probably. Does your stomach often send back its food?'

'No.'

'Can you enjoy being cold and have you learned to shield yet?'

'Yes. And no,' Clana returned.

'You can probably be a good windrider. If you really want to be.

It's hard work at first.'

'But they aren't windriding,' said Clana boldly, watching the inert balls of women, some bobbing now on wind lifts.

'They will soon. Floating is the first step. I have to get back to them. Come and see me, Clana, I live near the cella in the Kochlias with Li and Erika close by. You're almost there. Welcome Voki and Alaka. You can take the upper path after the oak grove. It's easily passable in winter. Go well.'

'And you,' Alaka sent before Manaje's touch moved away from them.

Clana was so ecstatic she almost forgot to apologise to the fern for dropping it so suddenly. Hastily she went back to the spot where first she had seen the women. The fern seemed none the worse for her rough treatment. She knelt lightly to finger its flat leaves, thanking it for helping her. She rubbed her cheek against it in a last-hold before she sent it off downhill into the draw where it began to grow happily.

What the older women observed was strange calisthenics: Clana hastening to an unremarkable spot, kneeling, caressing thin air, pushing her head to and fro, then finally leaping up and flinging her arms back in the direction from which they had come.

'She can teach us a lot,' Voki stretched to Alaka as Clana rejoined them. They set off following the ridge and keeping a steady south-southeast direction. As they passed the drifting bodies to the east Clana saw that one of the figures was whiteheaded.

'If you're never too old, you're never too young,' she assured herself and happily followed Voki and Alaka.

It was near dark when they at last reached the upper western entrance to the Kochlias, near the top of a low mountain just above its timber line. One-by-one they lay flat on the ground and scooted for several metres under solid rock. They emerged into a softly lit passageway, into the Kochlias, that magic place Clana had heard about all her life. As she walked with the women who had gathered to greet them Clana was sure she would never have spaces enough in her memory to keep all the wonder of it. Even so, she knew she was passing through only a small part of the endless underground tunnels and workrooms.

Tired child who dropped to sleep over supper took new

companions with her to dreamland: women who skated only a few centimetres above the floor; women who collected blood and ground strange-smelling herbs; women who carved stones with their minds or lifted huge burdens without ever touching them; women who practised big walks and low voices so they could be disguised as men, Voki had said.

She barely felt Alaka lift her into a nest of comfortable straw. A moment later she floated in a tiny ball just above a green field where she could watch the diggers and the brush-nesting birds as they tucked themselves away for the night.

The Remember Rooms

Clana could not love the foul smell of the Kochlias' bathing
waters. Even now, all dry and ready for her first rememberings, her
soft palate snapped shut at the thought of that water. It might be
warm and healing, and it was wonderful to be soothed and bathed
by other people like she had been this morning, but her preference
was still the cold clear springs of the ensconcement. She scrunched
into the niche she had built for herself: a large heap of small
pebbles which made a backrest and a mound of pebbles and coarse
sand that curved around to rest each of her arms.

'Why bathe anyway?' she asked herself, finding at last the magic
form-fitting movement that made her suddenly completely comfortable. Her bare body was almost reclining now, cushioned by
the remember room's custom seating accommodations. Around
her in the windowless chamber were nearly a dozen other girl-
children who were digging out and settling into their places amid
giggles and chattering.

Ranged around the room on a continuous ledge far above her head sat four cats. Another joined them even as she watched. Each one lay crouched with closed eyes but with its body in an alert position as if ready to spring. Clana reminded herself that the cats knew it all better than any of the women. They were the most regular attendants at the rememberings. And they were necessary, too. They filled in missing connections in the stories and added portions that the remember-guides occasionally forgot. Sometimes, it was said, as many as thirteen cats (and sometimes kittens) came to a remembering. Ordinarily, though, there were four or five and sometimes only two. If none came then the rememberings would usually be postponed, for few remember-guides trusted even their special training without the help of catwatch.

Clana thought she recognized the cream calico from last evening's ministrations. She enfolded it with a question. 'Do you enjoy remembering?'

To her surprise the cat responded, 'Do you enjoy breathing?' Clana withdrew, tiptoeing her enfoldment back to herself. She had overstepped. Everybody knew that remembering was in fact what a cat *was*, except for hunting, of course, and grooming and eating, all of which a cat also *was*. Joining in the intensified remembering with the women must have been for them just a special high. Clana surrounded the calico with an apology for the interruption. There was a brief acknowledgement before the cat closed off once more.

A number of adult women moved about the room now, apparently oblivious to the cats. Among them were Alaka and Nova, the remember-guides for today. She saw Britta, from the Eastern Ensconcement, with whom she shared a mother, and some other girl-children that she had seen but did not know. Some of the women were returning for a second or third or tenth time for the rememberings. Voki was one of those. Clana watched as Voki helped smaller ones to find the proper indentations and paddings for their bodies.

Clana's excitement was mounting again. She forgot all about the foul-smelling water and concentrated on making a memory of this very experience. As she absorbed every detail around her she was also aware of some of her own impatience. It had certainly taken long enough to come to this moment. First you had to travel all the way to the Kochlias and then you had to spend the whole morning in ritual singing and dancing and bathing and all the other getting ready. And then you had to hear all about what was *going* to happen in the remember rooms, how the guides would shield you and then teach you to shield so that you didn't feel all the stories in your hardself.

Clana had known all that before from her conversations with Alaka and she'd been anxious to get on with the stories themselves. One of her mothers was fond of saying that Clana loved a story better than brown beans and cornbread. It was true. When she couldn't cajole someone else into telling even an old tale, Clana would make up her own stories, peopling them with any living thing, stringing together scenes and events with chaotic abandon. She had looked forward for most of her seven years to this week, to the time when she would learn the rich history of the hill women. No wonder she bristled at the delays. No wonder she had resisted even the majestic Naming of the Names – the chanting of the long list of women who had given their stories to the remember rooms. She had paid respect to them all by joining in the recitation, but her heart was leaping ahead to the seeing of the episodes about the City, the Purges and Hunts, to the understanding at last of the Revolt of the Mother.

Alaka and Nova were beginning now to enwomb the entire group. They drew together each separate energy centre into a new matrix, inviting each to new meaning-making. Clana felt gently swayed. She felt safe. She felt well-loved and excited. The rememberings were about to begin. Nova was settling onto a well-worn sand pallet and was leaning against the far stone wall. Alaka picked her way carefully around the sitting and reclining bodies and knelt beside Nova. The two guides, enwrapping the whole group, also sought assurances from each girl-child and woman and cat that each was ready. As Clana opened to the questions, she was astonished at the difference between this and other group stretches. There was an immediate centre here and that centre was clearly Nova. Already the rememberer was immersed in a swirl of history. Already Clana could feel the heavy reinforcement of five cat memories. As each child or woman joined the enfoldment, the breathings also joined one another, seeking a rhythm, a unity. Nova seemed to drift deeper, to hold more seriously all the sensations she was about to share. The concern for the listeners was Alaka's job. Clana could sense her friend's weaving in and out of the open channels, assuring each that any listener could receive as much or as little as she wished of the narratives.

'Once upon a time,' Nova's sending began, 'before the Purges, once upon a time . . .' As Clana found herself repeating with the others the 'once upon a time,' she eased over the top of her preparatory breath and stepped off into the past. Her last hardself thought was of moving into dreams with an itchy nose.

At first there was only the tumult of sounds, voices, colours, scraps of a thousand memories in swift succession. '. . . the mask immediately to your face. Cover your mouth and nose with the mask and breathe normally. Again, we welcome you aboard Flight . . .' Sandalwood and wine, with the purple candle spilling its yellow insides all over the phone bill and the dresser cloth. The wires outside my window intersect at small and large angles all over the sky. A man calls my name and I answer. He is at the door smiling. A tall bearded smile. He lies down beside me here on the low bed . . . 'At a speed of ten point six times the square root of the air pressure in the tyres a car will hydroplane on wet or frosty pavement . . .' Inch high steaks. Fat and dripping grease. High flames and waves of heat. 'I'll quit if he doesn't get the fan going by tomorrow . . .' 'Liz, Rosie's won! The Amazons are city champions! I was out stealing third but we recuped. The party's tonight . . .' There he comes again stumping through the hall with that walker. I can't stand it another minute. I'll tell Jim we have to call the nursing home tomorrow . . . Heavy rhythms, roaring ears, flashing coloured lights, a hundred sweating undulating bodies, bending, turning, stomping, clapping, rushing, shouting. Next time I can't wear this damned brassiere . . . Firelight making pale faces pink. Short blue pants and day's end white shirts stamped 'Camp Mikatusi.' Treble voices hugging each other. Smiles and joy and longing. A spark flies upward. The velvet sky extinguishes it . . . It is midnight and he has not returned. I sit and spin these beads waiting for him. The child is crying in the hot night . . . 'Don't play with the doggie, dear. He's not very clean. See? His ears are all matted and he has fleas. This man is going to take care of him. Leave him alone now. We'll go see the clowns . . .' Green shit. Her panties are full of green shit. And running like mustard. I wonder if I ought to call McIntyre . . . '750,000 March for Free Abortion.' Busy newsprint, shots of laughing women, shouting women. Signs. 'Why reproduce in captivity anyway?' 'It's *My* Body.' 'No Forced Sterilisation!' That mounted policeman does not believe the signs . . . Other pages, other print: 'Rhodes Scholars Say Women's Lib Didn't Help Them a Bit', 'Clarke Chooses Female Running Mate', 'Nobel Scientist Refuses Woman-of-the-Year Award', 'Lesbian Priest', 'Corporate Power Moving to Women'. Papers, inks, funnels, brushed cotton, ski lifts, resins, commodes, caresses, slick walls, sketches, fireworks, forceps, buttons, wrenches, antiseptics, placards, glasses, foams, weeds, skates, cuts, keys, tags, beers, drains, drinks, shouts, shrieks . . .

'Too fast! Too fast!' Clana found herself calling aloud.

'Breathe, Clana,' Alaka was saying. 'You're all right. We'll focus now.'

Immediately Clana felt her own control enter the rememberings. She inhaled once more with the others, allowing her breath to be a long time falling. With her softself she reached out and embraced an armful of scattered sensations, set them all aside, gathered another, set them aside. There was in the remembering now a movement towards a particular place, a particular person: each of the girl-children and women stepped behind the eyes and ears of a long-dead hill woman and made her memory their own.

'A story at last!' thought Clana.

'. . . makes us just like him. Count me out.' Lynn's anger shook the heavy table. She shoved her chair back, breathing loud. Without looking at the other three women she threw a dime on the table, picked up her pack and headed towards the cashier.

'Fuck you, Lynn!' Amy thought to herself. Her own anger kept her from speaking aloud.

Ellen broke the stunned silence with her heavy voice. 'Wait a minute!' Lynn turned. Ellen was on her feet now. She spoke low so that other women in the coffeehouse would not hear. 'Who're you going to talk to?'

Lynn turned so that she cut off any view from other groups. She spoke directly into Ellen's livid face. 'I'm going to talk to nobody.

Nobody! In fact, I'm leaving town in the morning like I started to do before you got this off-the-wall idea.' She turned to Amy and Jan, almost hissing in her effort to keep her voice down. 'Jesus, I thought we were getting together a harmless night ride with a little purple prick painting and at the most a branding. I didn't bargain for killing the guy!'

Jan spoke. 'And who else do you figure is going to put him out of the way! Eight women for sure we know he's raped and he's *already been* on one of your 'harmless little night rides', for Christ's sake. You think that stopped him?'

'We don't know that –' Lynn began.

Amy felt her stomach churning. She was overly aware of her past closeness with Lynn and now her own anger was warring against the outrage that she sensed in the other woman. 'Lynn,' she said, trying to talk calmly. 'Sit down just for a minute. Then you can go.'

'Looks like we're all going,' Ellen muttered. They turned to see Barbara coming towards them making the gesture with her hands that told them the house was closing.

'It's only seven-thirty,' Jan protested loudly.

'Don't hassle me right now. Just get out. There's three guys who're raising hell because we won't serve them. We're closing up entirely.'

'So what happened to all the safe-space-for-women rhetoric?' Ellen wanted to know.

'Look.' Barbara was pissed. 'We gave them the whole rundown, told them they could go to the bookstore or the bar or to almost any other part of the building. They're looking for trouble and I'm on alone. So just go.' She gathered the dishes in one hand, mopped the table top with the other.

'Come on,' Lynn was saying. 'We can talk at my place while I get my stuff together.'

'Helluva way to run a business,' muttered Jan, pushing her part of the tip towards Barbara's heavy rag.

Amy followed the three women to the cash drawer, straining to see through the doorway if the men were still outside. 'Watch out, boys,' she thought. 'We're not in the mood tonight.'

Nova was leading them through Amy's story, then the ins and outs of Ruth's, Linda's, Helen's, Dorinda's, Priscilla's, Sourcera's, Modutu's, Erika's and more, a hundred episodes all lived in a few hours, all retold and re-remembered, recalling the days when life in the cities was a freer thing for women. The stories were still going on when the sun above the Kochlias finally left the sky and Clana was roused by Alaka from the high energy of a women's dance. All the others save Nova had one-by-one been lifted out of the past and carried or guided from the remember room. As she drew back to her hardself Clana protested aloud. 'Wait! I have to –'

It was Nova who spoke next, shaking herself out of the rememberings. 'We'll pick up the dance again another time,' she sent. 'Promise.' To Alaka she stretched, 'I'll wait here for ministrations. Will you join me?'

'Yes,' sent Alaka, lifting Clana to her shoulders. 'The River Singers from beyond the plains are still here. They have offered to do our ministrations tonight.'

'Good. They have wonderful hands. Hurry back.' Nova collapsed immediately into a deep sleep.

'How about some food?' sent Alaka to Clana.

'I don't think I can eat,' Clana replied, and before Alaka ducked her head through the door to the corridor there was a limp girlchild on her shoulder, joining Nova in an exhausted and dreamless sleep.

Then there were the other remember rooms the next day, the ones with the relics – corridor after corridor of strange items, each shelved and covered by a field of fixed-and-flexible patterns which could best be called an explanation. Clana did not understand the magic that the Kochlias workers had summoned in order to make it happen; she only knew that as she touched each artifact her hands and arms and even all the cells in her body were filled with the knowledge of – or speculation about – that article's use. She stood now, stroking a connected series of twelve iron pipes which her senses told her were once used for heating. Her forehead and lips were equally puckered in her effort to figure how the water must have got hot. Most of all she felt pressured and frustrated under her puzzlement, almost angered, in fact, that she would never be able to visit for very long with any of the relics. Even now it was almost time to go to the rememberings again – rememberings today of the Purges and the Hunts. And she hadn't even been yet to the rooms where all the books and hard pictures were.

She swept her eyes over all that she had studied just this morning – tea bag, lincoln logs, dixie cup, dog licence, spark plugs, skateboard, handcuffs, bolts with washers, bolts without washers, rheostats, bus transfers, pacifier, ankle reflector, hypodermic syringe, TV set, wine sealed in a bottle, vacuum cleaner, yardstick, obturator, high-heeled shoes, centrifuge. All of the military room: the pistols, the grenades, the rifles, the bayonets, the green-covered first-aid kits and K-rations, the uniforms and even the ancient cannon. Her hands left the radiator and went back to a handful of wires and electrodes which were attached to a small gauge. The aura told her that this apparatus was used in experimentation on rabbits and other small animals.

'Does it puzzle you, Clana?' Rhynna was standing beside her, speaking aloud. Clana smiled to see the relic-keeper. She had liked Rhynna's hair from the moment she saw her and now she all-of-a-sudden knew she liked Rhynna all over. The hair stood out from the woman's head for almost a foot all around. Rhynna had allowed Clana to try – in vain – for almost an hour to tame that hair, to squeeze it close about her head. 'Lots of people ask about that device,' Rhynna went on. 'These pads were attached to the animal's head and this needle probed its brain. Changes in the brainwaves were monitored by this gauge.'

Clana shuddered, but then drew her attention again to Rhynna. The relic-keeper was holding one of the electrodes in each of her hands, forcing the pointer on the gauge to flip to its maximum mark. Rhynna released the wires and the pointer dropped back to its original position.

Astonished, Clana almost shouted, 'Your hair! That's how you make you hair stay out!'

Rhynna laughed, 'My hair doesn't move.' She made the needle flip once more. 'You can do this too, when you learn to separate and see. We can do anything that the old machines could do. And with a good deal less effort.'

'Like the glow lobes?'

'That's one thing.'

'And windriding?'

'Yes. And lots more.'

'Bombs and nerve gas and disease pellets?'

'Easy.'

'Then why don't we do them, Rhynna?'

Rhynna laughed again. 'That's the mistake the men made, sisterlove, and made over and over again. Just because it was possible they thought it had to be done. They came near to destroying the earth – and may yet – with that notion. Most of us like to think that even long ago women could have built what's been called 'western civilisation'; we knew how to do all of it but rejected most such ideas as unnecessary or destructive.'

Clana thought about that. She and Rhynna were both silent for a bit, Clana taking in what Rhynna had said – that was as close to a lecture as she had gotten here at the Kochlias – and Rhynna pulling absently on one of her long curly hairs, also alone with some proliferation of those thoughts. After a few moments Rhynna shortstretched so as not to break the silence. 'There's a remember-rhyme we use here a lot. Want to hear?'

'Yes,' Clana stretched back.

The choice lies not in doing not the things I cannot do,
Or even in the doing of the things I know I can.
But choice lies in the poet's heart who knows the metre true,
And still refuses to allow, no matter how much she'd like to
  do it or how much it hurts her not to do it, the final line to
  scan

As she ended the verse Rhynna was laughing. Out of some deep understanding that she could not name, Clana was laughing with her. And all the way to the rememberings she repeated the rhyme knowing that some day she would understand it even better.

'Once upon a time, too many women became too wide awake. Once upon a time . . .' It was Alaka's rememberings today which drew Clana and her sisters into the past. She was dimly aware of the gentle mind assurances of another remember-guide who was the watcher today. Her name was Bessie and she had no teeth and very soothing hands.

'Once upon a time . . .' Clana whispered with all the others.

Kendra spun around when Jill touched her arm. As recognition dawned in her face she jerked back suddenly. 'Jill – '

'Kendra, I've got to talk to you. When can I call you?'

'You can't.' Kendra tried to pull away.

'Then come have a drink with me now. Or coffee. Just a few minutes. We can't stand here in the street –'

'I'll say we can't. Look Jill, we've said it all. It's changed. Can you understand that? Now just forget it and let me alone.'

'Changed. It certainly has,' Jill said slowly. She looked at Kendra, the new Kendra, fashion plate Kendra, from neat heels up to her lightly made-up face and the hair precisely cut to its casual fall. She was suddenly and awfully aware of her own big awkwardness in girdle and hose, the tightness of her skirt, her bra. How easy for Kendra to fall into the pattern; how hard, how impossible, for herself.

Kendra turned and started to walk away. Jill reached for her arm. 'Take your hands off me, do you hear?' Kendra's voice was rising. A young couple paused to stare.

'I beg your pardon,' Jill said formally. She fell into step beside Kendra now, shifting her bag to her other shoulder As usual, her feet were hurting, her legs were cold, and even the tailored lambswool coat could not warm her body or her spirits. 'Kendra, I –'

'Steve!' Kendra called, looking toward the corner with a shout and a wave. Jill stopped short to see the overcoated man wave back in recognition as he came towards them. Kendra turned only long enough to whisper, her eyes burning, 'Go away, Jill. Do you hear? I can't afford it. And neither can you. I promise you if you ever try to reach me again I'll call the police. I promise you!'

Jill stood alone, too stunned to register the warm eyes that Kendra turned to the man, the upturned smile, the light hand tucked through his arm. She knew that she was very cold and that she could not be caught loitering.

Melva pulled the fluffy quilt up over the sleeping stranger. She turned to the woman in the big leather chair. 'I wouldn't have believed it, Cissy. They shot them.' She rose, went to the silver lighter on the desk and lit a long cigarette. She paced back and forth in front of the closed draperies. 'They shot them down in the street, right near Jefferson and Twenty-fifth. Shot to kill, Cissy!'

Cissy dragged on her own cigarette. 'I've seen them use the needle guns. They do that just to stun them so they can get them under control –'

'Machine guns, Cissy! That's a bullet wound!' Melva jerked back the covers from the small sleeping woman and pointed to her thigh. 'Blood in the streets, real live honest-to-god blood running all over the sidewalks and cars. I'm paying my goddam taxes to have them spill women's blood!'

'I hear you, Melva. You don't have to shout.' Cissy stubbed out her cigarette and walked to the heavy curtains. She peeped out briefly. 'And I believe you.' She suddenly felt very cold.

Melva tiptoed toward Cissy. Drawing her shoulders together and shaking her finger she whispered, 'And do you know who the women were, Cissy? They were politicos. Like Nancy. Like your own sister, Deborah. The libbers. All of them in pants, no men with them. They'd all come out of some meeting and the police just opened fire. Right in the middle of a residential district, Cissy! Without any warning to anybody! Everybody in the block could have been killed.'

'No. Not if they were observing curfew. They'd all be in bed,' Cissy observed grimly. 'They didn't stop you?' She raised her head.

'I had my yellow flag up. I couldn't get through for all the police cars so I turned around. I found her,' she pointed to the sofa, 'moaning between two cars nearly a block away on a side street. She must have run that far. I pulled her into the wagon. There was so much crazy confusion nobody saw me roar out of there. Cissy, what are we going to do?'

Cissy didn't answer. She lit another cigarette, trying hard to make the hot fire warm her shaking bones. She sat back down in the chair and held her head. Was Deborah one of them tonight? Cissy choked back the silvery taste of oncoming vomit. Do? There was only one thing to do. She straightened. 'You'll have to decide, Melva, if you're coming with me. I'm going to load this woman up and take her to Eleanor's where Harry can take care of her leg. If Harry will . . .' she mused. 'That's a good bit south, even from here in the suburbs. So then from there I'm driving as hard and as fast as I can to get away from this city. If we can trust Jack's short wave some crazy things are happening all over lately and the only safe place will be in the hills. I'll risk one call to Deborah first. If I can't get her I'll go without her. And if you want to come with me then go back over to your house and leave a note for Jack – or don't even leave him a note. Just come. Right now.' Cissy had walked to the kitchen and as she talked she began throwing cans of food into a box. Suddenly she stopped. She stared at Melva. 'I know it's different for you. You've got Jack. And a man's no small item these days. I won't blame you if you don't go.'

The two women stood facing each other. Melva turned away, looking down at her bare legs, her sandalled feet. Then she seemed to remember something very important. Her eyes met Cissy's again. 'I'll go,' she said. As she broke for the door she looked back with something close to a smile. 'I've needed to go for a long time. Give me twenty minutes.' She was out of the door.

Cissy put out her cigarette and went to the couch. Kneeling as she gathered up the woman she said to no waking ears but her own, 'Well sister, here we go.'

'Tammy, you do like I say now, do you hear? It's a game, honey. We put you right here in this old duffle bag, in with all the laundry. There. That's my sweet baby. That soft enough for you? Now hush, child! You just got to hide real good while you go away for a little trip. Me and Zelda will be coming on soon after. But you got to go like the other little girls in the bags. Yes ma'am. Every one of you is in a laundry bag just like this one – Jackie and Ethel and Elizabeth and Lu, all of them. Now that's just plain fun, huh? What you got to do is just be real quiet, quiet as a mouse, even when Old Man Casey heaves you in his truck tonight. And don't you move more than your big toe then or make a single sound and don't you let anybody else giggle or talk either. Because then they'll find you and you got to be *It*. You understand? That's my sweet baby.

'Now when you're all in that truck, that's when Casey's going to roll you right out of town. Right out of town, Tammy! And when he lets you out you going to be in the country. Out there where we all went one time, you remember? Where you said, 'Oh, Zelda, where is the houses?' Out there where old Spot ran away to. What? No. Me and Zelda won't be there for a while. We got a summons to go down to the Commission. But Doris – you remember her? – Doris will be there when Casey takes you out of the truck. She's going to get you out of them bags and give you some cakes and take care of you all, you hear? And you do exactly like Doris says and don't give her your comebacks. Now lay there quiet, you hear? That's a sweet baby. We got to go now. You just go right to sleep. Nobody's going to hurt my Tammy, not my sweet baby. 'Bye now, sweet baby, sweet baby . . .'

Someone was screaming. Some two were screaming. Clana thought at first it was simply a plunge into another horror. But the screams were too close. She put her hands to her ears and brought herself back to the stone and sand chamber. The rememberings had ceased for a moment and hung suspended somewhere between the now and the then, between old screams and new screams. Clana felt particularly the suspension of cat history and the effort Alaka was making to hold steady while Bessie attended to one of the adult women. The woman was sobbing now, her contact with the past and with the rememberers completely broken. As she opened her eyes Clana realised that the second set of screams had been coming from Dallo, the girl-child just beside her, but Dallo was calm now, still in the deep past, her outcries only a resonating response to the contagious cries of the older woman. Bessie's hands were cradling in her lap the head of the screaming woman, and Clana – along with all the others – heard Bessie's shortstretch to Nova, elsewhere in the Kochlias.

'Nova. Come.'

Nova's response: 'To shield?'

'Yes. She dropped her own shading very suddenly. She's all right and wants to go back now. She needs your shading and holding, though. Can you come?'

'I'll be right there.'

Throughout the room a low hum had begun, a continuous, even harmonic, joining of the human and cat voices gathered there. The wordless rhythm pulsed softly, enfolding Bessie and the sobbing woman. Alaka was calmly waiting, her voice linked with those of the rememberers and the cats. As she joined in the humming herself, Clana felt strangely at ease, just as Alaka seemed to be. She was ready to shield herself again, ready to rejoin the past. The humming took on extra textures, colours and chords of cooling consonances. Clana felt rather than saw Nova enter the room and stretch out beside the moaning woman. The remember-guide gathered the unresisting body full-length against her own, taking the damp head from Bessie's lap and setting it in the stroking place between her own head and shoulder. As Nova soothed and rocked, as the humming diminished into silence, as Bessie touched each rememberer again in reassurances, Clana moved again towards Alaka's centre. They were all going back now to the dangerous days . . .

'Do you know whose cabin this is?'

'It's empty. That's enough.'

'And it's got food. Look here.'

'Marilyn, take this and go and relieve Michelle down at the foot of the path. She needs to get warm.'

'I don't know how to use that thing.'

'Maybe you won't have to. Just hold it like you would if you did know how. Like this.' The slight woman demonstrated and then urged the taller woman out of the door.

'I still don't think we should have this fire . . .'

'You want us to freeze our asses off? If it brings anybody this late we'll be able to take care of them.'

'Jesus, I thought I was through playing revolutionary.'

'Honey, we just began.'

'Here. Hold Renee closer to the stove. Could someone see the light from over on that other mountain?'

'They'd figure Mr Fisherman was here to thaw the trout.'

A sudden silence fell over all the women, as if a door had opened into each of their lives, revealing otherwise secret fears to outsiders. The woman holding the sleeping child blurted out, 'Well, here we all are.' The tension broke. There was laughter. Bodies moved again. There was a sound outside. Five women started to their feet and then relaxed as Michelle opened the door.

'We need at least two people to watch,' she said. 'The path splits and anybody could reach us from the upper way. I'm staying out.' With a quick look at the sleeping Renee she was gone. The thin woman, Diane, started to protest, then thought better of it.

In all this Judy had said nothing. She sat huddled near the stove rubbing her hands, listening to the others. She knew all but one of these women: knew that Shirley hated yogurt and bean sprouts, knew that Carolyn would rather not be holding Renee, knew that Diane would be fighting an unholy urge to take charge of everything, knew even that Michelle outside was probably suffering more than anyone from the cold, and that Marilyn preferred a karate chop to the rifle she was carrying. Grind out a paper together for four years and you get to know folks. She wondered briefly if Anita and Kay had made it to Tucson.

Judy looked up at the older woman standing by the kerosene lamp. Bev. A friend of Shirley's from the east. She had on what looked to Judy like brand new jeans and a down jacket just out of the store. Lucky for them all, though, that Bev had been with them. They hadn't been stopped in her out-of-state car. Suddenly Judy was overwhelmed. 'What the hell are we doing?' she thought. 'Why aren't we all safe in our own beds? I can't believe they were that hot on our tails. There were no warnings, no –'

'You're being naive, Judy.' Carolyn spoke aloud. Then both women stared at each other.

'How did you –' Judy began.

'I don't know. I thought you were talking to me.'

'I guess I was,' Judy said tiredly.

Diane interrupted them at that moment. 'I want to hear about Minneapolis, Bev, and Cleveland and Philadelphia, if you know. We got only drifts of the witch trials out here. All the real news from the east has been blacked out for months. What happened?'

'I wish I knew. I thought for so long I was crazy. Now I know it's happening all over. Is it a good time to get into it all? I've got a lot to spill.' The women assured her they wanted to hear. 'Well, we didn't know what hit us. In fact, we didn't know we were being hit.' As Bev sat down, the other four women settled with her, a familiar and ancient gesture of telling and hearing. Judy felt a tightness in her stomach.

'You have to understand that I've never been big for women's liberation. Shirley's always been ashamed of me, I think. Her establishment friend in the double-knit pant suit who prefers chairs and comfortable sofas to the floor. I was working up to being Programme Director at a commercial TV station. We'd heard about the women's stuff, of course, bits and pieces that could be ridiculed. Not much, I know now, of what was really going on. There were stories of man-hating separatist women who took off to the country with the back-to-the-land freaks and of vigilante women in the mountains who attacked and disarmed hunters. We were never sure how far the 'disarming' went. Some of them near where I was farmed and lived in the hills with little contact with civilisation. Nobody worried much about them. Not as long as they didn't make trouble. The countryside has a lot of tolerance for offbeat people.

'Once some hunter found a whole homeopathic pharmacy – a cave full of herbs and potions. Then there were some tales of tribal gatherings of women, peyote circles, covens. And that's what did it. It was the reemergence of that word, *witch*, that sent the men at the station up the wall. They laughed the hardest of all at the notion of witches and then their eyes would become very narrow, very hard. About that time things got serious. That's when the New Witch Trials began. It's no wonder there was a news blackout. I've never seen the powers-that-be try so hard to keep anything quiet. We had FCC orders to hold a tight lid on the information.

'It began in a small town above Minneapolis. Over a period of several months three boy babies were found abandoned in cars and laundromats. The cryptic notes found with them were traced to a group of women and girls living out in the boonies. They were all arrested without much protest and then tried together for a trumped up list of misdemeanours and felonies. There was a lot of public interest, but even so they would have served only a minimum jail term. The wind changed and blew against them when one of the women insisted that the group's last three children had been by virgin birth, that there had been no male sires. That was the turning point.

'What happened next begins the worst of it. People, particularly religious fanatics, were outraged against the women. It all got so intense so fast that the trial had to be moved down to a smaller town. There all the women were sentenced to long terms at separate prisons and the children sent to state custody. Any people who tried to support the women got heavy doses of moralism.

Worse, men and women who tried to help them were quickly silenced, if not by money pressures then by physical threats both to themselves and to their families. Some people even wanted to burn all the women in public executions. It was so insane. I've never seen such hatred.'

Bev paused. After a moment she went on. 'When I left, state laws were being revised to require every woman to be married. Polygamy was even being sanctioned in some areas so men could have several wives. Curfews on women went into effect early. Any woman caught wearing pants went to a behaviour modification unit; she emerged wearing a dress and a very scary vacant smile. I saw two women, acquaintances of mine, after their visit to the local clinic . . .' Bev snapped her head as if to shake off the image.

'Women became more and more divided. All the freaky-looking ones were rounded up – you know, those who wouldn't wear even long hippie-type dresses, or those who didn't comb their hair, the kind that would rather be with women than with men, or the kind who gave their husbands any taste of a hard time. God, it was a nightmare. Only the ones who looked and behaved like ladies had a chance. And they weren't about to defend women who refused to conform. "Don't look at me. I'm no witch!"

'Then the misfit women began leaving the cities, heading for the hills, going towards rumours of country women who lived off the land, isolated and self-sufficient. Some found those women. Others probably didn't. All of them had to get away from police and state militias. All of them had to hide.

'If they were caught they didn't get a trial. Some say that hundreds were killed outright. Shot. Gassed. Burned, I didn't know whether to believe the stories or not. I think I do now. Anyway, a woman had a few options if she'd cooperate. She could keep her senses and be a whore or a wife or she could have a little tinkering done with her brain and be a whore or a wife anyway. If her body was too ugly or too old they could use her for maintenance work. I saw some of that, too.'

Bev looked at the other women. 'I'm telling you the truth. I know it sounds like some dippy science fiction story, but I swear it's true. It was weeks before I was really scared. I covered the New Witch Trials myself – all dressed in establishment drag, you better believe. And it was then that I knew I had to get out. The only place

I knew to come was here, to Shirley. Then it took me weeks to plan the get-away. Like playing cops and robbers. When I managed to get sent out of the city on an assignment, I gassed up the car, had my dog and cat put to sleep, and headed west forever. I hit only small towns all the way out and took no freeways. They're doing checks on most of them so I stacked the car with maps and drove the back roads. The day I left all the state homes for children and all the adoption agencies were annexed by the Department of Corrections. I've been dreaming of the things they could do to those kids . . .' She looked at Renee.

Shirley put an arm around Bev. They all sat in silence for awhile, amazed and unbelieving.

Judy spoke first. 'I guess I am naive.'

Carolyn nodded.

'Jesus,' Diane breathed.

'We're all so fucking naive,' Shirley said. 'Who could believe it was really happening? We're as bad as the Jews in Germany. And here we are with only two of us who've ever shot a gun before and one of us who's had any wilderness training. Girl Scouts don't count,' she said to Bev, hugging her. Bev smiled just a little. But not for very long.

'Listen!' Carolyn hushed them all. A motor in the distance.

'Helicopter! Blow out that light!' Diane bolted for the door.

'The fire! They'll see the smoke!'

'Forget the fire,' said Diane. 'Just get out of there and into the trees. The five of you stick together. It's probably only a patrol. I'm going to find Michelle and Marilyn.'

Judy had Renee now, bouncing around in her arms as she ran with Carolyn towards the blackness beyond the cabin. She strained to see the source of the increasing roar and realised with concern that there were two sets of lights coming towards them from a distance. 'Jesus!' she swore. Then to Carolyn she whispered, 'Where are Shirley and Bev?'

Before Carolyn could answer Bev crept through the low brush with Shirley behind her. 'Went back for water and wet cloths,' she said. 'If they're really after us they'll cover this area with tear gas.'

'That doesn't sound much like a middle management lady to me,' Carolyn teased. Judy felt the other woman smile.

'I saw a campus riot once,' Bev said.

They were tense now, cramped together on a soft floor of pine and redwood needles. That was the only thing comfortable about their circumstance, Judy observed. Berry bushes were ripping at her jacket and the sticks and branches from a long-felled tree seemed to poke at her every effort to settle. 'There are two 'copters,' she whispered. 'Both are coming from over there. The west, I guess.'

'If they're looking for us they can find us.' Shirley was grim.

'Not if we're well-concealed,' Bev said.

Shirley denied it. 'Ever hear of Kirlian plates? They actually track you down by your body heat, your aura. Shhh!' Shirley hushed herself, listening.

Renee was frightened now, wiggling and trying to protest Judy's holding her so tight. Placing her lips right against the child's ear Judy whispered, 'You mustn't make any noise, Pooh. Just hold onto me and stay still.'

The helicopters were almost directly overhead now and passing on to the east. Carolyn sighed aloud. 'Coast guard, probably,' she noted.

'This far in?' Judy doubted. But the sound was receding now. 'Let's see if we can reach the others,' she urged. 'Michelle will be worried about Renee. And Renee for sure wants Michelle!' She gave her heavy bundle a little double shake and tried to smile down through the darkness to Renee's face. Judy shifted her weight.

'No!' Bev cautioned. 'They're coming back!'

'My god, they are,' Carolyn said in dismay. 'And they're much lower!'

'Just sit tight,' Shirley was saying.

'Shit! They've got searchbeams!' Carolyn's voice was rising with the approaching sound.

'Get down!' Judy ordered. 'It's happening,' she told herself. 'It's fucking happening. How could it be happening?' She found herself crooning in Renee's ear. 'It's happening, it's happening.' They clung together now, all of them crouched, with Judy trying to cover all their heads with her arms. If she moved her head an inch her left eye could see a dim light bathing the cabin. 'Damn! We left the door open!' The light grew more intense as the motor noise increased above them. She could see the hovering 'copter now, its blinking lights outlining a bulk as big as the cabin itself. Now another light played on the little house. And another. She buried her head, praying that the thick trees would hide her white hand and Shirley's wheat jeans.

Suddenly, somebody shouted nearby, a cry barely audible beneath the din. At the same instant there was a burst of gunfire. Splat-splat-splat-splat-splat-splat-splat. All the women shook. Judy hugged them harder, almost smothering Renee. The child began crying, loud and hard. 'Shhh, Pooh!' Judy whispered frantically. 'They're doing it,' she thought wildly. 'They're doing it! They're doing it they're doing it, they'redoingit! . . .'

During the next moments the whole world erupted. Judy couldn't tell what happened when. She only knew that there was another burst of machine-gun fire and that all of them now, even Renee, were shaken out of their hiding and driven towards some kind of movement. All of them there in the underbrush got to their knees and looked towards the cabin, while above them the noise became more and more deafening. The searchlights made moving lattice-work patterns over the clearing, over the cabin, over the far trees. Suddenly, as if in a distant silent movie, Diane rushed into the crossing lights, her lips shrieking some words inaudible probably even to herself. She put a rifle to her shoulder and fired upwards at the hovering aircraft, flipped the bolt and fired again. And again. And again and again. Then she fell, fell and twisted, as the rifle jerked from her hands and landed across her body.

Carolyn and Bev both starting to rush to Diane. Shirley holding them back. Somewhere a woman's voice shouting, 'Run!' Shirley picking up Renee and leaping deep into the trees, urging them all to follow. The peppering of bullets just behind them as they ran and thrashed and fell and got up and ran again. Renee calling 'Mimi, Mimi!' and bawling her fear to the heavens. Somebody saying, 'My god, it's going to be dawn!' The lights still moving over the trees above them and beyond them, dipping into small clearings. The motors fading, returning, fading again. Breaking a path down the mountainside, Bev's shriek. Her pale face looking up at them as she bent over Michelle's body. Bev shaking her head. 'No!' as Shirley started to bring Renee. Bev motioning them on, running to catch up, her whole body shaking. The resting, the wondering about Marilyn. The 'copters again. Another peppering of the trees about them. Getting separated from Carolyn and Bev.

Darting, running, climbing, falling, running, slipping, falling, running again. Spelling Shirley in carrying Renee. Renee still sobbing.

Then, that scene in the late dawn. With Renee toddling between them Shirley and Judy were attempting to cross the steep and barren end of a small canyon. They had just begun their upward climb, hurrying towards the trees some fifty yards beyond at the top. When she turned at the sound of a returning 'copter, Judy fell, twisting her knee and swearing. She tried in vain to walk. For a few yards Shirley was able to carry her in a fireman's hold – until they both fell sprawled to the dirt.

'That does it,' Judy panted. 'You and Renee get clear and I'll try to look like a rock. Go!'

'We'll all three try to look like rocks,' Shirley said, reaching for Renee. But at that moment the child broke free and began pushing her tiny legs up the hillside.

Shirley shot after her while Judy shouted, 'For god's sake make her be still! Don't let her move!' She could see the 'copter now, a growing dot coming from the north-west. 'Jesus, let the sun blind him,' she muttered, and then, in spite of the sharp pain in her knee, she scooted close to one of the rare bushes that defied the hillside's desolation. She could hide a little maybe. Shirley had caught Renee now and was heading with her for the sun side of a large boulder.

'Get down!' Judy shouted, trying to stay still. 'Get down where you are and stay there!'

The 'copter was fully visible and huge now, flying a course a bit south of them over the other side of the canyon. At that moment, just when Shirley had shoved Renee down beside the rock and was attempting to duck herself, she made a misstep and with a cry went sliding down the steep incline. She reached out with her hands to stop herself, to regain her footing, but her momentum threw her instead into a full body roll. Judy lay transfixed and watched helplessly as Shirley's rolling body flailed down the hill. Renee, too, was apparently stunned into immobility. She did not even cry out.

As she knew it would, the 'copter turned. As she knew it would, it descended and cut a course towards Shirley's movement, so low now that Judy could see two men standing in its open door. As

Judy knew she would, Shirley finally broke her fall and immediately began limping for cover. And as she knew it would be, her own voice was drowned out by the roar and she was left whispering to herself, 'Stay still! Stay still!'

But she did not know what would come from the 'copter. As the thin nets dropped from its door, Judy could not believe her eyes. The first net fell short and was hauled up empty, to be dropped again. But the second one fell full on the stumbling woman. Shirley's arms were fighting the mesh, her legs still propelling her away from the 'copter, down towards the draw where the hills met.

Long ago Judy had read – was it in *National Geographic*? – about how wild animals were captured for zoos. She had been enraged. Enraged at the arrogance of those who took without asking and took so greedily, as if their brutalised technological power were the only significant thing on earth. Enraged at the fear and helplessness of once-majestic spirits trapped now – not for food, not even for what some tried to call 'educational uses', but for profit or the thrill of conquest.

Now on this grey morning just at sunrise Judy was seeing Shirley trapped and carried away like a wild animal, and her own raging impotence buried itself in one of her soul's deepest parts, never to be dislodged, she knew, even at her death. For the rest of her life she would be forgetting Shirley's wide and screaming mouth, her near escape from the corner of the mesh only to fall and be covered again. Every hour of all her remaining days Judy knew she would be forgetting the hovering machine, the shouts and howls of the men as they manipulated the net and drew it under Shirley, enclosing her at last, and with rude jerks lifted her up, a bound and subdued ball of flesh, into the mouth of the 'copter. She would be forgetting always the lurch of the helicopter as it suddenly turned and swept off into the west, its tiny lights still blinking, insolently trying to compete with the sun. She would set herself rituals for forgetting it all, a litany of forgetting every morning, a keening of forgetting every night.

It was long after the motor roared away that Judy heard Renee crying. 'The survivors,' she thought, trying to move her throbbing knee. 'What will we do now?' To Renee she called, 'Pooh! Come here!' But the little girl just stood on the hillside, tears pouring down her face, sobs rasping out of her throat, crying out her desolation to Judy and the empty canyon.

'I'll be forgetting that, too,' thought Judy, as she began pulling herself up the hill.

As she went to the last of the rememberings, Clana's head was already full of the strangest imaginings she had ever known. She was still mentally digesting all the hard pictures she had examined this morning – covers from old magazines with women clad only in high-heeled boots and a thin crotch band or being whipped into apparent ecstatic submission by a masked man ready to enter her, photographs of women on their knees servicing men, women and men in a hundred varieties of sexual postures.

The guides had been careful time and again to tell them how it was not always like those pictures. They had said there was a difference between abusive sex between women and men and the kind which was a mutual expression of love. But Clana was still confused. How could you let someone enter your body that way and not be a victim? How could you ever want that to happen? She tried to go back to the remember room memories of women loving men before the Purges, how rich some of those stories had been, how good such feelings had felt. That helped her to understand only a little better. When she told Alaka about her confusion Alaka had suggested that at some other time she come back to the remember room and live through those particular stories with less of a shield. Perhaps then, her friend had said, she would better understand how some physical expression between women and men might have been good.

Clana was still feeling upset and puzzled as she settled into her sand-and-pebbles seat. Other girl-children who had chosen to see the hard pictures with her were looking equally queasy. There was none of the usual playful cavorting among them today. Rather, each girl-child seemed locked into some misery all her own, meeting no one's eyes, moving slowly to her place. 'We all seem like very tired old women,' Clana thought to herself, 'or else the left-overs from somebody's unhappiness box.' There was hardly a word spoken as Nova and Bessie began drawing them into the rememberings of the Revolt of the Mother.

'Once upon a time,' began Bessie, 'there was one rape too many.

Once upon a time.'

Clana was relieved to be able to spin back into the past, hearing for a while a firm narrative voice from Bessie. 'The earth finally said 'no'. There was no storm, no earthquake, no tidal wave or volcanic eruption, no specific moment to mark its happening. It only became apparent that it had happened, and that it had happened everywhere.'

'Nell!' Sylvia was whispering almost in her ear. 'I just had this fantastic daydream, real as life!'

Nell rolled over towards the other brown body, much thinner than her own but equally sweaty under the afternoon sun. They were lying nude, soaking up some rare heat by a slow creek. Nell had just managed to get into her own fantasy. 'Yeah?' she said sleepily.

'There was a rodeo –'

'Wait.' Nell leaned across her to dig her wristwatch out of her pants. 'Okay.' She flopped back.

'What time is it?'

'Lots earlier than I thought. Not three yet. Go ahead.'

'Well, there was this rodeo. Texas or Oklahoma. Probably down by the old Rio Grande,' she grinned.

'Yeah.' Nell grinned back.

'Right in the middle of the fanciest quadrille you ever saw, all the men, every one of them, fell off their horses.'

'And the women too?'

'Nope. Just the men. Well, the whole figure stopped, music and everything, while the men tried to remount. But the horses were having none of it. They bucked and reared and wouldn't let the men back on.' Sylvia was laughing now. 'Some of the women dismounted and got the horses calmed down. But every time a man tried to climb aboard a horse it would go wild all over again. Well honey, the flags were all mixed up and falling and the crowd was hollering, and the men were all rolling in the dirt in their fine white cowboy suits – and the ladies were clean as a whistle, riding just as smooth –'

'What was going on?' Nell was caught up in Sylvia's laughter.

'I don't know. It got bad though, because one big red-faced guy couldn't stand the idea that his horse wouldn't carry him and when he got thrown a third or fourth time he whipped out his old fortyfour and shot at the horse. But the gun jammed or something so he began beating up on the horse with the butt of the gun. Then all hell broke loose. People grabbed him and officials poured into the ring. That was about the end of it. Horses rearing and bolting, men cussing and fighting. Mass confusion.'

'I was having some pretty heavy flashes myself,' mused Nell. She brushed off the shirt and socks that she was lying on, protecting her from the hot dirt beneath her. 'Logging trucks falling off the sides of mountains, car wrecks, airplane crashes. The moon must be in something crazy. Then I saw field after field of grain and in every one of them there was a big rusty farm tractor or combine, looking like it hadn't been used in years. Can you dig leaving expensive machines out to deteriorate like that?'

'Well, if they didn't work . . .'

'Yeah. Maybe so.' Nell sat up and stretched. 'Maybe it's the sun. It's supposed to give some people hallucinations. Jesus, we're spaced out, Sylvia. To nearly go to sleep like that. And the others don't know where we are. Anything could have happened.'

'But it didn't.' A pause. 'Are you going to stick with them, Nell?'

'For sure. It's the safest thing I can think of. Together we can find food. Together we can make shelter, and together we've got some protection. If we can hold out through the first hard weather then maybe we can go south. In the meantime I have a hunch we'll find other groups of women doing just like us. Aren't you going to stick?'

Sylvia had pulled on her pants and boots and now was tying her laces. 'Sure. I don't have any choice. I'm not –' She stopped suddenly to listen. There was the sound of a motor on the road high above them. 'Duck!' Sylvia whispered. In a second both women had gathered their clothes and pulled back from the edge of the stream to within the thin trees nearby.

Wheels ground on gravel and the motor stopped. Loud men's voices poured down the hill to them. Two truck doors slammed. Nell couldn't make out what the men were saying but she knew all too well what they were thinking. Since large numbers of women had started escaping from the cities a new sport had become popular. Nell and Sylvia – and all the women they had been hiding with – knew about such activities. *Cunt Hunts* they were called: small bands of men, usually three or four at most, packed up what gear they would need and set out for the day or the weekend to see what womanflesh they could find in the hills. Sometimes they got permission from the owners of the land who – with a quiet wife hovering in the background – usually granted it for a price. Other times they roamed the back roads indiscriminately, night and day, with spotlights and 'scope rifles, often drunk, often loud, always together, and always dangerous. Eileen had described for them all an encounter with such men. She had been raped again and again, beaten, teased, tortured and disfigured, then left alive only because the men had passed out long enough for her to crawl away. Most others who were caught weren't that lucky.

Now as the heavy bodies came thrashing and shouting down the hillside, Nell realised how foolish they had been to leave the large group, even for an hour or two. As she was cursing herself for that she heard something that made her sick all over. 'Dogs!' she whispered. 'Mother of god, they've got dogs!' Sylvia heard it too – several barks joining the tumult and yells of encouragement from the men.

'Come on!' Nell said. 'They've seen us.' She tugged at the other woman and the two of them began running back over the lightly broken path they had come by. Sylvia was in the lead now. When she felt Nell fall behind she turned. 'I gotta put these boots on,' Nell said. 'I can't get anywhere.'

'They're gaining on us. I think the dogs are already where we were,' Sylvia urged. Nell rose again and followed her. Her bootstrings were flapping but she made faster progress now through the brush.

Nell knew where Sylvia was headed: the low narrow place in the creek where they had crossed earlier. If they could make it to the other side before the men rounded the bend then they had a chance. 'But the dogs,' she thought, as she shifted her bundle of clothes to her other hand. 'We won't get away from the dogs.'

There it was. Sylvia had reached the narrow spot and was looking downstream to see if their pursuers could see. 'Come on!' she called softly, already stepping from stone to stone and then wading through water up to her knees. Nell, close behind, gave up on the rocks and splashed immediately into the water, desperately

174

watching the downstream bend. As she touched dry land again she heard the dogs on the far side, following exactly the route they had come.

'Hide!' she whispered to Sylvia, looking frantically around the small clearing, then literally she dived on the other woman, throwing them both over a fallen log, uphill and to the right of the open space. Even as she dropped on top of Sylvia she saw two loping dogs, white with black spots, pause in indecision only for a moment as they smelled a few feet up and down the stream and then plunged into the water. 'Jesus, Mary and Joseph, we're in for it now,' she whispered, but even as she said it the lead hound heaved out of the water, shook itself and then without a sniff or a glance, darted right by them and up the path into the trees. The second dog did not even shake itself but went happily bounding after the leader.

Before their astonishment could turn to relief, Nell and Sylvia saw the second dog stop short – almost as if it had forgotten something – turn, and head back towards them. It leapt over the log, pushed its excited face right next to Sylvia's and licked her twice very lovingly. With that it leapt over the log again and disappeared up the path.

'Well I'll be damned,' said Nell.

'Come on,' said Sylvia, shaking herself out of her surprise. 'We have to get further up and back this way. They'll follow the dogs.' They pulled each other and noisily crawled and scooted under a cover of ironwood trees until they could no longer see the clearing.

'Mamie!' A man's voice bellowed. 'You goddam jacktoothed hound! Where'd you go?' There was a splash.

'. . . about the damn dogs. Just find the girls, Arnold. They couldn't get far.' The voices were very close now. Sounds of stamping feet, splattering water.

'I tell you, they're around here somewhere. I saw 'em cross right here and after the trees that path's clear all the way up to the bluff.' There was an abrupt silence. Three men were just below them now. In a sudden panic Nell saw that the left foot that she was bracing herself with was sticking out from the low trees. The men were now looking at her boot with its untied laces.

The silence continued. Finally Arnold's voice spoke again. It sounded menacing. 'Well now, ladies, why're you being so unsociable? You come on out now.'

Another silence. Then a much nastier voice. 'You come out or we fire right into the bushes and kill you outright. Get down here.'

Nell had been holding Sylvia's hand. As they looked at each other she knew what Sylvia knew: that the men weren't bluffing, that they would certainly shoot; she also knew that under the shirt she was holding Sylvia had unsheathed her hunting knife, and she knew that whatever else happened, at least one of the men was probably going to die within the next few minutes. Sylvia nodded to her as if to affirm all that, and then, moving almost as a single person, the two women slid out from under the low trees. One bare-breasted woman and one woman naked except for her boots confronted three men.

Something in Nell wanted to laugh when she looked at them, not because she saw no danger, but because it was danger couched in a parody of military conformity. The three thick-shouldered figures all looked to be in their late twenties or early thirties, each with the same sunburned face and the early beer-belly roundness pushing at his shirt. They stood close to each other in a line facing the women. The far two held rifles while the first stood with his feet apart, thumbs hooked in his belt. All three of the men wore boots, work pants, flannel or cotton shirts of a plaid design. Their hair covered their ears and in each case it was topped by a blue baseball cap.

In that short moment before anyone spoke, as the tableau was frozen there on the creekbank in the autumn sun and shadow, it occurred to Nell that these men were scared; that, given the choice, each one of them would rather be anywhere else in the world right now but here.

That moment passed quickly. The middle man, the blond one with the nasty voice, sneered. 'Well,' he said. 'Two senoritas.' With that cue the atmosphere changed and all three men snapped into broad movement and a confusion of loud competitive voices.

Nell wasn't sure whether the unarmed man first grabbed Sylvia or whether Sylvia stepped first towards him. But when she saw the knife blade flash she threw her own bare body high upon the man's back, her arm in a stranglehold around his neck. Sylvia, free now from his grasp, was shouting. 'Ha-Ya!' with every plunge of her knife into the man's arm. 'His arm? Why isn't she killing him?'

thought Nell, still choking with all her strength. Then she saw that Sylvia's knife arm was being restrained by one of the other men, the dark one, and at that same moment she felt herself thrown forcefully to the ground. The scuffle that followed involved them all. She heard a cry from Sylvia, as if she'd been struck, but she could not identify the other confusion of sounds.

She herself now was on her back and pinned down by a mountain of brutal movement. The blond man was heaving back and forth on top of her, his sweaty hair falling over her face, his eyes closed tight in an agony of effort. Through gritted teeth he was panting with each of his thrusts, 'C'mon, baby! C'mon, baby!'

'My god, is he in me?' Nell thought. She tried to move her arms from under her but the man only bore down the harder. She realised that he had not yet come into her, that in fact he was still trying for an erection. Just as she registered that idea, her assailant's weight shifted. In a desperate move he shoved his hand between their two bodies and began savagely massaging himself.

Nell was aware then of huge guffaws above her, of taunting voices. 'Bejesus, he can't even get it up! What's the matter, Skunk?' 'Didn't you eat your Wheaties, Sport?' 'Hey Skunk, you need a little starch?'

The man – Skunk – seemed momentarily disoriented by the laughter. In an almost involuntary move, Nell took advantage of that. Arching her back she threw all her weight towards the unbalanced body above her. He fell to the side and she rolled out from under him. As she moved to a kneeling position she was aware of Sylvia's crumpled body by the water and of two big men looking in disbelief at their companion.

As for him, her would-be rapist, he sat like a child staring down at his open pants. Then slowly he looked at the other men, nobody laughing now. 'She's a witch,' he said, looking back at her with a growing fear and disgust. 'A witch! That's not ever happened before, not ever. Not ever!' He scrambled to his feet, bravado colouring his voice. 'Your turn, Arnold. You try her and see.'

Arnold paled. 'Not today,' he said. 'Not for me today. I'm bleeding pretty bad and I gotta get this arm taken care of.' He held his wounded limb like a baby. Nell waited. All eyes turned to the third man.

'I don't know what the hell you want with that one anyway,' he growled. 'I say let's shoot 'em both and take the tits back for proof.'

'You mean you don't want her, Howie?' This from Skunk, zipping up his pants and reaching for his gun. 'You were the one so hot for pussy today. Or is it that you can't get it up?'

Howie turned in rage and started towards the insult. 'Fuckin' sonofabitch –'

In an instant Skunk had levelled the rifle at the oncoming man. Nell watched while Skunk shouted, 'I'll shoot, Howie! I swear to god I'll shoot your balls off!'

'Howie! Skunk!' Arnold's voice rose above them. He tried to place himself in front of Howie but the enraged man pushed him away and continued his lunge towards Skunk.

'Howie!' Skunk shrieked as he pulled the trigger. Howie stopped, expecting to be dead. Skunk threw the bolt and fired again, point blank. Still nothing. He threw aside the gun in time to ward off Howie's leaping body, now pushing him into the trees. Above them both was Arnold, shouting their names, trying to separate them. Nell crawled and scooted over to Sylvia, careful to skirt the flailing men. To her relief, Sylvia was unconscious, but as far as she could tell, unhurt.

When she looked over to check on the progress of the fight Nell's eyes suddenly beheld the most welcome sight of her life: coming quietly down the path and almost surrounding the scuffling men were eleven strong women. 'Angels from heaven!' Nell thought gratefully, grinning at her friends. The women stood now with no words, no sounds, patiently waiting like weary schoolteachers for the boys to finish their recess. Two of the women had picked up the rifles and held them casually aimed at the men. Another woman was moving towards Nell to help her with Sylvia.

Slowly the scuffle began to subside. 'You need a nursemaid, you big horse,' Arnold was saying, on his knees now pounding on Howie. 'Be damned if –' He broke off abruptly to stare at a pair of boots a few feet away. Beside them was another pair of boots. And beside them another. And another. Arnold dared to raise his head. 'Lord!' he whispered. Without taking his eyes from the ring of silent women above him, he punched his companions. When they failed to respond he set his hand in Skunk's hair and wrenched his head to one side. Skunk then saw the same boots. And Skunk dared to raise his head. Without a word he climbed off Howie and knelt by the bushes, his jaw hanging loose, his eyes roving slowly from one immobile figure to the next. Relieved of the weight, Howie sprang into a sitting position. His eyes moved left to right and then settled with the rest of his body into a stunned expectancy.

The absolute absence of sound and movement went on for an eternity. Then, as if by some signal, all the standing women moved exactly one step closer to the crouching men. Nell saw genuine terror spring to their eyes. Then noiselessly one of the women, Eileen, raised her arm and pointed across the creek to the path to the road.

This time the silence was not so long. Howie was the first to his feet. He picked up his cap and tried to be casual in brushing his shirt but his eyes never left Eileen's. Arnold rose, too, his eyes riveted on Eileen. Skunk, still hitching up his pants, got to his feet beside him. Arnold shoved him towards the path. Two of the women stepped back to allow them through. Without a word the men raised their hands like robbers under arrest and began backing towards the spot where Nell and the other woman were holding Sylvia. Without even glancing at their intended victims, they slowly waded into the water, sometimes moving sideways and at other times glancing over their shoulders as they edged forward. When they reached the other side they turned and hesitated, as if expecting the women to follow.

Eileen's voice tore through the silence. 'RUN!' she screamed. Before her voice died the three men were pitching and stumbling over one another in the fight to get to the path and up the incline.

Again without a word the women moved, this time downstream and into the centre of the creek itself, there to watch and to remain visible while three stocky hard-running figures scrambled up the path and into the cab of a truck. When the truck motor failed to start, two of the men hauled out to push. The last that the women could hear was the crackle of tyres on gravel, slow at first but then more urgent as the truck picked up momentum and coasted down the far hill.

They waited until the last sound died before they quietly went back to the clearing. There they collapsed into relief and laughter.

'My god, I was never so scared in my life!' 'Scared, honey! I got no nerves left!' 'But I never felt so strong either!' 'Did you see them run?' 'They won't be back.'

Then one woman's voice rose above them all. 'We've got to get out of here. We can talk later.'

Another voice said, 'Sylvia's just coming around. We'll need two people to carry her.' Again the tone changed and the women began a businesslike filing up the path, Sylvia managing to walk a bit between two of the women.

Nell was one of the last to leave. She put her arm around Eileen. 'You never looked so good to me.'

Eileen was carrying Nell's clothes. 'You look good to us. We were afraid when we heard the shouts. Did they get to you?'

'No. No, they didn't.' As they turned to go Nell stopped to retrieve something from the bushes. 'Looks like Skunk dropped his cap,' she said, setting it on her own head with a grin. Then she and Eileen climbed up the path towards the camp.

Through her reverie Clana decided that all the others had left. They were probably already at the final bathings and holdings and were probably waiting for her. She concentrated, trying to send herself back to the remember world. No good. She pinched her eyes tight. Maybe they wouldn't find her. Maybe she could turn into sand and pebbles. Round, like a pebble. Hard, like a pebble. Smooth. Nestled against other pebbles.

She stopped. Very slowly she opened one eye. There were two eyes calmly staring at her. The cream calico blinked from the ledge. 'Isn't it time for your bath?' sent the cat.

'Will you bathe with me?' Clana stretched back.

The cat stood, arching her back. With a dignified leap she was beside Clana. 'I have no need to cleanse myself that way.' As Clana slowly sat up, the cat yawned, pushing her front legs forward. 'Besides,' she said, 'I can't stand the smell of that water.'

'Then will you let me carry you to the resting rooms?'

The cat considered. 'Yes. That would be nice.'

With a smile Clana scooped up the armful of fur and said goodbye to the remember room. The cat let her stroke her soft fur all the way to the doorway of the bathing rocks.

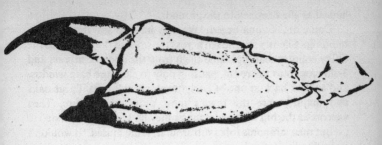

Meeting the Gentles

Evona's boot explored the flat top of a table. She put her knee down and moved her body completely through the window. 'An office,' she sent, sliding off the dusty surface. She could barely make out the walls of a large room dotted with clumps of furniture.

Behind her she heard Falstaff and Feste flapping their wings. She caught Chthona's shortstretch to them: 'It's all right to stay out here. But we may be inside a long time.' She could feel the crows' approval of that plan. Nothing in them wanted to enter the dark building. 'But none of your conversations,' Chthona was warning. 'We need quiet.'

'It's a good thing all the rest didn't come,' Evona thought, remembering how Chthona's whole loud menagerie, particularly the racoons, had insisted on joining them. In the end the prospect of windriding had discouraged most of the animals and Chthona had been able to convince the rest that there'd be more adventure right there where they were, at the edge of the Wanderground.

'But I didn't bargain for that whole escort of crows.' Another mindstretch came from above them where Tulu was hovering at her ride's end. In fact, none of them had expected that escort, and had been worried at first that those gregarious friends of Falstaff and Feste's might awaken the whole countryside as they rode through the night sky. 'But all's well,' Tulu reassured herself as she dropped to the ground.

'Come on,' Evona urged. 'We may have to search the whole building.' Silently she moved across the smooth floor towards the bulky counter that separated them from the doors. Chthona and Tulu crept into the room, pausing only to close the bare window and to look back at one of Earlytown's silent streets. Large oaks and maples were the town's most prominent feature. They welcomed the hill women, alone as they had been for so long.

'But there are some folks still around,' Tulu mused. 'It wouldn't be bad to live here –'

'Not at all,' Chthona agreed, at the same moment hushing both Falstaff and Feste outside the window who wanted to voice their own approval.

'Someone's near,' Evona stretched. She had found her way to one of the doors.

'A gentle,' sent Chthona.

'How do you know?'

'I know.'

'It's a gentle,' affirmed Tulu. 'We both can tell. He's at the door.'

As if on cue the door opened slowly. Evona's eyes, more accustomed now to the darkness, could see a figure a few inches taller than herself. His face was not distinguishable but Evona could tell it was set inside an explosion of small ringlets which made a perfect globe of his head.

The head turned towards her. 'You're the hill women?' His words broke the silence.

Evona cleared her throat. 'Yes,' she said. 'I am Evona.' Without second thought she did what she would not have done in the City. She held her left hand towards him.

He hesitated only a moment, then extended his right hand to enclose hers. 'And I am Pasquale. We were afraid you might not come.' He dropped her hand.

'And so were we,' said Tulu aloud and a little grimly. She moved with Chthona around the counter to the door. 'I am Tulu.'

'Tulu,' said the gentle, not moving.

'Chthona, brother,' said Chthona. She and Tulu each held out a hand. Pasquale accepted the invitation, closing for a moment one of his own hands over each of theirs.

'You have crows with you?' he asked.

'Yes,' said Chthona. 'Two. They are content to stay outside.'

'And there are others from this area,' he smiled. 'We call them the Earlytown Flappers. They claim the territory from here to our farm.' He beckoned them. 'We are in the courtroom. The windows are covered there.' Slowly he led the way through the door. Evona fell in behind her sisters as they followed him down a pitch dark hallway. She risked a full spanner check all around the courthouse, finding a number of safe but strange presences. Other gentles, she assumed. Then she swept northwards in wide reach to Koa at the nearest outpost. 'All well. Stay in brushtouch.'

'Yes,' sent back Koa.

They were turning now to another part of the building. 'Steps,' stretched Tulu, waiting so the three of them could mount the wide stairs together. High windows were outlined above them as they rose four flights into a large hall with sets of double doors. Pasquale threw open one of the doors and a shaft of light pierced the darkness. Instinctively the women moved aside and into the shadows.

Another man's voice spoke from within the lighted room. 'There are four of us in all. You have met Pasquale.' Deliberately, as if to demonstrate their harmlessness, two men stood silhouetted together just inside the door, their arms slightly outstretched. Tulu was the first to move into the light. She walked past Pasquale at the door and greeted with handtouch the two gentles. They were dressed much like the hill women, in soft shirts, work pants and boots. The dark tall one was Tony. It was he who had spoken.

Labrys, the thicker and clearly older man, spoke as Chthona greeted them. 'I know you, I think.'

'Perhaps,' she replied. 'Some years ago near the sea I shared a covenant with women and men like yourself.'

'Are you a scrier?'

'Long since.'

'Then I know you from a gathering on the Bald Hills. Welcome.'

Chthona nodded. Evona was stretching her softself out into the room beyond. The patterns she met were not too different from her own. She picked up low but sharp cusps of anxiety and tiny stripes of fear, but there were no stiff blockages, no frantic pressures. 'I'm Evona,' she said, joining the group at the back of a large and formal room.

'From the City,' said Tony. 'You carried the message of the meeting.'

'Yes,' she said. Now she could see every corner of the huge courtroom – the dark wainscoting, the high plastered walls with curtain-blackened windows, the judge's bench, jury box, witness stand. Towards the front of the room beyond the rows of benches, two highly polished tables – walnut, she guessed – had been pulled together and surrounded with captain's chairs. Abruptly she recognised the source of the room's anxiety: facing them in one of the chairs, his features enlivened by the play of candlelight, sat a stocky, much older man, his wild grey hair framing a sharp-lined, clean-shaven face.

'That's Andros,' Labrys told her. Then smiling and as close to the brink of humour as he apparently dared to go, he added loudly. 'He is a heavy, gentle man. We told him how heavy up four flights of stairs.'

'He's not able –' Tulu stopped herself. 'You carried him here?'

'We all came here,' Labrys answered, sobering quickly, 'Pasquale and I bearing his weight between us. No. He's able. Rather, we are able. We have a saying among us that a disability is anything that three men cannot do together. Yes. We are able to come here.'

They were all moving now down the aisle between the benches towards the grey-haired man. They could see that he had one leg extended, his foot propped up on a chair. He spoke as they neared. 'I made the unfortunate error of exceeding my capacities a week or so ago, and injured myself even worse than is my normal condition.' Though he did not smile, Evona sensed behind his small dark eyes an openness that was practised and disciplined – not a gift of nature, but the product of some painful growth. 'You are Evona. And Chthona. And Tulu,' he said with a hint of strain. 'I greet you all and I'm grateful for your coming.'

Tulu was pulling out one of the chairs. She stretched briefly to the other two: 'Well, here we go. Let's lay a blessing on us all.' Aloud she said, 'We don't come as representatives of the hill women, but only as ourselves.'

'I understood that might be so.' Pasquale sat with the other men while Evona and Chthona settled next to Tula. Without any fanfare and with unexpected ease the meeting with the

184

gentles was about to begin.

Evona was suddenly frightened. She opened her mindstretch to Chthona and Tulu, finding them both steady and unalarmed. She swept wide again to Koa and was reassured by that distant light-touch. She briefly brushed Falstaff and Feste, perched now in the top of a skinny tree just beyond the courthouse.

'We're here, lots of us,' returned Feste.

'And quiet,' reassured Falstaff.

'Still,' Pasquale was continuing, 'you will be able to bear messages?'

'Of course,' said Tula. 'But we could not find a unity among us on the matter of meeting with you.'

'That's familiar,' said Andros. Evona glanced at him to see what sarcasm accompanied the remark. She discovered instead a genuinely pained expression.

Tony spoke. 'We had the same struggle. None of our brothers wanted to come to such a meeting. Many felt that not even we should come.'

Evona's shock must have registered in some grotesque expression, for Andros suddenly exploded. Almost leaping to a standing position he leaned heavily on the table towards her. 'What did you expect, woman? That we'd fall over our dimpled toes for the almighty privilege of your company? That we dream women through our nights and envision them through our days? That we have no other occupation in the world than to slobber our precious enzymes in a vain hankering after the magic healing presence of the handmaidens of the great mother?' His fist hit the table.

Before she knew what was happening Evona's own fist struck the table, so shortly behind that of the stocky man that they almost fell in unison. 'I don't expect to be screamed at,' she shouted, back on her feet, 'by a doddering old man who can't keep his temper or find his manners!'

Andros' smile was wicked. 'Ha! She speaks of manners, gentlemen! She who has disdained the chivalry of a hundred centuries to claim her own sweet selfhood and independence! She begs my cape once more for the puddle, my strong arm for her support.'

They glared at each other over the table, seeking in vain some refinement of their rampant energy. Evona's throat was a fury of words, all of them fighting to be said at once. She could barely feel Tulu's strong ritual enfoldment: 'I wait by the well of your anger.' Another warmth flooded Evona. She no longer needed to shout.

'She wants neither your cape nor your arm, Andros.' Pasquale was speaking. 'She probably wants, as we all do, no more digging into old and deep wounds.' Andros straightened. He inhaled deeply.

Evona's eyes thanked Pasquale. Her voice was more even now and she tried not to speak unkindly. 'But you're right, Andros. I am surprised. Twenty years ago, ten or even five years ago, any man among you would have given a month's food for the chance to meet with hill women, or so our history tells us.'

Andros' face leapt into another contortion of rage. Then suddenly he frowned, clenched his teeth, squeezed his eyes tight. As if shaking off some body-riding demon, he threw himself back into his chair, holding his head in both hands. Nothing stirred. The grey head finally lifted, seeking the eyes of the other men. Andros started to speak but Labrys' wordless gesture stopped him.

Tony spoke instead, reaching as he did so to take Andros' big hand in his own. 'You're making no room for change, Evona. What you say is true. But we don't seek you now.'

'That's a thin line,' Evona muttered.

'A thin line?' Tony's dark eyes were puzzled.

'Between hating us like men have always done and learning to stay away, out of –' She faltered. 'Out of –'

'Out of respect?' Tony finished. 'You don't believe we can do that?'

Evona looked at him squarely. 'No. I don't believe you can do that. Not yet. Maybe never.' She pushed back her chair and walked away from the table into the darkness. 'There's a gentle in the City right now,' she continued, 'who needs strong women's companionship. He stays in the City, there in that cock-centred energy that he hates, not because he's a mother-fucker, not even because he's a man-fucker, but because he craves the tiny bit of company he can get there from hill women. Even hill women in disguise.'

Tony nodded. 'That may be true for him. But it's far from the whole story.' His voice had a sharp edge. 'Will you come back, Evona, and hear us through?'

Evona's fingers rubbed the railing of the jury box. She opened to an enfoldment from Chthona and Tulu. 'We stand with you,' it said. Evona glanced at them, then at the men. With a nod she walked back to her seat.

Tony waited as each person at the table shifted in some small or broad way. He released Andros' hand and spoke to all three women. 'In the beginning we kept ourselves from you in spite of our needs, out of respect for your wishes. And because we knew that women and men can do nothing but violence to one another. We also knew that the work the hill women were doing needed our protection though not our interference. That's no longer the case.'

Both Chthona and Tulu stirred in some alarm, Pasquale's gesture reassured them. 'We still will not interfere,' he interposed. 'But it's no longer out of respect, he means, that we hold ourselves off from you.'

'By refusing to teach us,' Tony went on, 'you have taught us well.' He looked at the other men. They looked straightforwardly back at him. Tony's dark eyes fell on Evona, then on Tulu and Chthona. 'We do not need you now. We can live without you,' he said. As if in some ritual assent the other three men each singled out the eyes of each of the hill women. Labrys nodded. Pasquale nodded. Evona knew she did not grasp the full impact of Tony's statement. She would be considering it for a long time to come. As her eyes met Andros', he too nodded, almost imperceptibly.

Labrys spoke. 'Can you see that this meeting, though there was great need of it, terrified many of us? All of us, even the youngest who have never seen hill women, fear that deep inside we are capable of betraying ourselves, of needing you again.'

'And sometimes,' added Andros, 'we protest that need too much.' What played over his face was both sheepish and grim, but it was a smile. Chthona smiled back. Tulu laughed aloud. In the next moment there was low laughter from them all, even from Evona. The tension eased.

There was another motionless silence before Labrys spoke. 'Very simply,' he said, 'there has been an increasing drop in the number of hill women on rotation in the City. It is imperative that you maintain at maximum the number you have on rotation there.'

The words fell like tiny blows on Evona. All the ease of the moment before fell away into a newly gathering tension. 'An unjust accusation,' she thought. While her sisters relayed to Koa far away the gentle's saying, she concentrated on her growing indignation.

'It may not have to be permanent,' Pasquale put in, rounding out Labrys' explanation. 'Perhaps only for a year or two. Ten years at most. We've recently discovered among ourselves a very happy thing, something that will allow us, when the time comes, to do more than protect you.'

Evona was about to speak. Chthona's shortstretch stopped her. 'Let him finish it all first,' Evona waited.

Labrys continued. 'We're almost certain now, though we can't explain it, that there is a relationship between the number of hill women working in the City, and the incidence of rape, of machine and firearm functioning outside the City.'

Evona erupted. 'That's impossible,' she blurted. 'There's no connection whatsoever. We keep a constant complement of women there. We are very careful –' She broke off, looking at Tulu and Chthona.

'Then we've misjudged,' Labrys said thoughtfully. 'Or –'

Chthona started to speak, cleared her throat, then began again. 'I know what you are talking about. It's the women from the south valleys and eastern mountains, Labrys, who have been cutting off their rotations. We've known that at the outposts for months. But we've thought little of it and haven't inquired the cause.'

'Let's ascertain, then,' Andros broke in. 'These names. Have they returned to you?' He threw back his head and closed his eyes. 'Odyssey, Adria, Jocelyne, Madrone, Lavina, Patricia, Harlequina, Sno, Shaiyu, Lowey, Uxa, Leslie, Mandalay, Luna, Hora, Grete, Daniella, Ollie, Keiko, Tasha, Mindy, Cynthia, Kwo, Paula, Lyndalli, Ijeme, Nesta?' He opened his eyes.

'Only Ijeme is familiar to me,' said Tulu. The other women nodded.

'They are all women who have left their rotation in the City within the year. Is that right?' Chthona addressed Andros. 'And they are all, with the exception of Ijeme who has been replaced, women from communities far south and east of us.' A note of amazement coloured her voice. 'Do you know each hill woman who lives in the City?'

'We try to keep track. Shall we name them?' He threw back his head as if to recite again but Chthona cut him off.

'No, no,' she said. 'I don't doubt you.'

'The rapes,' Tulu broke in. 'The shotkillings. Are they really happening?'

'They are,' said Labrys. 'Not many and only at particular times, but enough to fan the rumours that men could be potent again outside the cities.' He reached towards her. 'If you could find the cause of the eastern and southern women's withdrawing, if you could convince them that they must not weaken their network in the City, then the City would contain the violence again and the rumours would have no hope of proof.' His voice held an anxious plea.

'No!' said Evona, pushing back her chair again and stepping away from the table. 'It makes no sense. How could fewer women in the City have anything to do with the outbreak of violence in the country?'

'Fewer women like yourself,' Andros corrected.

'Then why not fewer men like yourself?' she countered, moving toward him. 'Why isn't the presence of gentles in the City just as important? Maybe your own men are disappearing, running from the City. Why does it have to be the women? Always the women!' She strode back and forth between Andros and the darkness of the jury box.

Pasquale was on the edge of his chair. He had turned, his eyes following her pacing as if begging her to listen. 'We don't know for a certainty. Maybe some delicate balance of energy. Maybe some supernatural message to keep us all toeing the line. Our judgement is purely of symptoms, Evona. Every time there is some abuse of energy outside the City we only have to check on the women in rotation. Every time there will be some irregularity in the rotation pattern.'

'Item,' Andros announced. Evona stopped her pacing. 'Several years ago when three hill women were caught and killed in the City whole parties of celebrating men and their women poured into the countryside. They revved up deserted farm machinery and hauled truckloads of copulating couples around a field all night long. Things stopped rather suddenly, a cessation that corresponded precisely to the arrival in the City of the hill women's replacements. Item.' Andros drew the chair holding his leg closer to him. 'Last year when some crisis called four of your women home without warning, some would-be hunters holding rifles that had not fired for generations found that live ammunition worked. There were several rapes at that time too, – country men of their wives or of women living alone who thought they were safe. When the hill women returned or were replaced, the effect took hold again. No shots. No rapes.'

Tony spoke, addressing Chthona and Tulu. 'Once very long ago when you cut down on rotations, a factory far out by the river fired up its power units of its own accord and for a short time workers were able to manage minimal production there. When you resumed full rotations, the power units failed again, forever, as far as we know.'

'No causal link,' Andros said, 'but extraordinary correlation.'

There was a long silence. Each hill woman weighed what had been said. Chthona, aware that Koa had not been able to follow the gentles' speech, was busy reconstructing and projecting it for better understanding. Somewhere in the old courthouse a board creaked. A mouse scurried across the plaster. One of the candles flickered wildly. The figures at the table leaned inwards. Evona resumed her seat. She too leaned forward. Eventually Chthona sighed. The three women's channel-joining flowed in a strong assent.

Tulu spoke. 'Your request seems reasonable,' she said. 'We can easily carry it to the other hill women. We can as well reach our sisters to the south and east. They must be made aware of what their withdrawal is doing.'

'Or at least of what it seems to be doing,' Evona added. She looked at her sisters, then at each of the gentles. 'I pledge myself personally to a reaching of the valley and mountain women, to an explaining to them of your observations, and to an urging of their returning of women to the City.'

'I, too,' said Chthona. 'And there will be others who will aid us in that.'

'I add my pledge as well,' said Tulu. 'All of us, women and gentles, will be safer.'

The faces of the four men in the candlelight reflected both joy and incredulity. Labrys broke into a smile. Tony, also smiling, flung an arm around him. Pasquale rolled his eyes heavenwards and released a stream of air from his throat. Andros favoured them for a second time that night with a grin.

'There's one thing more,' Chthona was saying to Pasquale. 'You spoke of some happy thing you've discovered.'

'Happy indeed,' he replied, standing up. 'It may seem to you a small accomplishment but for us it is a triumph. Will you help us?' The women nodded, puzzled. 'Then excuse us a moment.' Pasquale leaned across the other three men and there was an excited whispering among them.

Labrys broke from the group. 'We were going to ask you to mindreach to the Earlytown crows. But since you brought your own companions, would all three of you reach to them with some piece of knowledge? Preferably nothing secret.'

Instantly the three women channel-linked. 'I don't like it,' Evona sent. Something nagged at her consciousness.

'Shall we refuse?' asked Chthona.

'No,' Evona replied. 'I've been too much on edge all night. There can be no harm in this.'

'Then what message?' Chthona was clearly enjoying the game. 'Use a remember rhyme.'

'I've got one. An original,' Tulu volunteered. 'Stay open with me.' Aloud she said, with scarcely a moment's pause between Labrys' question and her words, 'Of course'.

Chthona had found Falstaff and Feste at the top of Earlytown's highest maple. 'Be ready for some crazy words,' she sent.

'A song?' Feste asked eagerly.

'Not quite. Just remember the sounds.'

'We'll be very quiet,' Labrys was saying. 'Tell us when you'll begin.'

'We've begun already,' Evona responded. She heard Tulu say to the birds, 'This is dedicated to you, sweethearts.'

'We're ready,' testified both crows as Tulu trotted out the pattern of an ancient poem:

> . . . *on the pallid bust of Pallas just above my chamber door,*
> *And his eyes have all the seeming of a demon that is dreaming . . .*

The crows loved it. They caught the rhythm and were repeating the entire verse. Evona knew the metre but had not heard these particular words. The gentles had hardly settled into being quiet when Tulu announced, 'There. They have it.'

'Amazing,' murmured Tony.

Pasquale was gesturing to the other gentles as he said to the women, 'We have to ask you to be very quiet now and not use your mind talk.' With combined eagerness and shyness all four men were rising to stand behind their chairs, Tony and Labrys supporting Andros.

'You look a little like a chorus line,' Tulu suggested gingerly.

' 'Tis more than coincidental you should remark that,' Andros said, 'because this thing works only if we stand in a line. Like this.' He nudged his brothers, and all four men turned profile to the women, each holding onto the waist of the man in front of him – Labrys, Andros, Tony, and Pasquale. Caught up in the spirit of the performance Evona found herself laughing with the others.

'Actually a conga line,' Pasquale explained, looking at them over his shoulder. 'Labrys, you lead.'

Evona half expected the old courtroom to ring with the merriment of song and dance. Instead a remarkable quiet descended upon them all. She watched transfixed as the four gentles closed their eyes and raised their heads. They seemed to hold their breaths, to be waiting for something. They waited without breathing for a long time. Evona and her sisters waited as well. The sight fascinated her: four large bodies, so foreign to her experience, standing almost as one man, waiting. Then it was clear that this was not waiting at all. This was the thing itself. Evona was suddenly embarrassed. She was afraid she was missing the whole point, that she was supposed to see something that she wasn't seeing. She was about to enfold Tulu and Chthona when the gentles broke their trance. Andros first – laughing aloud and muttering, 'Wonderful!' and clinging to the shoulders of the other men to maintain his balance – then Labrys, Tony, and finally Pasquale, all exclaiming and sighing as if some great effort had been expended, and all leaning with laughter and relief on chairs and each other. Andros was declaiming,

And the lamplight o'er him streaming throws his shadow on the floor;
And my soul from out that shadow that lies floating on the floor
Shall be lifted . . .

'Nevermore!' The four men chorused. With childlike glee they hugged one another in congratulation.

The significance of what had happened burst upon the women. Evona's heart pounded. A pressure in her chest lifted her from her chair and drove her away from the group. At the same moment Tulu and Chthona were on their feet, propelled towards the gentles, their voices loud with questions and praise, the men's voices loud with answers and gratitude.

'When did you discover this?' 'Can you do it only with crows?' 'With each other?' 'Do they speak to you in words? How does it happen?' 'Gentle brothers, what a wonder!'

'. . . worked together for ten months just to get a chicken hawk's attention.' 'It's got to be in sequence.' '. . . always takes at least four to do it, to lay each strip on top of the other.'

Evona rocked back and forth on the rail of the jury box, trying to ease her surging stomach.

'It's not enfoldment, then?' she heard Tulu ask.

'No. It's like a bridge, not a circle.' She suddenly hated Tony's deep voice. 'We think it is a different form altogether,' he went on, 'a form unique to men. If only we can develop it –'

Evona's lips tightened. 'Just a minute,' she said loudly from her isolation in the shadows. Six astonished heads turned her way. The candles dimmed as she walked back towards the light. She stood sedately by the corner of the polished table. 'You can communicate with the crows, is that right?' She addressed the whole group of men.

'That's right but –'

'And you don't enfold them to do that?' Evona ignored Pasquale's answer.

'No,' said Tony. 'I was saying it's more like a bridge –'

'More like a sword?'

'No, Evona. Not a sword. Like a bridge between two people. I build a track to come to your space –'

'You don't build anything to my space, mister.' Evona felt Chthona and Tulu's mindstretch surrounding her, not pressing, but offering ease. 'Drop it,' she said aloud to them. Their prompt obedience left her feeling naked and alone. She threw her words out with all the more vigour. 'And how do you intend to use this wonderful new-found gift?'

Labrys started towards her. 'Evona –'

'Wait!' Andros held him back and staggered to lean on the table. 'Where's all your trust, woman?'

'You've given me no reason to trust you.' Immediately Evona knew the lie of that. Yet she was compelled to push on. Her voice was rising. 'How will you use that power? To pry into the lives of others? To conquer them?'

'That's not worthy, Evona!' Labrys was angry.

'When have men ever used their power for anything else?' Evona challenged. 'The whole raped world is a testimony to that.'

Labrys was holding back some explosion. 'We are not like other men,' he said tightly.

'Until tonight I had believed that, too.'

'But what has happened tonight to change that?' Tony broke in. 'What have we done but given you the knowledge of our work?'

'That's it, Tony,' Andros answered him. 'It's that sharing that wrecked it.' He edged towards Evona, supporting himself by the table. 'You see about as far as your self-righteous hand and no further, Evona. Does it occur to you that we might have some humanity too? That as a special breed of men we may be on the brink of discovering our own non-violent psychic powers?'

Evona could touch only stark loneliness. She desperately wanted Chthona and Tulu to enfold her again, to give her comfort and ease, to take away her rigidity, her drivenness. There they stood, strangers to her just like the men beside them. Yet she could not ask. Instead she scoffed. 'Non-violent? Never. You know what will happen. You'll use your own new power all right. You'll use it, perfect it, manufacture it, package it, sell it, and tell the world that it's clean and new because it comes from a different breed of men. But it's just another fancy prick to invade the world with. And you'll use it because you can't really communicate, you can't really love! Of course it's not an enfoldment. You couldn't enfold an ant if it crept into the middle of your hand!'

Andros did not flinch. But her words had reached him. He spoke quietly. 'You still want it all, don't you? Just like every woman since the dawn of time. You demand your holy isolation from men so you can develop your unique female powers, but you are threatened to the core by the suggestion that we have equally unique powers – don't even whisper that they might be equally valuable. You want us out of your life so you won't have to deal with our so-called violent energy, but you'd perish tomorrow on your rotation if gentles were not in the City aiding you.' He pushed himself up until he was squarely in front of her. 'Face it, Amazon woman. We're not just your protectors anymore. We begin, just barely begin, to live without violence, to learn what you started learning long ago. Very slowly we are following a healthy hope, a life-giving possibility, a pathway that will make us your strong allies when the day of reckoning comes. You have to trust us now, lady. You may sicken at that thought, but you've got no choice.'

Evona turned again into the darkness. A shiver ran over her. She spoke with her back to them. 'We can withdraw our women from their city rotations.'

'Yes. You can do that,' Andros answered.

'And then you will have no time to develop these new skills.'

'And there will be helicopters over the ensconcement, raping parties in the Wanderground.'

Evona's head swam. The top of the judge's desk was just at her eye-level. She leaned there a moment, fighting complete fallaway. With an agonised effort she released her shield. Strength flooded towards her.

'We share your misgivings,' Tulu was sending.

'And we wait by the well of your anger,' Chthona finished.

'But you trust them.'

'It's not a matter of trust. They will do what they will do. We can't stop them,' sent Tulu. There was a long stretch-silence.

'They will do what they will do,' repeated Chthona. Another stretch-silence.

Great tears rolled down her face. She did not brush them away but straightened instead and turned to look at the gentles. They stood in postures of expectancy and pain. Pasquale was crying, his wet cheeks a mirror of her own.

'I am not scorning any one of you or your discovery,' she said, 'or even your intent. My mistrust is of a deeper thing.'

Labrys spoke. 'Our maleness.'

Evona nodded.

'Then only time will tell,' he said.

'Yes.' She met their eyes one by one.

Andros stood tall. 'I don't know how to bind an oath with you,' he said. 'Perhaps binding is not appropriate. But in all that has passed tonight, in all that will be our future, I do hereby pledge myself again to your well-being and to your ultimate victory. As I stand apart from you, my life lived for myself and my brothers, I shall stand always for you as well. You may rely on that.'

'I stand always for you as well,' repeated Pasquale.

'For you as well,' said Tony and Labrys together.

Something akin to gratitude flooded Evona, not quite dispelling the tumult inside her. She let herself be drawn into Chthona and Tulu's enfoldment of each of the gentles, into a holding and a rocking, into a warm and thankful parting for their having richly met.

'There's need for another gatherstretch,' sent Tulu. 'We know much more than we did before.' A south wind was aiding their ride home.

'But are we in danger?' Koa's stretch was anxious.

'We don't know yet,' sent Chthona.

'Let's say there's reasonable doubt,' Evona added. She looked down upon forest growth, clean new lakes. 'Actually, the earth looks wise and stubborn tonight. Like she's not about to be raped again.' Just ahead of her Evona heard a refrain from Falstaff and Feste.

'Nevermore!' they sang out to the night skies.

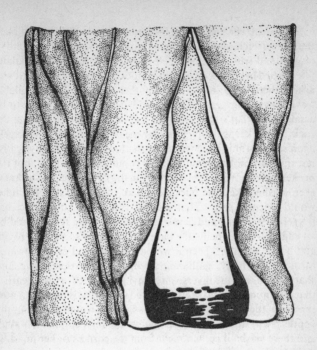

Voki at the Welling Place

Voki was alone at the welling place. It was late evening. No moon. With an effort she focused her close attention on the thin stream of water that oozed from beneath the cleft in the rock. Then, straddling the water's path she stood on the wet gravel and deliberately, as if to touch the magic of the place, laid the blackness of her hands high on the grey dampness above her head.

'Artilidea,' she mindstretched. Her channel reached out. No answer. Only her own openness. A waiting. It hung between her and the old woman. Voki concentrated. She held the sending very taut, still curling it gently around Artilidea, enfolding her, enwombing her.

'Artilidea!' she sent again. Still no response. Voki pulled back the mindstretch, shaking her head with some violence. A sound of disgust and frustration escaped between her tongue and palate. She pushed her cheek against the smooth stone. Then, there it was again, there deep inside her. Another of those uncontrollable waves beginning again. She braced herself. She was about to be assaulted. 'What's happening to me?' she whispered against the rock. 'What keeps taking away my meanings?' She was strangely agonised. Nothing in her young life had assailed her so physically, not the heat, not the cold, not the coming of her blood, not the broken collarbone when she fell from the narrow path. She knew even as she asked the question where the centre lay: Artilidea would die very soon. That was the embedded knowledge that triggered each long and devastating seizure. First there would be an edginess in her belly, the bare suggestion of something rough and uncomfortable. Then it would intensify and creep upwards through her body, gathering strength like a tidal wave and sharpness like some inverse intestinal pain. The first time earlier that afternoon she had been staggered with astonishment but now she knew the pattern, knew how each wave would rise from the depths, swirl upward to crash against the high cliffs of her skull and there wash all contentment from the corners of her mind. It would pulse through all the convolutions of her memory and over all the crevices of her awareness; it would pull every surface taut and suck it dry.

Only when she groaned aloud would the wave subside, leaving her empty and barren, hollow and utterly deprived. This time standing at the welling rocks, she sent her cries into the cleft itself, into the lining of the stone faces, into the interstices where in some restless shift of the earth ten thousand years ago they came together first. Voki felt the rocks moving. They parted ever so little yet so vastly to receive her pain; with sudden vulnerability they gave away before her face, separating to receive her cries, to enfold and welcome the vulnerability she brought to them.

How long she stayed pressed there against the damp smooth stone she could not guess. Her shaking ceased. Her arms outstretched, she stroked the stone in thanks. Then consciously she began a breathing. In and up and hold. Out and down and hold. Her sensibilities returned. The world crept back to her. She was aware again of the welling place, of the ancient smells and moistures soothing her, of the rock cheeks that cradled her own.

She straightened. She felt more in control now. 'Don't think of her,' she told herself. 'Don't let her in.' Even as she formed the thought an image brushed the outskirts of her mind, brushed by again from the other direction, and a third time stayed to claim her full attention.

Artilidea, one day long ago when the sky had broken and flooded the grain fields; Artilidea by the northern fence line, drenched and angry against the wind, beating the ground with her cutter and shrieking a curse: 'Sister goddess? Sister traitor! Damn your promises!' And then Voki herself running crouched behind the raging figure as it strode through the downpour. How the old woman banged gracelessly into her hut and turned a surprised smile to the girl on her threshold. 'Well, come in out of the rain, Voki. Close the door.' How, unbelieving, Voki had stared at the old woman. 'You cursed the goddess?' she said aloud. Artilidea laughing. 'The goddess? Well, of course. Such as she is.' Artilidea stretching her arm in soothing towards a nanny goat gnawing on a swaying hammock thread and with the other hand removing her wire-rimmed eyeglasses. How as she wiped them with a dry shirt she turned to Voki, puzzled, and shortstretched to the girl, 'Who's been dosing you up on reverence?' How, still shaken, Voki could not respond and how the old woman then laughed again. 'If she's real then she needs some irreverence, doesn't she? Halved the ensconcement's winter grain, she did.' Artilidea suddenly smiling but serious saying, 'I'm cursing our own closedness, Voki. We should have known, could have cut and gathered sooner.' How Voki had nodded, understanding something very important that day in the old woman's hut with the cold rain beating on the walls and the nanny goat bleating in the corner and her own muddy tracks forming puddles by the door.

As that memory returned, so did the surges of pain. All over again, up from the belly, searing through her head, wiping out, sweeping clean, leaving only emptiness and loneliness. Again she was moaning into the cleft, being received by the rock. Then a breathing again and the world returning.

Voki straightened. She was cold and strangely thirsty. She rubbed her arms. Opening her eyes she searched the darkness for the water beneath her. The flow there made no noise. She reached with her hand to touch the slow stream and then with one move she dropped face down into the wet gravel. Her mouth found the water, seemed to fit into the stream's movement. Her forehead rested on the upright stones. She drank. She cried. She was quiet. Her arms pressed the rougher rockface around her. Blackness everywhere.

She lay there soaking in the welling waters, moving her lips enough to breathe, enough to make the emptiness subside. She was no longer cold. In fact, she felt surrounded by a warm holding. Her long body heard the call.

'Voki.' It was Artilidea. Voki opened her mindstretch to meet the enfolding voice. 'I've chosen tomorrow to go, Voki. Will you go with me to the upland scree?'

Voki sent immediately. 'Of course. Who else will go?'

'Yelena. We're gathering now for remembering and holding. Those who wish and who can come in their hardselves will presence with me; all who can are welcome to join from afar.'

'It seems sudden,' sent Voki. She was aware of trying to shade herself from the other woman.

'You knew,' replied Artilidea.

'I knew,' Voki acknowledged.

'I chose to wait until now for telling. Less to-do that way.'

Voki found herself unable to answer.

'Are you there, Voki?' Not words, but an asking.

'Yes,' Voki sent. She didn't allow herself to say more.

There was a stretchsilence before Artilidea sent again. 'Will you open to me? Trust me?'

Voki no longer resisted. She lowered her shade and gave the channel its full breadth. She unlocked her memories of the old woman, her recent agonies, and as she felt them all again herself she allowed Artilidea to live through them with her. She cried aloud once more, not this time a standing heroic figure wailing into the rock but now an unashamed girl-woman, drenched and miserable, screaming some unleashed rage, slobbering grotesquely into the wet gravel, making unbeautiful, uncontrollable sounds like a helpless infant blubbering and angry in the midwives' hands. The channel to Artilidea had deepened the agony and made possible the release.

'What is it Artilidea? What's happening to me? Why can't I control this?'

Artilidea seemed to be remembering. 'It's called grief. Named as one of the obsoletes. It used to be quite common among us. Some of us still occasionally feel it, but it's counted a product of possessiveness.'

'What do I do with it?'

'It's yours. Claim it.'

'Possessive.' Voki felt stunned.

'I'm not sure of that.' Artilidea's doubt coloured her mindstretch. 'Often I think we may have lost a good thing when we left off grieving. But not if it racks you so, Voki. Do you need earth now?'

Voki laughed. There she was, sprawled all-embracingly on the wet ground, and a dying woman was offering earth to her. Artilidea read her and sent again. 'Obsolete notion. I've never been stronger. Do you understand what it means that I go when I am ready and at my will?' The tone of the stretch softened. 'Anyway, when have you ever waited for my strength to say your pain? I need to breathe with you.'

Voki acknowledged the gentle reminder. 'Where are you, Artilidea?' She needed some sense of the old woman's surroundings.

In response Artilidea began slowly moving her eyes; Voki saw through them that the old woman was not in her hut but outdoors, down by the grain keeps, there at the threshing circle where she had done her skilled work and where she had guided others. Voki could see other women already beginning to gather, carrying quietly the soft light of glow lobes. As Artilidea's eyes circled the scene, Voki could observe that the old woman was bundled in a quilt. Beside her, her hand at the small of Artilidea's back, Yelena sat visiting with two women from the Eastern Ensconcement. Artilidea was not presencing with those around her; rather, she spoke again to Voki.

'Breathe with me, Voki.'

'Breathe with me, Artilidea.'

Their outreaching channels still entwined but unshared, the two women began the contact, Voki lying flat upon the earth, Artilidea sitting upright among those gathering to greet her dying. The hard distance was short between them and Voki locked easily into Artilidea's diaphragm level. In. Hold. Down. Hold. Always open, ever enfolding one another, the channels came together, joined in knowing, making a third entity between the two, yet one at home with them both. The holdings lengthened. Voki felt a familiar centre: Artilidea's point of absolute balance, the source from which the old woman's life energy seemed to come. As she sought her own balance in her own source she knew already Artilidea's centre to be for that time her own and her own for that time to be Artilidea's. The knowing of that knowledge was the earthtouch, the strength-giver, the doubt-dispeller, the lover-loved. Voki remembered her grief and from her still place of understanding, stroked it like a kitten's neck; she claimed it, letting it be her own; she knew it would immobilise her no more. Whatever message she dared put into the holding was to her self from herself through Artilidea. To themselves they sang, to each other they sang, 'May we come again in loving, may we come again in learning, may we come again each to the other, each to herself. May we come again. May we come again.'

Small smooth stones rattled beneath her hand. Her wiry hair was cleanly parted by the water's stream.

'Well-received, Artilidea,' she sent.

'Fully given and well taken, Voki.'

'Deep and soon, Artilidea.'

'Deep and soon, Voki.'

'By the red waters.'

'Deep.'

'Soon.'

'Deep and soon.'

'Deep and soon,' Voki finished.

Voki rose from the welling place, sending her thanks to the rocks, the ground, the water. She moved through the lighter darkness of the trees and turned with sure steps towards the grain keeps. An old friend and lover was dying there tonight and she must join in the telling of the days of Artilidea.

The Telling of the Days of Artilidea

Even before she broke through the forest's edge above the grain keeps Voki heard the rhythms. She did not know the language of the singing; she never knew it until she joined her own voice. She could make out the lights now, the soft glow lobes clustered in a circle there on the circular threshing ground. On this clouded moonless night she could barely distinguish her own blackness from that which surrounded her. She was glad for the guidance of the glow lobes. 'Artilidea,' she thought, 'you old rebel. What other self-loving woman would choose to die at the dark of the moon?'

Her steps hastened as she drew closer to the growing group of women. By the keep and off to one side she noted several cats, uncommonly near to one another; they seemed to sleep. Occasionally a dog barked. There was a casual air about the way birds and chickens as well as larger animals seemed to come and go among those in the circle, as if to pay respect to one who could live a century, then as if bored – with age and human company – to wander restlessly away again only to return and listen with renewed surges of respect.

The women sat and stood in a patternless attention to a wildhaired woman who with several others was on one of the large wooden boxes scattered around the edge of the circle. The bony frame of a white nanny goat rested at the old woman's feet.

Artilidea was conducting her own dying. That was characteristic, too, thought Voki. Often a dying woman couldn't do that. Sometimes she would go without choosing to go and at the end others conducted the rememberings and the holdings. Some who died violently – in the City or being hunted – had not even time for rememberings and holdings and often were not even in earthtouch when they died. Then the ministrations had to be done after their death. Voki was uncomfortable with the inappropriateness of all that. She held taut in a moment of care for these women. 'We are getting better,' she thought, 'but we are only now learning how to die. When we really learn how maybe we won't need rituals, not even any holdings.' A strong feeling swept over her, stark admiration for the big-boned old woman who was dying this evening at her own will and because she was ready. 'It's the rest of us who are not ready for her to die,' Voki thought. That thought brought her to the edge of the circle itself.

Before she settled Voki dutifully sent a mindstretch over and around the neighbouring territory. There her softself encountered others, those not participating but who were instead greeting and watching; they were tonight's protectors of the scores of women who were met together for the telling of the days of Artilidea.

'Earthtouch to you, Voki.' It was Tulu's stretch-enfolding that caressed her.

'And to you,' Voki smiled back. 'Who is watching with you?'

Another personality swept over her. 'It's me, Voki. Earlyna. Why are you wet?'

Voki looked down at her soaked clothes. 'I was at the welling place.' She started to send more, to tell them both of the grief she had been fighting, to share with them yet another assurance of the healing waters of the welling place. She decided against it. She felt that they both thought her very young yet. She was not comfortable sharing now. Perhaps some day. She was suddenly brought back to her hardself as a heavy jacket was flung around her shoulders. Krueva stood behind her enfolding her in her arms.

'Earlyna says you are cold and wet,' Krueva whispered in words.

Voki nodded and beamed. Then in a surge of needs she turned to embrace the other woman. Krueva had been her learntogether, her closest one, a little less than a year ago. It was easy now to leap onto the old pathways between them, to tell Krueva in an instant of the agonies about Artilidea, about her shame at grieving, about the healing of the welling place. Krueva heard, rocked the girl-woman in a long holding, held and rocked. Then Voki allowed Krueva to guide her to an inner part of the gathering of women. Immediately she felt warm, embraced by the presencing; there seemed a minimum of mattering tonight, of anxiety or of unfinished cares; the women were full and ready for the evening's concern. Krueva sat behind her and girl-child Clana pushed close to her, offering a private shortstretch. Voki opened to it.

'We've just gotten through telling again about what it used to be like in the cities. Then we told about the searches and how she escaped to the hills,' Clana sent, 'and now the cats are ending their part.'

Voki began her tuning in, breathing onto the level of the other women and the cats, onto the plane where solo voices rang out in the story of Artilidea. One sang of how she took her name among her outlaw sisters, another of how she was one of the few left who had survived the purging of the strong women from the cities. Another solo sang of her gifts of history, of her knowledge imparted for the remember rooms – 'lest we forget how we came here'. One sang of her years of planting, of her schemes for greater yield, and of the day she lay in the deep lake without air and was not discovered by the flying machines.

Over all the singing Artilidea herself sounded loud and clear, affirming each memory, occasionally making mild revisions: 'That I did, that I did.' Or 'We certainly were. Yes.' Or perhaps, 'But only by firelight.'

The chanting continued a good while, for Artilidea was well known among the hill women. Short solos from a long line of singers, some recalling anger and struggle, some making laughter ripple throughout the gathering, each singer grateful for the life of old Artilidea. Women from afar, from the Eastern Ensconcement, the Kochlias, and the North Wanderground joined with their mindstretches in the weaving of an intricate narrative that would belong now to each one there.

Voki could not bring her own voice to sing. She sat instead braced by her sisters, open and hearing in the free-flowing rite. At last the solos ceased. Only a low humming now. Artilidea spoke aloud.

'We have remembered well. Thank you for recalling the days I've spent with you.'

'We take you with us, Artilidea,' Krueva's voice came from behind Voki.

'We take you with us,' others repeated.

'As I do you with me,' Artilidea chanted. 'I wish now to say in what way I've chosen to go.' A hush happened over the crowd of women. All breathing seemed to stop. Birds perched, insects ceased their drone, all the animals seemed to turn with the women towards the voice at the edge of the circle.

'I'll lie open to the wind. The weather and the wolves may have whatever of me is good for them. Yelena and Voki will go with me tomorrow to the upland scree to a place I have seen in my early morning dreams.' Artilidea reached down to touch the goat at her feet. 'Thelma wishes to go, too. We'll be companions as good in death as we have been in life. Yelena and Voki will hold us there, hold us into our passing. They will lean us back upon the earth, lean us back upon the sea, easy and long. Then the earth will bear us. Then the sea will bear us. Easy. Long. Easy. Long. Yelena and Voki will leave us there.'

In the silence that hung above the gathered women, whispers ranged in from great distances away, one woman even daring to stretch from the Dangerlands near the City. The separate whispers presenced in a chorus that blanketed the gathering.

Easy. Long.
Easy. Long.
Leaning back upon the sea,
Leaning back upon the earth.
She will bear you.
She will bear you.
Easy. Long.

There was another time of no words. Easy and long.

When the silence parted for the asking, Egathese formed the question, 'What can you tell us, Artilidea, that we can know?'

'Nothing, I guess, that you won't remember in your own time, learn in your own way. It comes to me now to remind you of the mirror in my hut behind the shutter. I hope some will find some joy in it. It was important to me once. My eyeglasses will return with Voki and Yelena in case there comes another among you who can't yet heal her eyes. I invite you to try them on sometime. They reveal remarkable things. What more can I say? The ground is ready for spring sowing. Watch out for the weak axle on the high-bedded wagon. We need to train toters for the harvest. Beans planted when the moon is Leo-borne will speck and rot. Scrapings from a cow's horn can clot wasting blood. The wind won't turn the barrels when clouds are in the east. When the Pleiades are murky there is unrest at sea. A brown dog with a white left hind foot can dance upright. The salamander by the bathing rocks knows all about the Salem trials. I'm reminded of no more.'

There were a few smiles, then a silence, and a closing of sorts while all rested on some shared plateau listening to the passing words, the passing influence of Artilidea. She spoke again, this time in a different voice. 'Before you hold me into dying we are invited to ask about the dying of the earth, the dying of the race.'

The words were somehow a cue. Even if she had never before been at a dying Voki would have sensed that some important shift had come. Things changed key. Each woman-channel presenced deeper; each animal-channel presenced wider. Every channel reached to join an other. Channels linked in threes, in fours, in tens, in scores. Each woman touched an other's centre and found it to be, as well, her own. One source rode among them all, and the knowing of that knowledge by all the knowers knowing was itself an other presence, an other being, freshly new yet as familiarly textured and odoured to each woman as her own nest.

Words seemed to rise from that which was newly-created among them:

'Why do you slay me? Why do you slay the mother?' A chromatic lift moved a group of voices to answer:

We do not slay you.
We do not slay the mother.

'Who is the slayer, then?'

Suddenly, the climbing ritual was shattered by a child's voice. It was Gynia. She spoke aloud and clearly out of rhythm. 'What's a slayer, Seja?'

The magic was stunned into suspension over the threshing circle. The women, all of them, save little Gynia had been engrossed in the channel-joining. Now they were brought down, brought back to their hardselves. What was their interruption? An uneasiness was gathering in the silence. It grew. At last someone laughed. The tension snapped. Other relieved voices joined the first, and others then until the circle seemed to wave forward and back, forward and back, in a mass of laughing women.

Voki was least of all good humoured. She worried that Artilidea must be impatient, perhaps even hurt with this annoyance. She was surprised and disappointed to see the old woman smiling with the rest. Voki set herself to formulating a neat definition of a slayer so the ritual could continue. The words were about to take an irritated bounce off the end of her tongue when another voice spoke first.

'One who kills without need, Gynia.'

Voki looked around her. Others were looking around as well. Then realisation broke on all their faces at once. Even Voki was filled with astonished pleasure. Whatever other presence they had created was still among them and was now herself attending to irregularity in the pattern. Gynia was speaking once more, 'Then I do not slay you. I do not slay the mother.'

'Good,' said the presence. 'Let's go on.'

They were back again, all of them this time, locked in the channel-journey, understanding anew the hidden flexibilities in ancient womanforms. Opposing voices now began, waging an agony in the sky. First the new presence would challenge and exhort; then the gathered women would respond. The presence sang: 'Who is the slayer, then? Who slays the mother?'

The women answered:

The Crown of Creation.
He is the slayer.
His is the litany.
We are the slain.

Separate voices among the women intoned the invasion litany:

If it moves: shoot it down.
If it grows: cut it.

It is wild: tame it, claim it.
If it flows: a harness.
It shines or burns: gouge it out.
It is female: rape it.

Then the presence again: 'You are not the slayer then? You do not slay the mother?'

The women together:

How have we shot for sport?
How maimed the growing?
How have we claimed the wild?
Harnessed the flowing?
How have we gouged the earth?
How have we raped?
His is the litany.
We are the slain.

Another chromatic change as the challenging voice came again: 'He is the slayer. You sometimes wear the crown.' A heavy silence, then affirmations from each woman wove themselves into the ceremony. 'She has said it.' 'It's true.' 'Right.' 'It's so.' In their hardselves now the women were on their knees or sitting. A kind of keening arose, a remorse under the refrain.

We have worn his crown.
We have shared the slaying.

The antiphon continued, the presence speaking: 'Throwing off his crown, then, will you slay the slayer?'

Throwing off his crown then,
Still we slay him not.

'How then will you deal with the Crown of Creation?' A shift. A movement to still another different level. A minor key. The women were still kneeling, heads bent, hands on their bellies. Then a repeated word, spoken by separate women:

Change.
Change.
Change.
Change.
Change.
Change.
Change.

'And if the slayer will not change, will not yield the crown?'
Another shift. Another level:

Death.
Death.
Death.
Death
Death.
Death.
Death.

'Aha! You slay the slayer, then!'

No! Changing not, he dies.

'Then you do not slay him?'
The rhythm moved just a hair's breadth:

We do not slay him
But aid him in his dying,
Show him how to bear himself
Into his own stilldeath.

Show him how to pull on the knotted sheet,
Show him how to breathe
How to push, how to cry.
Show him how to count between
The pains. How to die.

Bathe him in the blood
And the water of his dying,
Show him the way to give death to himself,

Cut the species human
From the cord of life,
That the species human
May at last let go.

With water and blood we can wash away the slayer.
With water and blood we can wash away the race.

Another movement, this time to a major key. Krueva stood up. 'Artilidea,' she said, 'ask the question.'

Artilidea was standing too, now. Her big voice had an anxious edge as she spoke. 'Will we save the earth, the mother? Stay the slayer's hand in time?' No answer. Only a silence, and underneath it, the keening.

A woman Voki did not know rose and asked the question again. 'Will we save the earth, the mother? Stay the slayer's hand in time?'

Still the silence. Abruptly the keening ceased. Even the hills seemed to wait. Nothing. No sound. Voki shook her head. She knew that in all the calls to the dying earth there had never yet been an answer. Never would there be, maybe. Every woman there could phrase the question: still there would be no answer. She could not remember what kind of movement happened next. She was aware, still, of the presence among them all, aware as well of the silence, of no answer coming from that presence, from anywhere. Only silence. Finally as a few more women began to rise, Artilidea took up the words of the challenger: 'Though you have no answer, still you have the task.'

The circle of women changed now from a low mass of kneeling figures to a more active pattern of rising women. As each woman slowly stood she intoned, *The task. The task.* The murmur of that phrase grew to a strong unison voice. *The task*, the women intoned. *The task.*

Above them all Artilidea's voice rose: 'What is the task?'

To work as if the earth, the mother, can be saved.
To work as if our healing care were not too late.
Work to stay the slayer's hand,
Helping him to change
Or helping him to die.

Work as if the earth, the mother, can be saved.

At that moment Artilidea leaned upon Yelena's arm and turned toward the centre of the crowd of chanting women. She spoke as she went: 'Yours is the task, then. Mine is the passing. And, although I may, I may not come again.'

> *If you so believe, then so it is:*
> *Ours is the task,*
> *Yours is the passing.*
> *And, although you may, you may not come again.*

The glow lobes hung in the air encircling all the women now. Artilidea moved to the centre. She approached a woman who was a stranger to Voki and stopped a few feet from her. The woman was younger, but only by a generation. Artilidea stretched out her hands. 'Are we at ease, Ara?'

The younger woman did not answer at once.

Artilidea dropped her hands. 'I am glad you came.'

Ara looked at the earth, then at the old woman. 'We are at ease, Artilidea,' she said.

So the holding began with Ara and Artilidea as they embraced and rocked together in the soft light. Yelena drew Voki to her and together they leaned in upon Artilidea and Ara. Slowly, others gathered, encircling, enwombing each other. Clana and Gynia rode the shoulders of bigger women. Layer upon layer, fold upon fold, the holding began. All the women leaned each on others, yet nowhere was there a burden – closely fitting, closely entwined, Artilidea at the centre held by all. A low level of humming came from everywhere; it seemed literally to support the mass of women. Animals crowded inward, mixing sometimes in the circle, more often providing a circumference beneath the suspended glow lobes. Their wild, domestic and barnyard noises blended into a concert of women's sounds.

The circle of humming rocking bodies held Artilidea, held each other, far into the darkest hours. Some left when the night was deepest, some stayed till dawn, holding and rocking, holding and rocking; most were still there when three women and a white nanny goat walked into the sunrise towards the upland scree.

JOANNA RUSS
THE FEMALE MAN

'A visionary novel about a society where women can do all we now fantasize in closets and kitchens and beds ... intricate, witty, furious ... savage' Marge Piercy

Joanna is from a present time very much like our own, where she struggles to survive and gain acceptance in a man's world; Jeannine, a romantic dreamer in search of the ideal husband, is from an altered past in which Hitler never took power, World War II never happened and the Great Depression continues. Janet comes from the planet While-away in the far future, where duels are fought and children born and brought up, but where no men have existed for hundreds of years. All three women are transported from their own times and united by a mysterious figure for an unguessable purpose.

Joanna Russ, Nebula and Hugo award winning author of such remarkable works as *We Who Are About To* and *The Adventures of Alyx*, today remains one of the most important writers ever to emerge from science fiction: she is one of the small number whose work may still be read by those future generations of whom she writes. *The Female Man* is her best known work.

0 7043 3949 8
£1.95